D0593125

Simple Justice

John Morgan Wilson

Simple Justice

A Benjamin Justice Mystery

D O U B L E D A Y
New York
London
Toronto
Sydney
Auckland

PUBLISHED BY DOUBLEDAY
a division of Bantam Doubleday Dell Publishing Group, Inc.
1540 Broadway, New York, New York 10036

DOUBLEDAY and the portrayal of an anchor with a dolphin are trademarks of Doubleday, a division of Bantam Doubleday Dell Publishing Group, Inc.

Library of Congress Cataloging-in-Publication Data

Wilson, John M., 1945–
Simple justice: a Benjamin Justice mystery/John Morgan Wilson.
p. cm.
1. Journalists—California—Los Angeles—Fiction. 2. Gay men—California—Los Angeles—Fiction. 3. Los Angeles (Calif.)—Fiction. I. Title.
PS3573.I456974S56 1996
813'.54—dc20 95-45207
CIP

ISBN 0-385-48234-5

Printed in the United States of America
August 1996
First Edition

10 9 8 7 6 5 4 3 2 1

For my father and for Jon-Noel—
two men whose gentleness and understanding
have meant so much.

Acknowledgments

Thanks must go to Alice Martell, my thoughtful and savvy agent.

To Judith Kern, my perceptive editor at Doubleday, and other Doubleday editors for their assistance and support.

To my friend and fellow writer, Brenda Day-Hanson, for her invaluable suggestions during early revisions.

To Irv Letofsky, my good friend and helpful newspaper sage.

And to Pietro, my partner in life, for enduring the demands of the writing life and the writer's ego while somehow remaining his wonderful, loving self.

Simple Justice

One

BILLY LUSK was murdered on a Tuesday, shortly after midnight, and Harry Brofsky came looking for me that afternoon.

It was mid-July. Hot winds that felt like the devil's breath blew into Los Angeles from the desert, rattling through the shaggy eucalyptus trees like a dry cough.

The city was golden, blinding, blasted by heavenly light. It was one of those days that made nipples rise and minds wander and bodies shiver with sensuality and inexplicable dread. The kind of day when the heat wrapped snugly around you but sent an ominous chill up your back at the same time, like the first sexual touch in a dark room from a beautiful stranger whose name you'd never know.

Harry found me in West Hollywood, bobbing my head to an old Coltrane tape and trying not to think about alcohol.

"Look who's caught up with me," I said to the empty room, when I saw Harry's car pull up. "My, my, my."

I was staying in a small garage apartment in a leafy neighborhood known for its irregular shape as the Norma Triangle, where quaint little houses crowded cozy lots and lush greenery crawled unrestricted over the rotting corpses of old wood fences.

My single room was up a wooden stairway at the deep end of an unpaved driveway, which ran alongside a neatly kept California Craftsman, one of those finely beveled, wood-framed bungalows that sprouted up by the thousands during the building boom of the

1930s and 1940s. The owners, Maurice and Fred, had purchased the property in the late fifties, when West Hollywood was a quiet community of middle-class families and well-behaved bohemians on the eastern edge of upscale Beverly Hills, and Maurice and Fred had been in the early stages of their four-decade relationship.

Thanks to their kindness, I was staying in the apartment rent-free, in exchange for performing odd chores. It wasn't the most dignified arrangement for a thirty-eight-year-old ex-journalist who had been awarded a Pulitzer prize. But not quite six years ago, in winning that coveted award, I'd destroyed any personal dignity I might claim, not to mention my career, in one dark and reckless act of fraud, so where and how I lived didn't matter all that much.

Nothing really did now, except somehow getting through another day, until all the days were mercifully used up.

Through the unwashed window of my room, I looked down on the rear yard, where a flowering jacaranda swayed like a lonely dancer in the restless breeze. Three plump cats lounged in the tree's shade, their tails barely twitching in the oppressive heat, watching a hummingbird dart among syrupy pistils of honeysuckle while I watched them.

In the three months since Maurice and Fred had installed me in the apartment, I'd spent most of my time at this window, where I could see down the narrow driveway to the street without anyone clearly seeing me. When Harry finally showed up, unannounced, I felt as though I'd spent most of those hours waiting for him.

I watched him wrestle his Ford Escort into a space at the curb and struggle wearily out. He mopped his round face with a handkerchief, found a cigarette, and adjusted his bifocals to check a scrap of paper for the Norma Place address. When he'd confirmed the numbers, he glanced up at the apartment, just long enough for me to see what the years had done to him, and to feel the gnaw of guilt.

I briefly wondered how he'd found me after all this time. Then I remembered that Harry had once been a reporter too, and a good reporter knows how to find people who don't want to be found.

"Oh, Harry." I listened to Coltrane blow the final jumpy notes of "My Favorite Things," the fourteen-minute version, then heard the machine click off. "I do so wish you'd left well enough alone."

As he crossed Norma, passing a trim young man with a gym bag and a perfect tan, Harry could not have looked more out of place.

Although West Hollywood as a whole was predominantly heterosexual, with a sizable population of older residents and Russian Jewish immigrants, the makeup in this neighborhood was distinctly different. The Norma Triangle was situated only a couple of blocks off Santa Monica Boulevard near the section of West Hollywood known as Boy's Town, where gay businesses proliferated and single male adults were presumed homosexual until proven otherwise.

Harry was thoroughly heterosexual, and looked it in a dull, stereotypical way. Close to sixty, he was dressed in a musty-looking blue-gray suit appropriate for the funeral of someone you don't really care about; he had the rumpled, unfashionable look of a transplanted Midwest newspaper editor, which he was. His brown loafers needed polishing, his gray mustache needed trimming, and so did his waistline, all of which marked him as a man who didn't care much about his appearance. And if there was a single obsession in Boy's Town, other than the endless search for a new sexual conquest, it was the constant cultivation of one's physical image, a kind of fraternity row mind-set pumped up with gay flair.

With my thinning blond hair and ex-wrestler's body going paunchy and slack, and a fashion sense that ran to old jeans and sweatshirts, I didn't fit in too neatly myself. But there was still some muscle on my six-foot frame, and my blue eyes remained alert to the sight of an attractive face or body, marginal indications in Boy's Town that I might be a practicing homosexual. Harry, on the other hand, looked like anybody's heterosexual uncle from anywhere that wasn't too exciting.

I listened to his hacking smoker's cough as he climbed the stairs. He'd always had trouble with hot weather, and by the time he reached the top, oily sweat pebbled his forehead, and his pale face was blotchy. It was the first time I'd seen or spoken to Harry Brofsky in five years.

"You can't afford a phone?" he asked, squinting at me through the screen. "Things are that bad?"

For a moment, I considered asking him to leave.

Jacques had lived in this apartment when I'd first met him ten years ago. He'd been waiting tables and writing poetry and I'd been a hotshot young reporter at the *L.A. Times.* Jacques had stayed through the years until the virus got him and he became too sick to take care of himself, moving into my apartment the last months of his life, in his twenty-ninth year. After he'd died, Maurice and Fred had never rented the place again. They'd loved Jacques like a son, and I think they missed him nearly as much as I did.

I could feel his presence in the room, fragile and fading with time like my memories of him, and I didn't want intruders.

"Hello, Harry."

"I have to stand out here like a salesman?"

I felt the guilt again, flushing through me like a sickness coming on. I opened the screen door and stepped aside to let him pass.

Harry took a final, nervous drag on his cigarette, crushed it underfoot on the landing, and shuffled in. His sad gray eyes, bright and mischievous not all that many years ago, surveyed the small room.

He saw an unmade bed, an ancient dresser piled with books, a small TV set with rabbit ears, a few dozen jazz tapes scattered beside Jacques's old stereo. Sitting on a shelf were two framed photographs: one of Jacques I'd taken a year before he died, when his large brown eyes were clear and deceptively healthy and his narrow, boyish face was rosy and brown, full of sun, full of hope; another of my sister Elizabeth Jane, snapped at her eleventh birthday party, smiling for the camera with a sadness I'd been too blind to see. There was also a framed one-sheet from *East of Eden* hanging on a wall, signed by James Dean; it was a memento from Maurice's youthful days with the Sal Mineo crowd that Jacques had liked for some reason, so I left it up. Not much else.

"Lovely," Harry said, looking around. "Early Salvation Army, if I'm not mistaken."

"What's on your mind, Harry?"

"Where the hell have you been?"

"Around."

"Doing what?"

"Living in the backseat of the Mustang. Trying to drink myself to death."

Harry had never had much time for self-pity.

"I guess you fucked that up too," he said.

"I guess I did."

I could have told him more: that Maurice and Fred had rescued me from the backseat of my old Mustang convertible, just as they'd once rescued Jacques as a troubled teenager from the streets. That they'd moved me into the apartment and shamed me into pulling myself halfway together, telling me that I owed Jacques at least that much after he'd fought so hard for so long to hang on, before slipping away from us.

But that was intimate stuff, and Harry and I had never been too comfortable with intimate stuff.

"Cut to the chase, Harry."

He perched himself on the only chair in the room and asked for a glass of water.

Then he told me about the murder of Billy Lusk.

Two

WHEN HARRY BROFSKY came to see me about the violent death of Billy Lusk, fifteen to twenty residents were being murdered each week in Los Angeles, with gang activity accounting for roughly half the killings.

At the same time, reported hate crimes were on the rise, especially those targeting lesbians and gay men, which, for the first time, outnumbered even those directed at blacks and Jews.

As Harry explained it, the murder of Billy Lusk bridged both categories: A young gang member had selected a victim outside a gay bar in Silver Lake and gunned him down in cold blood.

"From what Templeton tells me, it's pretty cut-and-dried," Harry said, referring to Alex Templeton, his top crime reporter at the *Los Angeles Sun.* "A witness heard a gunshot a few minutes after midnight, then saw a Mexican kid kneeling over the body in the parking lot. Turned out it was some kind of gang initiation deal."

The door and windows of the apartment were open wide, and the hot wind rattled the screens like a mad person trying to get in. I sat cross-legged on the lumpy bed, hugging my chest with my arms. The few feet that loomed between Harry and me felt as wide as the Santa Monica Mountains.

"Exactly which part of Mexico is the suspect from?"

My question drew only a peevish look.

"You mentioned that he's a Mexican national," I explained,

scratching reflexively at an old sore point between Harry and me, although my heart wasn't really in it.

"I didn't say he was a Mexican national."

"Yes, Harry, you clearly used the term *Mexican.*"

"Pardon my political incorrectness. A Mexican-American kid. Chicano, Hispanic, Latino. Take your pick, because I can't keep the fucking nomenclature straight anymore. I leave that to the more enlightened souls on the copy desk."

There had been a time when Harry wouldn't have spoken so callously. During the 1980s, which had spanned the primary years of our working relationship, I'd raised his consciousness to a marginally sensitive level, where he'd begun to see people unlike himself as actual human beings. He'd obviously relapsed in the years since, and I suppose I should have cared, but I didn't.

He took out a cigarette and stuck it between his lips without lighting it.

"The kid—pardon me, the eighteen-year-old young man—fled the scene. A witness got his license number as he drove away. The cops traced it to his parents' house in Echo Park. Found him in his bedroom, listening to rap music."

"I believe that's a capital crime right there."

Harry gave me another look, more smug this time than irritated.

"There was blood on his shoes," he said. "Also on his clothes."

"Maybe he cut himself shaving."

"From what I hear, he doesn't shave yet." Harry raised his eyebrows, waiting for a rejoinder.

I didn't have one. I was thinking what Central Jail must be like for an inmate with a boy's face. With nearly seven thousand suspects and convicts packed into one building, Men's Central Jail was the largest in the world, and more violent than any California prison. The kid was lucky, I thought, to have a gang affiliation for protection.

"For what it's worth," Harry went on, "the blood type from his clothes matches the blood type of the victim."

"What about a weapon?"

Harry and I had fallen into a once-familiar pattern, perhaps to avoid matters not so easily discussed. It was a game we'd played many times, with well-defined roles. Harry was the brusque, curmudgeonly editor, skeptical as all good editors should be, but essentially a product of his conservative Midwest roots, a believer in well-established systems and institutions. I was the bleeding-heart reporter, raised in the East in a home where alcohol and violence provided the most vivid memories, who distrusted authority as a rule, convinced that life is fundamentally unjust in a world ruled by the privileged and the powerful.

The undercurrent of tension and competition between Harry and me had been a constant, keeping us from ever being truly close. In spite of it, or perhaps because of it, we'd hammered out a couple of dozen award-winning articles when we'd been at the *Los Angeles Times,* "damn fine articles," as Harry used to call them, after he'd loosened up with a drink or two.

What was different now was that Harry was no longer employed as an editor at the mighty *Los Angeles Times,* but instead at the barely profitable and far less respectable *Los Angeles Sun,* struggling to put his career back together; and I was no longer a reporter and had no interest in much of anything beyond my private thoughts and extending as much time as possible between drinks.

I also had no idea why Harry was here, telling me about the murder of a man I'd never heard of outside a gay bar halfway across town. Perhaps he thought I could provide special sources or contacts for Alex Templeton's story, but I didn't want even that much involvement with Harry or the newspaper or anything else beyond these walls.

"Templeton says the cops have all the evidence they need," Harry said. "The weapon's a moot point."

"A moot point."

My voice was faintly mocking, as it had been a thousand times in conversations with Harry.

The corners of his mouth curled into the slightest smile. He played his best card, saved for last.

"The kid confessed," he said.

"Ah."

"He even bragged about it. Like I said, some kind of gang ritual. You know how those people are." Harry was so offhand, so blatantly offensive that I should have sensed what was behind it. "Templeton's putting the story together for tomorrow's paper."

"Let me guess," I said. "Banner head, front page. *Gay Man Gunned Down by Rampaging Gang Bangers.* A dead faggot, ripe for exploitation. Then forgotten by tomorrow."

"My, aren't we on a high horse," Harry said.

"The *Sun* has a grand tradition for sleaze and sensationalism, Harry. You can't deny that."

"As a matter of fact, we plan to treat the story with the utmost respect. I'm even planning long-term follow-up, to see how it plays out."

"A queer, murdered outside a gay bar in a working-class neighborhood that's largely Latino? Since when has the *Sun* considered such things worthy of respectful coverage?"

"You haven't read the *Sun* recently, have you, Ben?"

"It's been awhile."

"I've been making some changes," Harry said. "Moving gradually away from the hothouse stuff. I figure this murder gives us a nice hook for some in-depth reporting. Maybe even a series."

"Because of its socioeconomic implications?"

"If you want to use five-dollar words."

I'd worked with too many editors, Harry especially, to swallow a load that easily.

"What's the kicker, Harry?" I watched him fidget a little on the edge of the chair. "Why this particular story?"

He removed the unlit cigarette from his lips and rolled it thoughtfully between his fingers before finally looking up.

"Billy Lusk came from big bucks and breeding."

I smiled, but sadly.

"Wealth, social status, and the right zip code. That makes all the difference."

"It does make a difference, Ben. Poor people dying violently has never been big news. Whether you like it or not."

"What I like or don't like doesn't matter much anymore, Harry."

He ignored that and rattled off details like a salesman trying to close a deal he feels slipping away.

"The victim's stepfather is Phil Devonshire, the retired golf pro. Serves on half a dozen corporate boards. Mother's Margaret Devonshire. Comes from old Pasadena money, heavy into philanthropy. Country club people, up in Trousdale Estates."

I suddenly felt edgy, impatient. It was nearly five. I was getting closer and closer to needing a drink. But more than that, I didn't like having Harry here, didn't like playing the old game with him. It served no purpose; Harry Brofsky was part of the past.

"Why are you telling me all this, Harry?"

He slid off the chair, went to the window, and stared out across treetops and rooftops at the Pacific Design Center: a bold glass monolith in two sections, one cobalt blue, the other money green, jutting dramatically into a sky scoured clean by the Santa Anas.

When he spoke again, all the combativeness was gone from his voice. It was the voice of a tired man, not tired from the day but from the years.

"I want you to put together a short feature," Harry said.

Three

IT WOULD HAVE BEEN less a jolt if Harry Brofsky had told me he was secretly a transvestite, or planned to join the priesthood.

"I don't think I heard you right," I said.

Outside, scrub jays and mockingbirds filled the warm air with a cacophony of chirping and screeching, as they often did during morning and early evening hours in this part of town. Mixed in was the chatter of an angry squirrel somewhere up an avocado tree, and a distant horn from down on the boulevard.

Yet Harry and I seemed frozen in a moment of utter silence.

Half a minute passed before he turned to face me. I hadn't seen him look that vulnerable since his third wife left him eight years before, on the day he turned fifty; she'd tucked a note under the cake and taken the dogs.

"All I want is a sidebar," Harry said. "A short piece to go with Templeton's story for Friday's paper, covering the arraignment."

I realized then that he was serious.

"How long have you been delusional, Harry? Taking your medication?"

"I don't need much, Ben. Fifteen inches would do it. A perspective piece on gay-bashing, anti-gay violence. Why it happens, what it means. That kind of thing."

"Let Templeton write it."

"Alex Templeton's barely a year out of grad school," Harry said. "A good reporter, but . . ."

"Straight."

"Inexperienced."

"You've got plenty of seasoned reporters at the *Sun* who can handle that piece."

"Not the way you would," Harry said. "Maybe you focus on the victim, humanize him. Maybe you try to get inside the head of the killer. You can work it any way you want."

"Forget it, Harry."

"It wouldn't take you that much time. You could wrap up a piece like that in half a day. Less."

"I'm not talking about time, and you know it."

I slid off the bed, agitated, and angry that it showed.

"Even if I wanted to write that piece, which I don't, you'd never get it in the paper. Not even the *Sun.*"

"We'll run it deep inside. With the jump."

"You can't put my name on an article and expect it to have any credibility. Besides . . ."

"I've already cleared it with management. If it's handled correctly, the guys upstairs think it's actually got some good promotional value."

"Running an article by a reporter who won a Pulitzer for a series he fabricated? That's good promotion?"

"Handled right." Harry smiled grimly. "Up against the goddamned *Times,* we need every edge we can get."

"Readers would scream, Harry."

"This is a town of new faces and short attention spans. Most of our readers won't even remember."

"Enough will."

"Fuck 'em."

"That's not good enough, and you know it."

"Then we'll deal with the issue directly, take advantage of it. We'll write an editorial that recaps the whole Pulitzer mess and puts it in a new light."

"Let it lie, Harry."

His eyes followed me as I paced the room.

"Everybody makes mistakes, Ben. These are the 1990s. We live in the era of Ollie North and Marion Barry. Michael Jackson, Tonya Harding. O.J., for Christ's sake. If they're entitled to another chance, so are you."

I whirled to face him, using my words like a whip.

"Don't you get it, Harry? I don't want another chance."

I saw him wince, and had to look away.

I ran a hand across my chin, feeling thick stubble. The last time I'd been at the market I'd come up short of cash, forced to choose between wine and razor blades; it hadn't been a difficult decision. I couldn't remember when I'd showered last, either, and wondered if I smelled as bad as I looked.

"Listen," I said, "I just want to be left alone."

Harry's eyes scanned the unkempt room.

"To do what? Rot in this dump?"

If he meant to get under my skin, he succeeded.

"Jacques lived in this dump for nine years," I said, letting my anger out slowly, like dangerous radiator steam. "He wrote some of his best poetry in this dump."

Then, to make Harry squirm a little: "We made love a couple of hundred times in this dump. This was his home, Harry."

I didn't expect him to apologize; it wasn't Harry's style. But beneath his emotional armor, Harry Brofsky was a decent man. When he spoke again, his tone was soft, almost comforting.

"We'll bring you back slowly, Ben. An occasional freelance assignment. No big investigative pieces, nothing heavy. Until readers get accustomed to your byline again."

"You're not listening to me, Harry."

"Benjamin Justice."

He spoke my name forcefully, letting it hang there. The last time I'd heard my full name spoken aloud had been on TV and radio news reports, right after the scandal had broken.

"Readers used to look for that byline, Ben. It meant something. It can mean something again."

I hadn't seen Harry so worked up since the day the Pulitzer was first announced. Then, it had been jubilation. Now, it had the unsettling feeling of desperation about it.

"I'm not a reporter anymore, Harry."

"You'll always be a reporter, dammit."

"The fire's gone."

"It's never completely gone."

He sounded as if he was trying to convince himself as much as me.

"Forget it, Harry. It's not going to happen."

Our eyes met, longer than before. Then he sighed heavily and turned away, his shoulders slumping so that he became pear-shaped.

I looked beyond him, out the window, and down at the house. Fred, a retired truck driver, was away on a fishing trip. Maurice, home from teaching classical dance, had decided to weed the front garden. After eating, the cats had wandered out to be near him, sitting in the shade like three overfed supervisors while Maurice toiled on his knees.

He was somewhere in his sixties, slim and graceful, a beautiful old man. His long white hair was soft and silken, held back with a lavender bandanna. Bracelets and rings festooned his bony wrists and fingers like those of a gypsy. From time to time, he glanced appreciatively at younger men in shorts as they walked briskly by, heading down to the bars and gyms. It wasn't yet evening, but warm weather drew men out of the neighborhood early and down to the boulevard in swarms, like June bugs. That's when Maurice liked to do his gardening; he especially admired legs.

"You must be doing some kind of writing," Harry said quietly. "To pay the bills."

"Odd freelance jobs. Press releases, that kind of thing."

"Press releases. Jesus."

I wanted a drink badly now, and for Harry to be gone.

"This isn't just about the Billy Lusk murder, is it, Harry? Or about raising the level of reporting at the *Sun?*"

He waited tensely, like a doomed man about to be executed with the truth.

"You might make some changes at the *Sun,*" I said. "You might even turn it into a halfway decent newspaper, if the electronic superhighway doesn't kill it first. But life can never be like it was, Harry. No matter how much you want to bring the old days back."

"You were the best reporter I ever had."

He turned to face me, raising his voice hopefully.

"You always gave me more than I expected, Ben. You always surprised me. We shook the paper up. We shook readers up. It was a damn good time."

"That was a long time ago."

"You're thirty-seven, for Christ sake!"

"Thirty-eight."

"Do you know how young that is?"

"I can't do it, Harry."

"I'm talking about a fucking sidebar." Bitterness crept into his voice. "A thousand words. A few hours out of your life."

He looked away, reddening, and squeezed out his next words painfully.

"A chance for us to be a team again."

I was reminded suddenly that the newspaper was all Harry had. No kids, no mate, no pets, not even a garden to tend. Then I realized I was probably the closest thing to a son he'd ever known, or ever would; I was surprised I'd never thought of it before.

But there was something else, something Harry wasn't telling.

"What is it, Harry? Why do you want me back so badly? After what I've done to you."

He stepped out on the landing, fought off a coughing spasm, and lit a cigarette.

He smoked awhile, looking north toward the hills that rose up beyond Sunset Boulevard.

"I want you to work with Templeton. Pass on what you know. Leads, sources, document searches, interviewing, rewriting. The whole enchilada. I'll pay you from my freelance budget. There's not much, but there's some."

"From what I've seen, Templeton's doing fine without me."

"I thought you hadn't been reading the paper," Harry said.

Score one for Harry. He turned to face me.

"Alex Templeton has the chance to be as good a reporter as you were," he said.

"That's your department, Harry. You did it for me. You can do it for Templeton."

"I don't have that kind of time anymore. It's not the velvet coffin we worked in at the *Times.*"

"I've heard things aren't so cushy at the *Times* anymore, either."

"I'm still working at a newspaper with a fraction of the budget, where everybody does twice the work."

"I operate solo, Harry. You know that."

"One more shot at the big prize. That's all I want, Ben. A chance to get back on top before it's all over. You can help give me that. But it means you have to crawl out of your hole and rejoin the world for a while."

I felt dread rising in me like nausea.

"I'm sorry, Harry. I can't."

I saw muscles tighten along the jawbone of his soft face, and his eyes turn to cold stones.

Then he spoke the words that for nearly six years I'd hoped I'd never hear from Harry Brofsky.

"You owe me, Benjamin."

Four

WHEN HARRY was gone, I poured a glass of wine and drank it fast, standing right at the kitchen sink.

I began to feel better, and poured a second glass as the six o'clock news was coming on.

There was no hard liquor in the apartment; it was too dangerous to keep around. For self-medication, I relied on an economy jug of white wine kept cold in the refrigerator, with a reserve bottle in a nearby cupboard so that I was never without. It was a gutless drink, no soul or muscle, and I didn't like the thin taste, all of which helped keep my consumption in check.

The City of West Hollywood had cable television, but only if you paid. I adjusted the rabbit ears on Jacques's old TV set and sat through a thirty-second commercial that reminded me we were at mid-summer in an election year. The spot was on behalf of U.S. Senator Paul Masterman, a former lawyer who managed to soften his notorious misogyny and homophobia each time the microphones and cameras were turned his way. I'd once interviewed Masterman about his well-documented record of flip-flopping on human rights issues, a meeting he'd abruptly terminated when my questions had turned toward his history of marital strife, specifically the charges of spousal abuse that his wife had suddenly dropped after he'd offered her an unusually generous divorce settlement.

In the ensuing years, media scrutiny had done some damage to

Masterman's image, but he had still engineered two close reelections. He was the quintessential Nineties politician, a shrewd manipulator of public sentiment who used the medium of television especially well, which was pretty much all that mattered these days.

"Senator Masterman," I said, as his telegenic face appeared on screen. "And where will we find you exploiting misery today?"

His current series of commercials was a brilliant demonstration of cynicism and ambition masquerading as public concern. Each spot found him in a new section of Southern California, delivering a potent anti-crime message targeted at a specific voting bloc, but cleverly fashioned to tap the fear of violent crime that preoccupied a broad cross-section of voters. So far, I'd seen commercials taped at a Jewish convalescent home, where a burglary and murder had recently occurred; at a family-owned Mexican restaurant in east Los Angeles, the site of an armed robbery; and at a barbecue in upscale Malibu, where money was being raised as a reward for the capture of a child molester who was preying on local children.

In the ad airing that night, Senator Masterman stood on a street corner in South Central, the scene of a recent drive-by shooting, with his comforting arm around a weeping black mother whose young daughter had been killed in the cross fire. Like his other spots, this one had been shot quickly and cheaply, with a handheld camera, giving it the look and feel of a news report. It was another deft touch that had kept Masterman even in the polls with his opponent, in what was shaping up as his toughest fight yet to retain his Senate seat. If he repeated his previous pattern of campaigning, he would flood the airwaves during the final weeks with a series of negative ads filled with innuendo and half-truths about the other candidate, winning over as many ignorant or undecided voters as he could.

At 5:59 P.M., *Eyewitless News,* as L.A. print journalists preferred to call it, blasted into my room with shameless electronic fanfare and a blitz of crass promotional teasers for the evening's upcoming stories. Harry had made me promise to tune in. I figured I could give him that much.

The producers led the show with the Billy Lusk murder, starting with old sports footage of Phil Devonshire, when he'd been a money leader twenty years earlier on the professional golf tour.

Then the director cut to a photograph of Devonshire's murdered stepson, zooming slowly in on Billy Lusk's pretty face. It was a head shot, taken from a modeling portfolio, that showed a clean-cut young man with soft blue eyes, an upturned button nose, and a curly crown of hair tinted surfer blond. Completing the portrait was a practiced smile, about as fresh and natural as processed cheese.

In short order, viewers were informed that the victim had died instantly from a single gunshot to the face from a .38 revolver; that it had happened a few minutes past midnight in the parking lot of a gay bar called The Out Crowd; that a teenaged gang member named Gonzalo Albundo was in custody; that Albundo had signed a confession, and was being held on half a million dollars bail.

A shot of The Out Crowd bar was followed by footage of the handcuffed suspect as he was transported from a patrol car into downtown Parker Center for booking. He wore baggy pants but no shirt, just as the detectives had found him at his parents' Echo Park home, and he appeared younger than his eighteen years. He was of medium height but slightly built, his coal black hair cut short and a soft mustache just starting to show against his copper-colored skin. I thought I saw the potential for a handsome face, if he lived long enough for his boyish features to develop, which at that point seemed unlikely.

Then I saw something that caused me to sit forward in the chair, and to feel my first spark of interest in Billy Lusk's murder.

As two detectives led Gonzalo Albundo into police headquarters, he wheeled around to flash angry eyes and shout defiantly at the camera, a brazen display of teenage machismo. But as I zeroed in on those dark eyes, I sensed that Gonzalo Albundo wasn't feeling angry or defiant at all. He looked seriously scared, close to trembling. His outburst was an act, badly performed, and I wondered what that meant.

There was also something else in that brief footage, something insisting to be noticed, that I couldn't put my finger on. And when Albundo was gone from the screen, I found myself seeing the ghost of his image in my head, as I tried to figure out what I'd missed.

Next came a taped interview with Billy Lusk's roommate, conducted in the mid-Wilshire apartment they'd shared for three years.

Physically, the two men couldn't have been more different. Derek Brunheim was tall, husky, and dark-haired, with an oily, pockmarked face and a coarse beard that no razor could hope to even temporarily erase. The news report failed to note his age, and it was difficult to guess. He might have been forty, but Brunheim was one of those heavily bearded, prematurely balding men, not unlike myself, who often appear older than they are.

On-camera, however, a soft-spoken and effeminate manner belied his bearish look.

"Billy had his problems like everyone else," Brunheim told the reporter, "but inside, he was a good person. A beautiful person who didn't deserve to die like that."

The reporter thrust her microphone closer to Brunheim's scarred face, and asked why he thought his friend had been killed. Anger flared in Brunheim's red-rimmed eyes.

"Ignorance, bigotry, intolerance," he said, lisping more heavily as he spoke more rapidly. "What every gay man and lesbian faces every day of their life."

Sixteen seconds of sound bite; for *Eyewitless News,* an in-depth interview. And Billy Lusk was history.

I refilled my glass, grabbed the chair, and carried them out to the stairway landing, where I settled in and put my feet up on the rail to think.

Fred was home from his fishing trip; his mud-spattered Cherokee was parked in the driveway, looking solid and manly, like Fred himself. I could see his bulky form through the kitchen window as he cleaned trout at the sink, while the three cats mewed about on the countertop, sniffing wildly. Maurice puttered around the kitchen behind him wearing a silk robe, fresh from the shower, stopping once to peck Fred on his unshaven cheek. Beethoven's Seventh Symphony ascended from the open windows, and out on the street couples walked their dogs.

I thought of Jacques, because on an evening like this, if we'd been on speaking terms, we would have been out walking too. Sometimes remembering him felt good, but sometimes it came like a stab in the gut, as it did at that moment. I anesthetized myself with more wine, and watched the light change.

Dusk settled over the neighborhood like a veil dropping. The birds became quiet, and the air slowly lost its crackle of heat. Maurice and Fred came out to eat on the patio, with the cats following, and told me there was enough food for another plate. I thanked them but declined.

My thoughts had drifted to Gonzalo Albundo.

I let the news video replay in my head: I saw the suspect handcuffed and shirtless, his brown skin smooth and unmarked; his baggy pants riding loosely on his narrow hips, as he faked a macho swagger; his young face, not quite pretty, not quite handsome, somewhere in between.

Most of all, I saw the terror in his eyes that he'd attempted so manfully to conceal.

Then I tried to envision the inexcusable act of violence to which he'd confessed: the heavy revolver gripped in his slender fingers; the lanky arm extended boldly, just before he pulled the trigger; the mask of hatred on his young face as he blew Billy Lusk away. But no matter how hard I tried, I couldn't conjure up that vision, couldn't make it all fit.

Something was wrong with the picture.

I turned the whole thing over in my mind, formulating questions the cops might have overlooked. They had a prime suspect, identified at the crime scene, with blood on his clothes, who had quickly confessed. It wasn't a situation that would cause an overworked cop to put in much time or thought on the case, especially one who wasn't too concerned if another faggot had been eliminated from the population, or, for that matter, another gang banger.

"Don't do it," I said.

I could feel the curiosity surging through me like a drug taking over.

"Stop now, Justice. Don't get involved."

But it was too late, and I knew it.

I finished off my wine, slipped on an old pair of running shoes, and trotted down the stairs and out to Norma Place. A block east, I reached Hilldale, where I turned right, heading down past well-kept cottages and faded apartments to Santa Monica Boulevard.

At the corner, hundreds of stylish men paraded by like peacocks on their way from club to club. I could feel my heart pound against my chest, as insistent as the dance music that pulsated through a nearby wall.

I sensed a crack in Harry's "cut-and-dried" case, and I knew my mind wouldn't rest until I found out just how significant a crack it was.

Maybe Harry had known that all along, when he'd tantalized me with the background details. It was Harry, after all, who'd pressured me to watch the evening news, knowing that its superficial treatment of the Billy Lusk story would raise more questions than it answered.

Clever old Harry.

I slipped a quarter into a pay phone, punched in his number, and heard him pick up.

"Here's the deal, Harry. I'll help Templeton with research, and I'll offer suggestions as the Billy Lusk story develops. That's it."

It was more than I wanted to give, more entangled than I wanted to become. But Harry was right about one thing: I did owe him, big time. He'd been more than an editor to me at the *L.A. Times.* He'd been my mentor, the one who'd let me find my voice as a writer and my courage as a reporter. And I'd repaid him by filing a series that had won a Pulitzer and then, when my story was found to be fraudulent, had cost us both our jobs and our reputations.

I'd work with Templeton just long enough to pass along what Harry had taught me, so Templeton could take my place and get Harry off my back. Meanwhile, maybe I'd find some answers to the questions about Billy Lusk and Gonzalo Albundo that nagged at me like an unfinished crossword.

Just this once, and that would be the end of it.

Harry tried again to sell me on a sidebar carrying my byline. I abruptly cut him off.

"Take it or leave it, Harry. It's all you're going to get."

He took it.

Five

THE AGREEMENT I'd struck with Harry left my mind jumpy and troubled, and I didn't get much sleep that night.

In the morning, Alex Templeton was on another assignment, with a noon deadline, so our meeting with Harry was set for early afternoon.

I welcomed the temporary reprieve, no longer so certain I could hold up my end of the deal.

I passed the morning in an air-conditioned Century City high-rise, grinding out press releases for a fiftyish lesbian named Queenie Cochran, who owned and operated one of the most powerful public relations firms serving Hollywood's stars. Fortunately, veracity has never been a high priority on most PR agendas, and Queenie had no qualms hiring someone with my blemished reputation.

In practical terms, I worked not for Queenie but for one of her assistants. Queenie had become so influential in the area of media relations, virtually dictating how print editors and TV producers covered her famous clients, that she no longer had time to deal directly with part-time freelance hacks such as myself. That task fell to Kevin, an amiable and efficient young man who moved through Queenie's offices in a classy Electric Wilshire wheelchair, and who was sometimes seen in Boy's Town club-hopping with his Chinese-American boyfriend.

Kevin had the lean, angular looks that invariably stirred my blood, along with the most intense pair of blue eyes I'd ever had the pleasure to look into; the frailness of his paralyzed lower limbs added an erotic dimension that I'd fantasized about more than once. His pleasant personality, however, cooled any genuine romantic heat I might have felt for him. He was much too normal and uncomplicated, with no apparent vices or compulsions other than his singular obsession with James Dean.

Framed photographs of the legendary actor adorned Kevin's desk, lobby cards from *Giant* and *Rebel Without a Cause* hung on his office walls, and James Dean's personal copy of the *East of Eden* screenplay was encased in glass on a side table, along with a 1955 edition of *Daily Variety* reporting the young actor's death. Kevin regarded James Dean as a tragic example of life lived in the Hollywood closet, something of an irony given Kevin's employment in a show business firm that helped create a cover for everything from drug addiction and infidelity to abortions and pedophilia.

For a few days each month, he paid me fifteen dollars an hour to reorganize, tighten, and punch up the rough drafts of the firm's flacks, many of whom were journalism school graduates who lacked the writing skill and backbone to succeed as reporters, and who apparently had never heard the truism, You don't get paid to write, you get paid to rewrite.

That morning, I found Kevin taking a break at his desk, sipping herbal tea and thumbing through a new book of James Dean trivia. He handed me a floppy disc that contained the rough drafts of several press releases in need of salvaging.

"Just do your usual good job," he said, and smiled his implacable smile.

Down the hall, I found an empty desk with a computer, inserted the disc, and scrolled through pages of mangled syntax and ludicrous hyperbole promoting one of the firm's clients, a professional tennis star named Samantha Eliason.

Eliason, who was in the later years of her career and attempting the transition to sportscaster, operated in a circle of attractive and successful lesbians who went to great lengths to keep their sexual orientation a secret from all but their closest friends and colleagues.

During the past year, the tennis pro had been on a mysterious sabbatical from competition and out of the public eye. Office scuttlebutt had it that she had been holed up at an ultra-private clinic somewhere in Europe, returning to the U.S. only recently, which generated rumors of chemical dependency or an emotional breakdown. According to Kevin, only Queenie Cochran, who moved in the same social circles as Eliason, knew the real story.

The press releases I'd been assigned that morning were the agency's latest efforts to convince the public that Eliason was in seclusion writing a book, and to keep her name current until she was ready to resume her highly public profile. Later, Queenie could announce that her client had changed her mind about the book—the kind of lie publicists purveyed as routinely as brushing their teeth.

Personally, I couldn't have cared less where Samantha Eliason was or what she was doing, as long as I got paid for my work. I dutifully polished up a dozen pages of shameless puffery and probable falsehood, taking my time to pad my hours.

Just before lunch, I left an invoice for sixty dollars on Kevin's desk, and had the receptionist validate my parking ticket, saving me the eight-dollars-per-hour charge downstairs.

I ran into Kevin as he wheeled into an elevator on his way to lunch, cradling the trivia book in his lap. We rode down together chatting while I gazed unabashedly into his Paul Newman eyes and secretly wondered who did what to whom when Kevin and his boyfriend were alone and feeling sexy.

"Did you know that James Dean had a heart tattooed on the inside of his thigh?"

Kevin's words came at me out of nowhere, triggering a minor landslide in my memory.

"A tattoo," I said.

"It was up high, hidden by his scrotum, where no one could see it. A doctor discovered it during an insurance physical for *Giant,* but kept it to himself for years."

I heard Kevin only distantly now; my mind was on Gonzalo Albundo and his image from the evening news.

"There was a letter *S* tattooed inside the heart," Kevin said. "Some people think it stood for *Sal.* You know, Sal Mineo, the actor. Of course, it's just hearsay. So who really knows."

I stared down at him, dumbfounded.

"A tattoo," I said.

He nodded. "Isn't that interesting?"

I ran a hand through his shaggy hair.

"Kev, you'll never know how interesting."

The elevator doors opened. Kevin rolled out, turning his wheelchair toward a group of coworkers who were waiting for him in the lobby. I reminded him to keep me in mind for more work, and to leave a message with Maurice if he needed me.

"It would be nice if you got a phone, Ben."

I told him I'd think about it as the doors closed. I pushed the button marked "P2."

In the news footage of Gonzalo Albundo being led to jail, he'd been shirtless, his upper body completely exposed. Ordinarily, gang markings were proudly displayed on the neck or wrist, sometimes the upper arm or chest; I'd covered gang activity for awhile at the *Times* and knew the basic profile. Gonzalo Albundo was supposed to be a hard-core gang banger, a badass *vato,* but there hadn't been a single tattoo marking his smooth, brown skin.

That's what I'd looked so hard for in the video without realizing it, but hadn't seen. Because it wasn't there.

Gonzalo Albundo. No tattoos. Why?

It wasn't much, but it was something.

The underground garage was cool and dim, filled with the squeal of tires rounding distant corners on smooth concrete. I handed over my ticket to an attendant with a thick Mideastern accent, who went to collect my car.

The murder of Billy Lusk was all that occupied my mind now. That, and where my impending appointment at the *Sun* might lead me.

As the attendant brought the Mustang around, my insides felt like walls collapsing, the way they did when I started needing a drink.

The Mustang was a '65 convertible, a classic I'd once restored to mint condition with my early paychecks from the *L.A. Times.* Now the red paint was badly oxidized, the grillwork showed more rust than chrome, and the tattered top fluttered like dead skin. Amid the glistening Mercedes and Lexuses of subterranean Century City, my neglected car reminded me of how far down I'd personally sunk and how little I really cared.

I drove toward the glare of sunlight and back into the heat, wishing Harry had never sought me out, wishing he had as little faith in me as I had in myself. It would have left everything so much simpler.

A minute later, I was on Olympic Boulevard, heading twelve miles east, downtown. Back to Harry's domain. Back to the newspaper world.

Each passing mile took me closer to a place I told myself I didn't want to be.

Yet I could have hit my brakes and turned around at any one of several dozen intersections.

I kept my foot on the accelerator, making every green and yellow light, and running each one that was red.

Six

I EASED THE MUSTANG into a parking space in the southside warehouse district, fed two quarters into the meter, and approached the headquarters of the *Los Angeles Sun.*

The ornate building, one of the most photographed in the city, rose to four stories and covered half a block. It had been an architectural showplace during the *Sun*'s heyday in the 1930s and 1940s; its facade suggested the Romanesque, with an abundance of sculptured corbeling and heavy arched windows supported by twisted columns, and statues of Roman figures gracing the corners of each level.

In the late Fifties, when the *Sun*'s fortunes had begun to decline, so had the upkeep of the building. Now it was faded and shabby; the statues were encrusted with years of pigeon droppings, and its once-proud stonework was marred at street level with graffiti and splashes of urine.

Outside the main entrance, a dozen nicotine addicts huddled, getting their early afternoon fix: management, editorial, and labor, puffing furiously, united for a minute or two by their common craving.

Harry spotted me and emerged quickly from the pack, sucking down a lungful of smoke before flicking his butt toward the curb.

He took my elbow and hustled me into the marbled lobby, as if he was afraid I'd change my mind. I hadn't been inside a newspaper building in half a dozen years, and as I pushed through the revolving doors, I felt a set of muscles tighten somewhere deep in my guts.

I signed in with the guard and rode the elevator up, standing rigidly beside Harry and staring at the tarnished copper doors. One or two passengers glanced curiously at my face, but no one showed any recognition. Maybe they were too polite. Or maybe it just didn't matter anymore.

We got out at the third floor and turned in the direction of Harry's office.

The four-story *Sun* building stood six stories below the highest level at Times Mirror Square, which housed the *Los Angeles Times* two miles north and occupied an entire square city block in the heart of Civic Center. The difference in the size and stature of the two buildings paralleled the difference between the newspapers themselves. The *Times,* with more than a million daily subscribers, was an institution in Southern California, a major force in its political, economic, and social affairs; whether it was a great newspaper was a matter of debate, but not its regional influence. The *Sun,* with fewer than 300,000 regular readers, had a good sports page.

For years, pundits had referred to Los Angeles as "a one-and-a-half-newspaper town," where the *Sun* attracted only two kinds of journalists: young ones on their way up, and older ones on their way down.

"How are you doing?" Harry said.

"I'm all right."

We passed along a corridor of buckling linoleum through the soft side of the paper, where the feature sections were put together, and into the hard-news area.

A couple of dozen reporters sat in their cubicles, separated from one another by sound-absorbent partitions, their ears pressed to telephones or plugged into tape transcription machines. They typed furiously on their keyboards as we went by, fixing their eyes resolutely on their computer screens; no one looked up.

"Fucking computer pods," Harry grumbled, glancing at his isolated reporters. "Nobody talks to anybody anymore, nobody knows anybody anymore. We might as well be toll booth operators."

I followed him into his office, where he picked up the phone and asked Alex Templeton to join us.

The morning edition of the *Sun* lay atop a stack of files on Harry's desk. Templeton's article on the Billy Lusk murder was the lead piece on the front page of part two, the City section. I'd read through it earlier that morning; it was a solid if predictable piece of news reporting, well organized and sharply written. It was also quite a few cuts above the flashy, sensationalist reporting the *Sun* had been known for in recent years, when it had been trying desperately to lure readers away from television and the more staid but substantial style of the *Los Angeles Times.*

Harry was right. Alex Templeton, though just out of graduate school, was a good reporter, with the potential to be very good.

"Benjamin Justice," Harry said, as Templeton entered the office, "meet your new partner in crime."

Alexandra Templeton looked me up and down slowly and critically before uttering a word.

She was a tall, sinewy woman, one or two inches shorter than my six feet, with an almost regal presence. Her beauty was startling: vaulting cheekbones; frank, almost fierce dark eyes; braids of black hair draped dramatically down a long, slender neck; flawless skin as dark and rich as deep obsidian, suggesting the force of volcanic fire beneath.

I put out my hand. She squeezed it perfunctorily, riveting her eyes to mine.

"I understand you're going to work with me on the Billy Lusk story," she said coolly.

"On an informal basis."

"Informal or not, I hope you'll get your facts straight." She narrowed her eyes. "Because making things up isn't my style."

"Templeton, cut the crap," Harry said. "We already talked this over." He gathered up some papers from his messy desk. "I've got a meeting. Get along, OK?"

On his way out, he stuffed some cash into my shirt pocket. "And, you. Get a phone."

When he was gone, Templeton slipped into the big chair behind his desk, leaving me to face her from the smaller visitor's chair.

Behind her, the latest editions of the *Los Angeles Times* were draped over racks for Harry's perusal, along with the *New York Times,* the *Washington Post, The Wall Street Journal,* the *Christian Science Monitor, USA Today,* the *Orange County Register,* and the *Los Angeles Daily News,* which was actually the newspaper of the city's San Fernando Valley.

Templeton looked quite comfortable in a newspaper setting. Barring the obstacles typically faced by those of her race and gender, she could no doubt rise to Harry's level and beyond, if she so desired, at one of the fifteen or twenty major newspapers around the country. That was assuming that printed newspapers survived long enough in the new age of video-shortened attention spans and electronic transmission. But Templeton was also exceptionally attractive, which probably meant she'd follow the dollars and the glory to television, reporting stories in a fraction of the time allowed by print, with a fraction of the depth and complexity, the way most of the world was already getting its information.

"Where should we begin?" she asked, with feigned politeness, folding her long, slender fingers across her lap.

"Why don't you fill me in on the case?"

"There's really not much of a case." She turned each word crisply, with the perfect articulation of someone educated at high-class prep schools. "They have their suspect and a plausible motive. Witnesses have placed him at the crime scene. He's confessed and intends to plead guilty. Open and shut, all the way around."

"You believe that?"

"The police certainly do."

"That's not what I asked."

She hesitated; her eyes flickered, suggesting a mind racing back through a notebook full of details.

Finally, she said, "I don't see much reason to doubt that Gonzalo Albundo committed the murder."

I wasn't sure if the tone in her voice was smug or just supremely confident.

"Weapon?"

"They haven't found one. He apparently disposed of it after fleeing the crime scene."

"Previous record?"

Once again, she hesitated. Then: "I don't believe so."

"You don't 'believe' so?"

She flinched.

"The police didn't mention a criminal record," she said tightly. "Perhaps it was automatically erased when he turned eighteen a few weeks ago. I'll check."

"What about the gang Albundo mentioned?"

"What about it?"

"That's what I'm asking you."

"I'll check into that as well."

She raised her eyebrows and smiled thinly; the expression bordered on insulting.

"Anything else, Mr. Justice?"

"Did the detectives check the boy's hands for powder traces?"

The muscles tightened in her graceful neck, and her eyelids fluttered rapidly. She may have been a good reporter, well educated, smart, ambitious; but she was twenty-five, and she was still green.

"I'm referring to gunpowder," I said.

"Yes, I know what you're referring to." Then: "I . . . I didn't ask them that."

"Well, it's an easy question to overlook," I said, as smoothly as I could. "Especially given the confession."

She sat forward and placed her hands firmly on Harry's big desk.

"Don't patronize me, Mr. Justice. If I make a mistake, I'll live with it."

The remark might have had a double meaning, aimed right at me; or maybe not.

"All right," I said. "I'll be more careful. On one condition."

"Which is?"

"That you promise not to call me Mr. Justice."

She looked at me quizzically, as only someone so young would.

"It makes me feel Harry's age," I explained. "And I'm not quite there yet."

I expected at least a smile; she wouldn't give me even that.

We agreed to address each other by our last names, then spent another twenty minutes discussing the murder of Billy Lusk, choosing our words and tone of voice carefully.

I conceded that Gonzalo Albundo clearly looked guilty, but reminded her that it never hurt to poke around with off-target questions, what Harry liked to call "fishing."

"But if Gonzalo Albundo didn't do it," she asked, "why would he confess?"

"*Why* is always the most interesting question, isn't it? And always the most difficult to answer."

She considered that in silence for a moment; I could almost see the finely tuned machinery turning behind her lively, intelligent eyes.

Then she told me she was working on other assignments, including one that was just breaking, which meant at least one urgent deadline. She'd already asked Harry to give her an extra day or two before filing a follow-up story on the Billy Lusk murder.

"What about the arraignment tomorrow?"

"We'll handle it as a news brief in Friday's paper," she said. "Then go deeper a day or two after that."

We decided that I'd begin gathering background from various sources, so she could put together the perspective piece Harry wanted as soon as she cleared some time.

When it seemed there was nothing more to discuss, I stood up to go. She stood with me, but stayed behind Harry's desk.

"If it were anyone but you," she said, "I wouldn't accept this arrangement."

"I'm not sure I understand."

Her voice and manner, which had been merely cool, dropped toward the arctic zone.

"When I was a freshman in J-school seven years ago, we thought you were hot stuff, Justice. I'm not saying you were the only reporter we admired, or studied. But you got information other reporters just didn't get. You wrote with such authority and commitment. Real passion. In a way, I felt I knew you."

She paused, and for a moment I thought I saw in her eyes an emotion softer than resentment.

"I clipped every major piece you filed for the *L.A. Times,*" she said. "Including the AIDS series."

The AIDS series. Sooner or later, it had to come up.

A chronicle of two men, lovers; one dying, the other caring for him in his final days. A saga not just of the disease and its impact on a particular generation of young men, but *A Story of Love and Loyalty and Loss,* as Harry had summarized it in the deck that he'd inserted just beneath the headline.

"It was the best writing you'd done," Templeton said. "It took readers beyond the statistics, humanized the issues. I was only eighteen, but that series reminded me why I wanted to be a reporter. I clipped it and taped it above my desk in my dormitory room, it was that important to me."

"And then," I said, "it won the Pulitzer."

I resisted the impulse to smile at the irony.

Templeton leaned forward on Harry's desk, closing the distance between us a little.

"I was so happy for you. I celebrated with champagne, and I

don't even drink. I was happy for all of us who care about the truth.''

There was nothing for me to say, except that I was sorry. I preferred to keep quiet and take the punishment. In a perverse way, it felt good.

''And when I found out those two men didn't exist,'' she went on, her voice growing not just icy but tough, ''that you made them up, made the whole story up, I felt betrayed. And I felt more contempt for you than I can ever express.''

''You're doing a pretty good job.''

''When Harry first proposed this arrangement, I flatly refused. I didn't care to be associated with the notorious Benjamin Justice, the reporter who had to give back the Pulitzer prize. But then I realized what I could get out of it.''

''And what's that, Templeton?''

''I'm going to learn everything I can from you. I figure you owe me at least that much.''

''It seems I owe a lot of people.''

''Yes, I think maybe you do.''

I reached for my notebook and jacket. Templeton came around the desk with a big envelope stuffed with her photocopied notes on the Billy Lusk case.

''There's just one thing I've always wondered,'' she said.

''What's that?''

''Why did you do it?''

She wasn't the first person to ask that question. Harry had been the first, followed by countless journalists from around the country and as far away as Australia, whose phone calls I'd never returned.

''Like I said, Templeton, that's always the most interesting question, isn't it?''

''And the most difficult to answer,'' she said, sounding very pleased with herself.

''That's right.''

She handed me the envelope. Her eyes were riveted to mine again, and alive with challenge.

''Maybe I'll try,'' she said.

Seven

I GRABBED a late lunch at Kosher Burrito downtown, paying with some of Harry's cash.

Then I caught a westbound section of the Hollywood Freeway, driving straight into the sun and jockeying for lane position in the afternoon rush.

The Santa Anas were still blowing hot across the city and tearing at the Mustang's battered top. I lowered it and let the air hit me full blast, like a furnace door opening.

My destination was the crime scene at The Out Crowd bar, another mile or two down the freeway. But as I approached Echo Park Avenue, I impulsively swung the wheel toward the off-ramp, heading into the neighborhood where Templeton's notes told me I'd find Gonzalo Albundo's family home.

At the bottom of the ramp, a squat, flat-nosed Guatemalan offered bags of oranges and unshelled peanuts to drivers trapped for a moment in the congestion of cars. I bought a bag of each, using two more of Harry's dollars, and peeled an orange as I drove along the eastern perimeter of Echo Park. Around its steak-shaped lake, stately palm trees were rooted at attention like sunburned soldiers in the blistering heat, standing guard over brown-skinned families who lined the shores with picnic baskets and fishing poles, and ragged transients who slept during the day because it was safer to stay awake at night.

I drifted right onto Laguna Avenue, then followed a network of narrower streets up into the hills. Modest older homes perched on the terraced land, which was supported by rows of low, thick concrete walls, many of them spray-painted with gang symbols or recently whitewashed to cover them over.

The Albundo house was near the crest of West Covington Road. It sat at the center of a hilly triangle bordered by the Hollywood Freeway on the south, Sunset Boulevard on the north, and Echo Park Lake on the west, close enough to Dodger Stadium, I suspected, for the Albundos to hear the cheering crowds on nights when the Dodgers were winning.

I made a U-turn, and angled my wheels into the curb before climbing out.

Nearby, on the flat where the road crested, a '52 Chevy pickup sat on jacks. It was beautifully restored, painted canary yellow, with stenciled detailing along the sides and gleaming moon-shaped hubcaps. Beneath the transmission, someone was wedged face up, their booted feet extended in my direction. I heard the clatter of a heavy wrench, followed by an expletive uttered in Spanish.

Squinting due west through dark lenses, I tried to pinpoint the general location of The Out Crowd. I guessed at less than three miles, no more than ten minutes by car late at night.

Above me, the Albundo house rested at the top of a concrete stairway that had grown crooked over time from the shifting earth and the intrusive roots of an enormous rubber tree that spread out above the house, providing shade. On either side of the steps were terraced gardens of vegetables and roses. The house was a simple stucco, forty or fifty years old but well maintained, with a broad front porch filled with old wicker chairs, not so different from the house in which I'd grown up.

"You need somethin', man?"

The voice came with an exaggerated Mexican accent and a hostile edge from a man in his late twenties whose skin was the color of brown sugar.

He held a beer in his right hand and in the other a greasy crescent wrench that he clutched at a right angle, suggesting trouble. I recognized his pointed boots as the ones that had protruded from beneath the yellow pickup moments earlier. He was a few inches shorter than me, with weightlifter arms but a belly going to fat, and a droopy, sparse mustache. A few thousand beers ago, he'd probably been a good-looking man.

"Do you happen to know Gonzalo Albundo?"

"Yeah, I happen to know him. He's my brother. You a cop?"

"I'm from the *Los Angeles Sun.* The newspaper."

"I know what it is. You think I can't read, man? Because I got grease on me, from workin' on my truck? You think I can't read?"

I glanced at the vintage pickup, propped up on jacks. "Nice machine."

"I'm not in the mood for talkin' cars, dude."

"I'd like to ask you a few questions, then. If you don't mind."

"Why don't you reporters write the truth? That my brother killed a fag that tried to jump his bones, man! You make it out like this dude who got blown away was some saint of the church. He was a fuckin' *puto!*"

He tilted back his head and guzzled the rest of his beer.

"You're saying the killing was justified, then?"

"I'm sayin' I'm proud of my little brother, man. He did what was right. Any fag looks twice at me, man, I do the same thing."

"Why was your brother in that part of town Monday night?"

"It's a free country. He can be where he wants."

"Can you tell me what gang he belongs to?"

"I don't tell you nothin'. Except get your ass outta this neighborhood."

"I thought it was a free country."

He flung the beer bottle to the curb, where it splintered with an ominous tinkling of glass, and shifted the wrench to his right hand.

"You don't want to mess with me, *pendejo.*"

A car door slammed and a woman's voice yelled, "Luis!"

The woman hurried toward us on pumps, clutching a leather briefcase hand-tooled with intricate Mexican designs. Her suit was attractive but all business, and seemed to add height and heft to her slight stature.

"Luis!"

She stood between us, glaring at him with eyes as dark as his, while blood flushed her dusky skin.

"He's from the newspaper," he said, his accent suddenly lightening up to only a trace, like hers. "Trying to get more things to write about *nuestro hermanito.*"

Nuestro hermanito, "our little brother." Which made her the sister of Gonzalo Albundo.

She turned to me with a questioning look. I removed my dark glasses, hoping to appear less guarded.

"I'm from the *Sun.* We'll be doing a follow-up story on the murder."

"If it is murder," she said.

"What else would it be?"

Her brother stepped aggressively toward me.

"I told you, man. Self-defense. What the police would find out if they did their job. But since it's a white dude who's dead, and they got a Chicano to pin it on, they don't do shit."

"They have a confession," I said. "How do you explain that?"

He took another step toward me, almost in my face.

"I don't have to explain nothing!"

"Luis!"

His sister wedged between us. He took a step back, but continued to grip his wrench like a weapon. She turned to me with suspicious eyes.

"Why did you come here? What do you want from us?"

"I wanted to see where Gonzalo Albundo lived."

"For what reason?"

"The more I know about him, the more fair we can be."

I felt her probing eyes on my face, and wondered what she saw that made her relax.

"I'm Paca Albundo, Gonzalo's sister. This is Luis, one of his brothers. The one who doesn't work and likes to make trouble."

They exchanged a flurry of sharp words in Spanish. I was able to make out references to family and honor, but not much else. When she turned back to me, I told her my name.

"Yes. I know who you are."

"How's that?"

"I work as a librarian at the central branch downtown. A Native American specialist, history section. Six years ago, I was finishing up my degree in library science, cataloging stories published in the *Los Angeles Times.* At the time, you were big news."

"You have quite a memory."

"It was your face I remembered. From the TV coverage. There was a great deal of pain in it. There still is."

Luis looked me over, as if he was semi-impressed.

"This guy's a big shot?"

She spoke to him in Spanish again. This time I heard the word *periodista,* for "journalist," and *SIDA,* for "AIDS."

I assumed she was telling him about the series I'd written, because when he looked me over again, he laughed contemptuously.

"Since you know my history," I said to her, "maybe you don't trust me."

"Maybe I don't have a choice."

She smiled like someone who didn't enjoy having so little power, but understood how it worked. She invited me into the house.

"Write about the perverts!" Luis shouted, as we made our way up the steps. "Tell the truth about what happened! Unless maybe you're a pervert yourself!"

Paca Albundo ignored him.

As we climbed, she talked about the terraced gardens, proudly pointing out her father's roses.

Eight

ENTERING the shaded house was like stepping into a deep cave. Window curtains shut out most of the light, and the air was cool.

I smelled soup simmering, maybe a sauce, and heard a television set tuned to a Spanish language station.

Paca Albundo led me through the living room, where an old woman with leathery brown skin knitted while she watched a South American soap opera. She looked up, smiled vacantly, then directed her attention back to the TV.

"My father's mother," Paca said. "She and my grandfather live in the small house out back. My mother's parents are still in Mexico. We go down every year."

"All alive?"

"Three generations. My oldest brother, Ramon, is about to become a father. So that will be four."

We passed down a hallway hung with dozens of family photographs, framed and arranged chronologically to show the children growing up. Interspersed among them were crucifixes and framed verses from the Bible. As we walked, I glimpsed Gonzalo as he aged from a tiny brown cherub to a slim, thoughtful-looking teenager, almost unrecognizable as the boy I'd seen on the nightly news.

"Gonzalo's room," Paca said, when we reached the end.

She stepped in and raised the venetian blinds for light.

"Does this look like the room of a gang member, Mr. Justice?"

I scanned the neat bedroom. An old Fernando Valenzuela poster, curling at the edges and signed by the former Dodger pitcher, was tacked to a wall by the bed. A rock collection filled a corner of the room, each sample labeled in tidy block handwriting. A set of Boy Scout merit badges, including several for first aid, decorated another wall. A personal computer sat on a desk below a shelf heavy with books.

A framed photo also sat on the desk and I again saw the face of Gonzalo Albundo, taken a year or two before. Beside him in the photo was a pretty girl about his age, with fairer skin but similar Hispanic features.

"Gonzalo was the baby of the family, but he wasn't spoiled," Paca said. "He's always been a model son. Not just a good student, but top grades in almost every subject. He wants to be a teacher, like his brother Ramon."

"Maybe he takes after his other brother, Luis."

"Luis has his problems, but he's never been in serious trouble."

"He has a temper. And he's homophobic."

"Gonzalo isn't like that. We're a traditional family, Mr. Justice, but my parents never taught us to hate anyone. And Gonzalo has never been in trouble. You can check."

"We will."

"And when you find out what I've told you is true, will you still believe he could do what the police say he did?"

"It doesn't matter what I believe or what the police say, Paca. Gonzalo said he did it and gave a plausible reason."

The conviction suddenly disappeared from her face.

"I don't understand that. That confession, that talk about a gang. It makes no sense."

She straightened a pile of school papers on his desk. The top sheet was marked with an *A–*, but I noticed the date on it was nearly a year old. Perhaps she'd set all this up, I thought, for a reporter like myself, or for detectives who might return for another visit.

"He was afraid of gangs, Mr. Justice. And he hated what they are doing to our community. I don't know why he said what he did, but I know he had nothing to do with any gang. And I know he didn't kill that man."

"That man's name was Billy Lusk."

"Yes, Mr. Lusk. I'm sorry."

She turned away from me, straightened the pillows, smoothed out a wrinkle on the bed.

"I'm so confused. It makes no sense. Any of it."

"Tell me more about Gonzalo. Any recent sign of drugs, drinking, anything like that?"

"I asked his girlfriend about that. Angela, a very sweet girl."

Paca handed me the photo from Gonzalo's desk.

"They used to be very close. She said nothing like that was happening."

"How long have they been going together?"

"They've been best friends since grade school. Gonzalo was always a happy boy, but shy, very quiet. Angela was the only girl he was ever interested in. We all thought, you know, some day they would marry. Then, about a year ago, he changed."

"When he turned seventeen?"

"About then, yes."

"In what way?"

"He suddenly withdrew from us. From his family, Angela, everyone. He seemed distant, moody. In his own world. He kept to himself a lot, his grades started to slip. Something was bothering him, I could tell. I tried to talk to him about it, so did my father, but it only made things worse. Gonzalo pulled away even more. It was like we were losing him, but we didn't know why."

"Who were his friends? Where did he go when he went out?"

"He didn't have a lot of close friends. Just Angela. Then he didn't even see her. Mostly, he just stayed in his room, reading."

I glanced out the window. The drop to the ground was only a few feet, and the screen was unlatched.

"Did Gonzalo have his own car?"

"Yes. The one they say he was driving the night of the murder. My parents gave it to him for his seventeenth birthday, because his grades had been so good. He had to pay the insurance himself, from a part-time job."

I commented on the heat outside, and asked her if I might have a glass of water, with ice.

She left to get it. The kitchen was all the way down the hall, through the living room and dining room, on the north side of the house. I figured I had close to a minute, and began to quickly but systematically go through the desk and dresser drawers.

I saw nothing unusual and turned to the closet. Shirts and pants, all neatly pressed, hung from hangers; half a dozen pairs of shoes were lined up on the floor. There was nothing remotely resembling gang attire.

I stepped out to the hall and found it empty. I stepped back in, kneeled down, and looked under the bed, but found only more spotless floor.

Then I lifted the mattress.

Tucked deep in the center was a copy of *Frontiers,* a local gay magazine, open to a page of bar listings. Next to it was a package of latex condoms.

I heard a floorboard creak from the direction of the hallway and quickly lowered the mattress.

As I stood and turned, Paca stepped in with a tall glass of water over ice cubes. I sensed from her averted eyes that she'd also seen the items hidden in the layers of her brother's bed but was pretending otherwise.

I drank the water halfway down, then asked her if she thought Gonzalo would talk to me in jail.

"He won't even see us, Mr. Justice."

She went to the bed and straightened out the wrinkles I'd created in my haste. This was a family, I thought, that would prefer to smooth over troubling matters than deal with them directly, if at all.

"I tried to speak with Gonzalo right after his arrest," she said, "but it was like talking to a stranger. He pretended to be so tough, all his talk about a gang, pretending to be a *cholo vago.* But I know my brother. That wasn't Gonzalo."

As we turned to leave, the last thing I noticed was a portrait of the Virgin Mary above the light switch, next to a picture of a praying Jesus.

In the living room, the old woman was still engrossed in her soap opera, talking earnestly in Spanish to the TV as if the characters were real.

"We haven't told the old ones," Paca said. "But they keep asking where he is."

I thought about where Gonzalo Albundo was at that moment, and Paca apparently shared a similar vision.

"He's just a boy, Mr. Justice. Gonzalo won't survive in a place like that."

She opened the door, and sunlight sliced across the dim interior.

"You said you know your brother, Paca."

"Yes."

"Perhaps you know more about him than you're willing to admit. More than you're willing to share with me, or even with your parents."

She dropped her eyes uncharacteristically.

"My mother and father are very religious, Mr. Justice. Their faith, their church, its rules are all very important to them."

"More important than the survival of their own son?"

She looked up at me but said nothing. I thanked her for her help, and said good-bye.

Down on the street, I found Luis Albundo sitting on the hood of the Mustang, flipping the wrench in his right hand, watching me as I approached.

He slid off and stood between me and my car.

"I'm not looking for trouble, Luis."

"Sometimes, trouble finds you, *pendejo,* whether you look for it or not."

The exaggerated accent was back, along with a nasty sneer that was more laughable than frightening. Still, the man had a two-pound wrench in his hand.

"Did you ever stop to think how much damage someone could do with a heavy tool like that, Luis?"

"Yeah, I thought about it."

He flipped the wrench menacingly again, but failed to catch it as it came down. It clanged to the street like a bell chiming to the world what a screw-up he was. As he bent awkwardly to snatch it up, I tried to gauge the depth of his humiliation, and how much more anger it might generate.

"Of course, a real man wouldn't hide behind a weapon, would he, Luis?"

The question cracked his surly facade. He cocked his head and waited.

"I mean, a five-year-old girl could probably hurt me with a weapon like that. Or even a *puto.*"

He slammed the wrench down on the hood, and left it there.

"I don't need no weapon."

He took a step away from the car, closer to where I stood.

"We're two grown men, Luis. This really isn't necessary, is it?"

"I say what's necessary, faggot-lover."

He shoved my chest with both his hands, leaving greasy prints. It rocked me a little, but my feet held.

I figured he was right-handed, from the way he'd gripped the wrench. I also knew that if I shoved him in return, and he came instinctively back at me, his momentum would be moving forward, with his weight on his left foot as he prepared to swing his right fist. The street's slope would propel him forward even more. At least that would be the natural motion.

"What's the matter, Mr. Reporter? All words, no action?"

"Tell me, Luis, how are you with basic physics?"

"What?"

"For example, the laws of gravity."

I thrust my hands hard against his solid chest, moving him back a step or two, then set my feet, with my knees slightly bent and my weight on my toes.

He reacted predictably, coming back fast, planting his left foot as he cocked his right arm. I dropped away to his left, sweeping his foot from under him as I skimmed the ground. In college wrestling terminology, it was known as a single leg pickup. It worked about as well as I'd hoped. His momentum pitched him forward, and he landed flat on his soft belly.

As he started to rise, I mounted him around the waist, like a rider atop a horse, slipping my legs under both of his, then spreading them as I raised my heels back and upward. It knocked his legs out from under him, flattening him again and holding him there.

With my right hand, I drew his right arm into a hammerlock. I snaked my left hand around his left arm, under the inside joint of the elbow, then up around his shoulder, cinching it tight in a hold known as a chicken wing. From there, I reached farther to secure his throat in a chokehold, the only move among the ones I'd just executed that would have been illegal on a college wrestling mat.

He struggled, so I cinched everything up tight, well beyond the allowable limit. It caused him to emit a high-pitched squeal. I lowered my mouth to his ear.

"Old wrestlers get out of shape," I said, "but we never forget our best moves."

He cursed me in Spanish and started squirming, so I cinched the hammerlock up so tight that another inch would have snapped his shoulder blade. This time, the pain was enough to make him scream. I could have broken either of his arms in a matter of seconds, or choked off the blood to his brain. It was a feeling of pure power, and I liked it.

I loosened the chokehold a little, before I started to like it too much.

"I told you, Luis, I don't want trouble. Understand?"

He sank his teeth into my arm, so I cranked up the chicken wing, forcing a thin, constricted sound from his throat and leaving him gasping.

"Don't ever threaten me again, Luis. I'm just as capable of inflicting punishment as you. *¿Comprende?*"

He nodded furiously, moaning; tears leaked from the corners of his eyes.

I let go of him all at once, leaving him facedown in the street to work the painful kinks from his twisted limbs.

I flung the wrench up toward the house, among his father's roses, climbed into the Mustang, and set the odometer at zero. Before pulling out, I glanced at the dashboard clock.

Luis Albundo was in my rearview mirror as I drove away, standing in the street and yelling after me.

"*¡Mata todos los pinches putos!*"

I knew enough street Spanish to make the translation.

Kill all the fucking faggots!

Nine

I DROVE DOWN out of the hills to Sunset Boulevard and a land of bodegas and *tiendas* and *taquerías,* where spirited Latin music drifted from bars and workers poured out of city buses stacked up at intersections three or four deep.

Late afternoon traffic clogged the street, pushing radiators and tempers toward the boiling point. When it came to a standstill, I passed the time eyeing handsome young men as they sauntered by in the crosswalk, their brown faces stained with the sweat of a hard day's work performed for dog's pay, yet somehow radiant with optimism and laughter. All around me on the sidewalks were mothers with children, old people with children, children with younger brothers and sisters, and yet I neither heard nor saw a child crying. It made no sense or perfect sense, depending on how you looked at it.

On the car radio next to me, I heard a Selena tune end and something by Luis Miguel start up. The light changed and traffic moved haltingly again, snaking past potholes deep enough to plant trees in and patches of asphalt made soft like cheese from the heat.

I edged along until Echo Park was behind me and I was into the Silver Lake district. When I saw the side street I was looking for, I forced a left turn through the stream of vehicles and found The Out Crowd a few blocks later.

As I parked across the street, I glanced at the Mustang's odometer and clock: The trip had covered 2.2 miles and taken seventeen minutes and change. I figured that late on a weeknight, when the streets were nearly empty, Gonzalo Albundo could have reached the bar from home in less than half that time and driven back just as quickly. It also occurred to me that his brother Luis could have made the same trip, carrying with him all his homophobic rage, and maybe the .38 revolver that had been used to kill Billy Lusk, but never found.

The Out Crowd was an inconspicuous, single-story place, painted flat black, situated near the end of a long block of warehouses and body shops. Directly behind it, a hard dirt cliff covered with clinging cactus stretched a hundred feet to its rim, where older homes perched precariously, looking out on Hollywood and the more affluent communities beyond. On a rare day like this, when westerly winds blew the basin clean of smog, the clifftop residents could see all the way across the Promised Land to the sea, where the exiled pollution hung like dirty linen on the far horizon.

I sat for a moment in the Mustang and surveyed the crime scene. Strips of yellow tape cordoned off the main parking lot, which was located on the bar's north side. A narrower section wrapped around behind, up against the hard slope. It was on that narrow stretch of asphalt forty hours earlier that Gonzalo Albundo had been spotted bending over the victim's body, before fleeing into the darkness. Or so the witness had told the police.

I wasn't the only one interested in The Out Crowd that afternoon.

As I crossed the street, Senator Paul Masterman stood on the sidewalk just outside the yellow tape, preparing to read lines off cue cards while a handheld minicam recorded his latest anti-crime message.

Masterman had removed his jacket, loosened his necktie, and rolled up the sleeves of his dress shirt to reveal thick forearms burnished with graying hair and a Rolex watch that must have set him back a thousand dollars or two. Under the watchful eye of the director, a female assistant carefully arranged the folds of Masterman's jacket, which he'd hooked on one finger and slung casually over his shoulder. With his luxuriant waves of silvery hair, broad shoulders, and sharply cut jawline, Senator Paul Masterman was a man worth looking at it, and he knew it.

My eyes moved from the senator to an intent young man nearby, who looked away from the activity only long enough to jot notes on a clipboard. Although he was on the wiry side, rather than broad-shouldered and barrel-chested, the resemblance to Masterman was unmistakable. The younger man had the senator's strong facial lines and flinty green eyes, and the same erect bearing that suggested an ease of confidence and authority.

Like Senator Masterman, he'd rolled up his sleeves, loosened his tie, and opened the top button of his shirt. A few strands of golden-brown chest hair curled teasingly at his neck, promising more but not too much. I had considerable trouble keeping my eyes off him.

"Quiet, please," the director shouted. "Everybody settle!"

The assistant stepped forward and held a hinged clapboard in front of the camera, marked with the number "9."

"Masterman gay bar spot, take nine."

With a loud *clack,* she slapped the two sections of the board together and stepped quickly back.

"Here we go!" the director yelled. "And . . . record!"

Senator Masterman peered into the lens, catching the rotating cue cards with the edges of his eyes, reading the copy with expert inflection and flawlessly placed beats.

"This time, violent crime took the life of a young man outside a gay bar. But his tragic death has meaning for us all. Because each of us, no matter what our lifestyle, deserves to live safely, free of fear, free of violence."

On cue, Masterman toughened his tone and posture, and the cameraman did a slow zoom to the senator's rugged face.

"It takes a special person, someone with real guts, to put the punks and thugs in prison where they belong, and return the streets to the decent citizens of our communities. I'm that man. But I can't do it alone. If we're to win the battle, I must have your support.

"Remember, in our fight to take back the streets, *every* vote counts."

He finished by looking steadfastly into the lens, never blinking.

The director yelled, "Cut!" And then: "We'll keep that one. Nice job, Paul."

The assistant handed the senator a cold drink and scurried off. The young man approached beaming, and Masterman put an arm around his shoulders, talking earnestly as they referred to his clipboard notes.

When he looked up again, Masterman noticed me standing a few yards away, my eyes focused not on him but on the younger man beside him.

The senator lifted his cleft chin to peer down at me with undisguised displeasure, and I was reminded of two things: He loathed homosexuals, and he knew I was one.

He took a few steps in my direction until we were face to face for the first time since he'd walked out angrily on our interview nearly seven years before.

"Benjamin Justice, I believe."

He didn't offer his hand, and I didn't offer mine.

"Senator Masterman."

We stepped aside as a grip hauled a light reflector past us to a waiting truck. Around him, a half-dozen other crew members scurried to pack up equipment.

"I don't suppose you're here taping a spot in support of gun control," I said.

"You know my stand on that, Justice."

His voice was faintly amused, but just faintly.

"Guns don't kill people," I said. "People kill people."

"As the vicious murder that took place here so well illustrates."

"As I recall, Senator, you sometimes carry a handgun yourself."

"For self-protection. And with a special permit from the sheriff."

The younger man had been standing a step or two behind the senator, but now moved forward so they were shoulder to shoulder, and the resemblance became even more striking.

"A man in Dad's position gets a lot of threats," he said, confirming their relationship. "He can never be too careful."

"Especially when an irresponsible press goes out of its way to portray me in an unfavorable light," the senator added.

"You seem to have survived."

What little humor had been in his voice was suddenly gone.

"I'll always survive, Justice. Whether the attacks come from the anti-gun crowd or the militant feminists or the proselytizing homosexuals." He smiled like a shark. "Or their media sympathizers."

"Dad?"

The senator reacted like a man being called back from a distant room. He and his son communicated briefly with their eyes before the senator turned back to me.

"Forgive my rudeness. This is my son, Paul, Jr." Pride suddenly softened his face. "Just got his law degree from USC, like his old man. Paul, Benjamin Justice."

Paul, Jr., shook my hand.

"The name rings a bell." His voice sounded cautious, but not unfriendly.

"It carries a certain notoriety," I said.

"Justice used to be a reporter with the *L.A. Times,*" Senator Masterman said. "Until he had a little problem with the Pulitzer committee."

His son studied me closely for a moment, recognition dawning on his face.

"I think I remember. A story about AIDS, wasn't it?"

"I keep running into people with good memories," I said.

"It was a big story on a serious subject. Not something one easily forgets."

"And not every reporter wins a Pulitzer and then has to give it back," the senator added. "Who could ever forget that?"

His son smiled awkwardly and dropped his eyes, a gesture of decency that surprised me. It made me like him a little, despite his bloodlines.

"So what brings you out this way, Justice?" the senator asked. "Don't tell me you're working parking lot security at gay bars now."

"I'm doing some legwork for the *Sun.*"

"Like hell."

"Strictly freelance, Senator. Nothing major."

"You're not serious."

He sounded incredulous. I nodded. His next words came from a clenched jaw.

"Nothing to do with me, I assume. Or I'll damn well stop it right now."

I was reminded that Masterman had social connections with the *Sun*'s publisher.

"You're safe, Senator. I'm working the Billy Lusk story."

"Who the hell's Billy Lusk?"

"Dad." His son gave him a look just short of reproach. "William Lusk is the murder victim. His name was highlighted in the news clippings I gave you this morning."

"Of course." The senator smiled with the ease of a man who

long ago stopped counting the lies he got away with. "I guess it slipped my mind."

Then, without the smile: "I find it hard to believe you're working in journalism again, Justice. Even for the *Sun.*"

Behind him, a crew member removed the yellow tape that surrounded the crime scene. I realized then that it wasn't official police tape at all, but a prop for the TV spot. The police had apparently removed their own tape earlier, considering the investigation complete.

"Just gathering some background," I said. "For Harry Brofsky."

"After what you did to him? He must be a bigger fool that I figured him for."

The senator and I stood eye to eye, two monumental male egos in a showdown that only the senator could win, given my well-publicized debasement.

Then something happened that neither of us expected: For reasons I didn't understand, the senator's son decided to balance the scales a bit, which made me like him a little more.

"Everyone deserves a second chance," he said, fixing his father with clear, unblinking eyes. "Don't they, Dad?"

The senator shifted uncomfortably in his wingtips and cleared his tight throat. I'd never before had the pleasure of witnessing him so unnerved, not even the time I'd grilled him about his messy divorce with a tape recorder running.

"A second chance," he said quietly. I wondered if his history of infidelity and spousal abuse was on both their minds. "Yes, I suppose we all deserve that."

The pride I'd seen a minute earlier transformed his face again.

"You see this kid's talent for diplomacy? When it comes to politics, he won't just follow in my footsteps. He'll leave me in the dust."

He caught his son's neck in the crook of his elbow, pulled him close, and kissed him roughly on one of his well-shaved cheeks.

As I stood there awkwardly, I felt a pang of envy that had nothing to do with the fact that I found Paul Masterman, Jr., so attractive, even likable. It had everything to do with the sudden warmth shown by his father. Maybe I didn't care much for Senator Masterman's politics, and I had no doubt he'd been a bastard as a husband. But any man who showed such open and unabashed affection for his son got at least a token of my admiration.

It troubled me to think what I would have traded, how much of myself I would have given up, for a single moment like that with my own father. I wanted to know how a son reached that place with his father, what the secret was. Most of all, I wanted to know what it felt like. I wanted the senator's son to tell me.

"Senator!"

From a big black Buick nearby, the assistant waved a cellular phone. Masterman excused himself, and I was suddenly alone with Paul, Jr.

Tension more oppressive than the heat filled the space between us. I didn't know what the source was for him—lack of trust, perhaps, since I had once written some damning articles about his father. From my side, it felt charged with sexual desire, along with something deeper and more complicated that I didn't yet comprehend.

"You're probably busy," I said. "I don't want to keep you."

It was the kind of thing we say when we mean just the opposite, and Masterman was perceptive enough to know that.

"I have a minute," he said. His voice was cordial but neutral, giving away little. "Why don't you tell me more about your assignment?"

"It's nothing, really. Background for a follow-up piece." From behind my dark glasses, I studied the pleasing textures of his face, and the way the pattern of his beard accentuated the sharp contours of his chin and jaw. He would have looked good with one or two day's growth, I thought. Especially in the morning, upon waking, in a bed warm with lust. "I'm actually more interested in your father's campaign. You seem pretty involved."

"I wanted some time off before I start preparing for the bar." He shrugged as if it weren't all that important. "Working on the campaign is good experience."

I remembered his mother's charges in earlier years that her then-husband had rarely made time for their son.

"It also gives you a chance to spend some time with him," I said. "That must be nice."

"Are you collecting material for a story, Mr. Justice? Like the one you wrote nine years ago about my parents' marriage?"

"You do have quite a memory, don't you?"

"You really hurt my father with that article. Not just politically, but personally."

"He never challenged me on my facts."

"I guess that makes it OK, then."

"Maybe you were the one it hurt." I saw his eyes shift uneasily. "You must have been, what, nineteen at the time?"

"About that."

"Your father was a public figure, Paul. He was denouncing homosexuals for their immoral lifestyle, coming out hard against crime. So we decided his own philandering and record of domestic abuse deserved looking into. I'm sorry if you got hurt."

His face relaxed, to a smile shaped by irony, and maybe a little sadness.

"I'm actually glad you wrote it," he said. "It made me face some things about him I hadn't wanted to see."

Then, after glancing at the notebook in my hand: "I shouldn't be talking to you like this."

"I'm not here to grill you about your father, Paul."

I tucked the notebook behind me, between my waistband and the small of my back, and left it there.

"Besides," I said, "I'm no longer in a position to get anything sensitive into print. I'm gathering background on a murder case, that's all."

"For a story someone else will write?"

I nodded.

"That must be tough," he said.

"It is and it isn't."

He looked away, as if thinking the situation over. I sensed a need in him to talk, and kept my mouth shut, letting the silence work for me. After nearly a minute, with the tension winding tighter, he turned back to me.

"Even before Dad divorced Mom," he said, "there wasn't much chance for us to be together. It's like you wrote in your article. He always had something more important to do than spend time with his family. Sometimes it was his career. Sometimes other women. I guess that's no big secret, is it?"

"And you resented that. Maybe even more than your mother."

"I wanted more than anything to feel close to him." Emotion found its way into his voice. "I didn't just want it. I *needed* it."

"It's what every son needs."

"Maybe I needed it more than most." He made it sound like a confession. "I acted out in some pretty inappropriate ways."

"So did I when I was younger." I looked straight at him as I spoke, trying to reel him in as close to me as I could. "For the same reasons."

For the first time, I saw trust in his eyes.

"You understand, then."

I nodded, and when he smiled it was like clouds parting.

Suddenly, Paul Masterman, Jr., seemed within reach, *attainable.* The rivulets of perspiration I felt trickling down my sides had more to do now with anxiety than the heat.

I wasn't ready for his next question.

"Are you and your dad on good terms now?"

"Not exactly," I said. I felt, memories rising to the surface like a corpse coming up from dark water. "He's been dead for twenty years."

"I'm sorry."

"I'm not."

It spurted from me like venom, and I instantly regretted it.

"Now it's my turn to be sorry," I said. "You didn't deserve that."

"I'll survive."

"Like your dad."

His smile widened. Things got brighter again.

"Yeah. Like my dad."

Our brief relationship had taken a seismic shift; in a matter of minutes, we'd become friends. At least that was how it felt to me.

I glanced at the crew loading up the last pieces of video equipment and getting ready to move on, then at the senator talking earnestly on his cellular phone.

"He covers a lot of ground, doesn't he?"

"Dad? Yeah. He's amazing."

"So what exactly is it that you do for him?"

"I'm in charge of his schedule. And I scout locations and do the detail work for the TV spots."

"They're very clever."

I tried to keep the sarcasm out of my voice, but I must have failed, because his smile disappeared.

"They help get our message out," he said. "That's the important thing."

His words were those of a future politician, but they sounded awkward and insincere, which I appreciated. Unlike his father, he wasn't all that good at deception yet; maybe there was hope.

I decided to push a little, to see how much hope there was.

"I guess this gay-bashing death is pretty convenient, then."

"How's that, Mr. Justice?"

"Your father's finally found a way to win the hearts and minds of gay voters, while still appealing to the mainstream."

"We weren't hoping that someone from the gay community would become a victim of violence," he said evenly. "But Dad wanted very much to find a way to reach out to gay voters before election day."

"How inclusive. And how smart, in such a tight race."

Caution creased his face.

"You don't like our TV campaign, do you?"

"Not much."

"Tell me why."

"My opinion isn't important, Paul. It stopped being important six years ago."

"Try me anyway."

"The hard truth?"

He nodded.

"The spots are shallow, cynical, and exploitative," I said. "They play on people's emotions while offering not a single specific about how your father intends to implement change. The entire TV campaign is symptomatic of a shabby trend to manipulate instead of enlighten. Your father and every politician like him should be ashamed."

"I see." He peered somberly at me with his remarkable green eyes. "Now tell me how you really feel."

Then the green eyes twinkled, followed by a grin that showed off his perfect white teeth, about as infectious a grin as I'd ever encountered.

We both laughed at exactly the same moment. I hadn't laughed in a long time.

"You're right," he said, growing more thoughtful. "The spots are everything you say they are." The look on his face deepened to a kind of sadness. "And what's worse, Dad knows it."

"Then why does he do it?"

"Because it works. And that's the worst part of all."

I think it was at that moment, as I heard the honesty in his words, that I realized how easily I could fall in love with Paul Masterman, Jr.

"Maybe, when your time comes," I said, "you'll find a way to do it differently."

I felt instantly foolish for trying so hard to make him like me. But I didn't really regret it, either. It felt good, to be taking a chance after so many years. It felt good to want someone again.

"Maybe I will," he said.

Our eyes locked.

It was only a moment, the kind between two men that may not mean much to a straight man but usually means more than it should to a gay man who's had no one in his life for too long, and who suddenly connects with someone in a way that makes him feel no longer alone.

I was about to tell him how much I liked him, to just get it said and to hell with the consequences, when the assistant returned.

She handed him a form to sign, and he turned to go over it while I looked on over his shoulder.

As he jotted his signature, I studied the lovely veins that ran the length of his forearms and stood out prominently on the backs of his hands. I'd always had a thing for well-veined arms. Jacques had made jokes about it during trips back from the hospital, telling me I appreciated good veins even more than his nurses, who always were searching for a new place to stick a needle.

I stared longer and harder than I should have, my eyes eventually going to the papers Paul was signing, and he caught me looking.

He smiled and raised his shoulders in his familiar shrug.

"It's just a form from the city's film permit office, Mr. Justice."

"Actually, I was admiring your ring," I lied.

I braced myself against the tide of disappointment I felt washing over me. "Married long?"

"A year last month." He held up his left hand proudly to show off the gold band. "Our first baby's due in September."

"Congratulations."

"Thanks. It's a girl. Mom's already got the nursery decorated."

The assistant, who was hovering impatiently, reminded him that they needed to stay on schedule. Paul extended his right hand to shake mine.

"I enjoyed talking with you," he said. "It's always nice to get a fresh perspective."

"Perhaps we'll have the chance to do it again."

"I hope so."

I watched him climb into the big Buick with his father, and pull the door closed without looking back.

Then he was gone, like all the other men I'd bumped into in my life who might have meant something but never would.

I went into The Out Crowd to talk to the witness who had fingered Gonzalo Albundo for the murder of Billy Lusk, feeling more than a little unsettled by my encounter with Senator Masterman and his beautiful married son.

Ten

JEFFERSON BELLWORTHY was the kind of man who created an instant and indelible visual impression.

Like Alexandra Templeton, he was African-American, but even darker; his skin had the rich, lustrous look of fine ebony, as if God had performed the final polishing.

Bellworthy looked to be in his early thirties, with a good face, and he stood an inch or two over six feet. His powder-blue nylon running shorts were split up the sides to accommodate massive, muscular thighs, and an apricot-colored tank top showed off a gym-sculpted upper body that could justifiably be called magnificent.

My personal taste ordinarily ran to men with lighter frames. Had he shown the slightest interest, however, Jefferson Bellworthy would have been an easy exception.

He was behind the bar when I entered, toweling glasses that looked tiny and inconsequential in his big hands.

The Out Crowd was air-conditioned and cool, with walls painted flat black, like the exterior. Here and there, a poster promoted an AIDS fundraiser or some other event of special interest to the gay community. A George Michael tune played over the sound system, and at opposite ends of the long bar, two older white men nursed drinks. In a side room, a well-dressed Asian man, thirtyish and nice-looking, practiced pool shots alone, sending balls about the table with clean, graceful strokes. Otherwise, the place was empty.

I slipped onto a bar stool. Bellworthy nodded amiably and asked what I wanted to drink. My rule was no alcohol before 5 P.M. It was close enough.

I ordered white wine and turned my attention to the dapper, dark-haired pool player.

He was close to my height and slender as a reed, wearing a dress shirt and pleated slacks that appeared to be tailored meticulously for his supple body. His necktie, a rarity in any Los Angeles gay bar, was neatly knotted inside a starched collar. As he moved around the table, deftly making his shots, his smooth, angular face remained expressionless. I guessed his background as Korean or Chinese, but I couldn't be sure.

"You a rice queen?"

I looked over. One of the older men had slid onto the stool next to me. He was bald and paunchy, with mottled skin on the backs of his hands and tufts of white hair sprouting from his ears like cotton. He smelled like scotch ordered cheap from the well.

"Rice queen," he repeated. "You know, partial to Asian boys."

Bellworthy placed a cocktail napkin in front of me and a glass of Chablis on the napkin. I laid three more of Harry's dollars on the bar. Bellworthy took two of them away.

"Or maybe you go for older guys," the drunk said, examining me up and down with bleary eyes the way a chef might study a side of beef hanging in a meat locker. "I could sure go for you."

He leaned closer and reached for my knee. I pulled it away, and he caught hold of the rail to keep from falling.

I drank half my wine, slipped off my stool, and carried my glass around to the middle of the bar, where Bellworthy was putting the two dollars I'd just given him into the register.

"I'm Benjamin Justice," I said. "I called earlier today. From the *Sun.*"

"Oh, yeah." He looked me over quickly. "I'm off in a few minutes. We can talk then."

I finished my wine, set the empty glass on the bar, and wandered over to the pool table. The player barely glanced up, continuing his solitary shots. I noticed two empty beer bottles nearby, and next to them, one that was half finished.

He took another shot and looked my way.

"You play?"

"Not really."

He finished clearing the table, caught the cue ball before it dropped, and slipped a quarter into the slot. When the balls clattered down, he collected them, racking them quickly and precisely.

He tipped and drained his bottle, put it aside, and drew the stick back to make another of his perfect strokes. The break was almost surgically clean, scattering balls in all directions and dropping one or two.

"I do not think I see you here before," he said as he moved around the table, sending balls into pockets. Though his English was fairly good, his accent was heavy, softening his diction to an interesting verbal mush.

"I don't get out to the bars much." I added that I was there on business. Not surprisingly, he didn't pry.

A minute later, he asked if he could buy me a drink. It was spoken like proper etiquette, without a hint of sexual interest.

"Thanks. White wine."

His eyes, already sparkling from alcohol, registered surprise.

"You do not look like the kind of man who like the white wine."

"I'm not," I said. "That's why I drink it."

He went away thinking about that and returned a minute later with my wine and a fresh beer for himself.

"To your good luck," he said, and finally smiled a little. His cheekbones arched so high that his eyes seemed to rest on them like dark moons rising over hilltops.

We toasted, touching bottle to glass.

"My name Jim," he said, like someone meeting formally for business. He put out his hand and we shook. "Jim Lee."

I told him my name, and that I thought he was very handsome.

"You very forward." He laughed uneasily and picked up his pool stick. "Americans, they very forward."

Then, diplomatically: "That can be good, sometimes, I guess."

He began circling the table again, chalking his stick between shots, which he continued to make routinely.

I asked him if he came to The Out Crowd regularly.

"I come maybe two or three days in week." The alcohol had begun to erode his diction further, and to loosen his tongue. "I not like the West Hollywood bars. I think here is more friendly."

"Monday nights?"

"Sometimes. Not many people here Monday nights."

"Is that good or bad?"

"That depends on what you want, I guess." He bent over to

better see the line of his next shot. "Sometimes, I like to shoot pool in the day, when it more quiet. At night, they turn the music up very loud."

As he leaned over the table, the thin fabric of his suit pants stretched tight across his backside, revealing the form of his lower body. I imagined my hands around Jim Lee's narrow waist, or sliding up his slender frame.

When he'd taken the shot, I asked casually, "Did you happen to be in on Monday night?"

His eyes searched the table for his next shot, taking longer than before.

"You ask many questions." He glanced over, not so friendly this time. "You policeman?"

"No."

"You say you here for some business." His eyes turned back to scan the pool table again.

"I'm gathering some information for a newspaper. The *Sun.* Do you read it?"

"I read only the Korean papers."

"Yet you speak English quite well."

"I am in this country since I am sixteen. But in our house, we were permit only to speak Korean." He took a shot. His sure stroke was gone, and he missed by an inch or two. "My father, he want to preserve the Korean ways."

"Did you know someone was killed in the parking lot early Tuesday morning? A customer named Billy Lusk?"

"Yes, I hear."

He took another shot, missing badly.

"I just thought you might have seen or heard something."

He stood up, ramrod straight, his head held high. There was an unwavering sense of decorum about him, even if he was unable to look me in the eye, and even while he was on the verge of being drunk.

"As I say before, I not here Monday."

He unscrewed his stick into two sections and placed them in a narrow leather case, which he zipped closed.

"Did you know Billy Lusk?"

"We play pool." He slipped into his jacket and slung the leather case over one shoulder by its strap. "One or two times only."

"Yet you remember his name."

"It the polite way, to know man's name." He shook my hand and said, "Excuse me, please, Mr. Justice. I go now."

I thanked him for the drink, but he was already gliding out. He passed Jefferson Bellworthy coming my way, looking even bigger and more imposing now that he was loose from behind the bar.

"I can talk now," Bellworthy said.

I watched Jim Lee slip through the heavy curtains that protected the entrance to The Out Crowd from the late afternoon sunlight.

A sudden sliver of brightness, and he was gone.

Eleven

BILLY COME IN sometime after eleven,'' Jefferson Bellworthy said. ''Sat at the bar, like usual.''

We faced each other on metal folding chairs in The Out Crowd's office, which occupied a corner of the storage room in the back.

I noticed a gym bag resting atop stacked cases of Bud Light and, next to it, a popular self-help book on anger management.

Bellworthy leaned slightly forward, placing his big hands on the knotted muscles that ran like a network of iron cord through his upper legs. His hands were dark on top, with palms the color of cooked salmon.

''Did you know him very well?''

''So-so,'' Bellworthy said.

''What was he like?''

''Pretty-boy type. The kind you see more of in Boy's Town. You know, real taken with hisself. Always lookin' around, makin' sure people are lookin' at him.''

''Were you attracted to him?''

It wasn't hard to see he didn't like the question.

''He wasn't my type,'' Bellworthy said, tersely. ''Not even close.''

''You said he sat at the bar.''

''Yeah. Near the light, like always, where everybody could get a good look at him. Only this time, he kept lookin' at his watch.''

''Was that unusual?''

"I'd say it was. Billy was more interested in lookin' at other dudes and havin' fun. I don't think time meant a whole lot to Billy."

"Maybe he had an appointment. Or a date."

"Maybe."

"Did he hustle, sell drugs?"

"If he did, he didn't do it here. We don't allow that shit."

"You see him talk to anybody in the bar?"

"Sure. He knew people, he was a regular. And guys were always hittin' on him, he liked that. You know, a tease, a regular little heartbreaker. But you never saw Billy leave the bar with nobody. He was funny that way. He liked to keep his affairs private-like."

"According to the police, he got a phone call right around midnight and left the bar shortly after that."

"That's what Randy told 'em."

"Who's Randy?"

"The night bartender."

"You weren't working that night?"

"I was on the door. That's my usual job. They like a big dude at the door, 'case there's trouble. Not so much from the customers, but from the street."

"They let you tend bar during the day?"

"Right, to learn my drinks. Sometimes I help Randy out at night, if it's busy. But Monday's our slowest night."

"So you work double shifts?"

"Pretty much. I can use the bread."

"And you work out at the gym, too?"

He ran one of his hands over a bicep the size of a healthy cantaloupe.

"That's where I'd be now if I wasn't talkin' to you."

"You must be pretty tired when midnight rolls around, maybe not as sharp as you might be otherwise."

"I can handle it," he said, bristling. "I know what I heard and saw that night."

"OK, after Billy got the phone call, what then?"

"I took a break while he was still on the phone. Passed by him on my way to take a leak."

"That was a few minutes after midnight."

"Must have been."

"What next?"

"So I'm standin' at the urinal, shootin' a bunny. And I hear the gunshot."

"How did you know it was a gunshot and not a car backfiring? Or a firecracker?"

He snorted a little, faintly derisive. "Where I grew up, you learn the difference real quick."

"And you could hear the gunshot over the loud music?"

"The music ain't so loud back there, especially if the door's closed."

"If the door was closed, how were you able to hear the gunshot?"

He suddenly stood up, glaring down at me.

"What is this, man? The fuckin' third degree?"

"Just questions, Jefferson."

His eyes flickered furtively toward the book next to his gym bag. He drew in a deep breath, followed by another, as if he'd practiced it.

He sat back down and took one more deep breath, exhaling slowly.

"OK, ask your questions. Whatever you want."

"Do you have a problem controlling your temper, Jefferson? A history of violence, maybe?"

He tensed, though not as visibly as before.

"You could say I've had some problems in that area. I'm workin' on it."

"You feel any special animosity toward Latinos?"

He glared this time.

"No."

"You sure about that?"

His next words formed a question that provided an answer but also carried a warning.

"I said so, didn't I?"

"OK. So tell me how you were able to hear the gunshot clearly from the closed restroom."

"There's a little window in there. It opens right onto the place where Billy got wasted."

"What happened after you heard the shot?"

"I shook my dick a couple times and zipped up and ran out the back door to check it out. When I got outside, I saw the Mexican kid, whathisname . . ."

"Gonzalo Albundo."

"Yeah, Albundo. I saw him down on one knee, bent over Billy, with his back to me."

"Was he on his left knee or his right knee?"

"His left knee, the one they found the blood on."

"How did you know that?"

His body coiled, and I saw his meaty hands tighten into lethal-looking fists.

"I read it in your newspaper. OK?"

"Glad to see somebody's reading it."

He didn't smile.

"You got any more questions? 'Cuz I got things to do."

"Just before the gunshot, did you hear anything? Something that sticks out in your mind?"

He hesitated, his eyes restless with uncertainty. "Yeah, sort of."

"What was that?"

"I heard Billy, at least I think it was Billy, cry out somethin'."

"Cry out what?"

"It was like, 'Hey, what are you doin'? Come on, man, I wasn't serious, man!' Somethin' like that. You know, real scared. Begging, like."

I sat forward on my chair.

"Did it sound like he knew the other person?"

Bellworthy cocked his head, surprised.

"Yeah, sort of. Like he was . . ."

He broke off, unsure of himself.

"Like he was what, Jefferson?"

"I don't know. Like he was . . ."

"Take yourself back to that moment. Listen to Billy's exact words in your head."

He closed his eyes.

"Like he was what, Jefferson?"

A half minute passed.

Then he opened his eyes and said, "Like he was tryin' to talk his way out of somethin'. Somethin' he'd maybe got hisself into. Maybe too deep."

"Did you tell the police that?"

"No."

"Why not?"

He shrugged his huge shoulders.

"They didn't ask."

Twelve

I FOLLOWED the undulating motion of Jefferson Bellworthy's muscular buttocks through the rear door of The Out Crowd and back into the relentless heat.

It radiated off the asphalt, even in the building's shade, and even as the sun was going down.

As we stepped out, my nose caught the sweet aroma from floral bouquets placed by friends and relatives near the spot where Billy Lusk had died.

On the back wall of the rest room was a tiny window right where Bellworthy had said it would be.

"That's where Billy got it," he said, pointing to the powdery white outline of a human form.

At the edge of the chalked head was a bloodstain the size of a basketball, barely visible after seeping into the gritty blacktop.

"He took it right in the face, straight on," Bellworthy said. "Lookin' right at death when it came at him. He shit his pants, he was so scared. The cops told me that."

I asked a few more questions, and he provided additional details about the night of the murder, but nothing that got me too excited.

"There's one more question I have to ask," I said.

"What's that?"

"Do you own a gun?"

He looked at me hard, more with contempt, I sensed, than anger.

"You think every dude who's black owns a gun?"

"No. Just asking."

"I don't own no gun."

I went back inside and talked to Randy, the night bartender, as he dumped ice into a small sink behind the bar.

He was a lean, well-chiseled 501 clone pushing forty, with short-clipped reddish-brown hair and a trim, thick mustache. He didn't tell me anything new at first, except that Billy had seemed tense, even upset when he'd talked on the phone shortly before he was killed.

I asked about the caller's voice on the other end of the line. "Muffled" was the only description Randy could give me, like the caller might have been talking through a handkerchief.

I thanked him and started to leave.

"There was one more thing," he said.

I came back, opening my notebook.

"When Billy split that night, he left an unfinished whiskey sour on the bar."

"Is there something unusual in that?"

"Not for most guys. But for Billy, it's, what do you call it, outta character."

"How so?"

"Billy never left a drink unfinished, not once in all the times I saw him in here. We used to kid him about it. See, when he was ready to split, he'd always raise his glass and say, 'Waste not, want not.' We figured he did it so people would take one last look at his pretty face. You know, that cute little nose of his raised up in the air while he emptied his glass.

"Anyway, I just thought I'd mention it. Seems kinda funny, if he was takin' off for the night, that he'd leave behind his drink, barely half-finished."

"You think maybe he planned to be gone only a short time."

"Yeah, maybe. You know, maybe to meet somebody outside."

"Somebody who was on the other end of that phone, who might have called to lure him out."

"I'll leave that kind of speculation to the cops." He raised his heavy red eyebrows. "Or you media guys."

I went out the back way and ran into Bellworthy doing the same, with his gym bag slung over one shoulder.

"Thanks for your help," I said.

"Some of your questions I didn't dig too much."

"I noticed."

"I almost popped you one."

"Thanks for sparing me."

He grinned, embarrassed. "Yeah. OK."

"What you told me could be important."

"Yeah?"

"You've got a good mind for observation and detail. Maybe you should have been a reporter."

"Maybe I shoulda been a lot of things."

We crossed the parking lot toward the street, leaving behind the chalk outline of Billy Lusk's body and the fetid smell of cut flowers going bad in the heat.

Bellworthy crowded me with his massive body, and searched my face with his active eyes.

"You don't think somebody else killed Billy, do you? I mean, somebody besides that Mexican kid?"

"I'm not sure, Jefferson."

"But the dude said he did it, right?"

"Stranger things have happened in matters of the law."

He laughed a little.

"You got that right."

As we approached the curb, he looked my body up and down.

"You ain't built too bad, man. You ever in athletics?"

"I wrestled."

"College?"

"Some. You?"

"Football."

"College?"

"Yeah." Then, almost reluctantly: "And a little pro."

"How little?"

"Half a season."

"What happened?"

"Life."

He squeezed my bicep, which was thick but going soft, and pinched me here and there for body fat.

"You need to get under some iron, man. Do some aerobics. Get the fat outta your diet. A few months in the gym, you could be an OK-lookin' dude."

"I'll consider that a compliment, Jefferson."

He laughed.

"No, really. I do some personal training. I'd give you a discount." He grinned. "Sort of as a favor to society."

I laughed for the second time that day and told him I'd think it over. I started across the street, while he headed another way.

As I climbed into the Mustang, I noticed a pay phone on the corner.

It was less than fifty yards away, with a clear sight line to The Out Crowd. If someone had called from that booth, they could have hung up and been across the bar's parking lot within seconds.

Then I noticed a familiar figure huddled in the phone booth's shadow, looking in my direction.

Jim Lee lurched from the shadow toward the car. He clenched a paper bag wrapped around a stubby bottle in one hand, and gripped his coat in the other; half his shirt was untucked at the waist and his tie was loose.

As he staggered up to the car, he tried to pull himself together, which made him look even more inebriated than he was.

"I think maybe you want some company with me."

He slurred his words badly but invested his voice with a sexual frankness I hadn't expected.

I reached across and opened the door.

Thirteen

I KNEW, when I first kissed Jim Lee, that if I were to remember nothing else about him, I would never forget his lips.

They were large, soft, wonderfully succulent.

Freed by whiskey and desire, he used them with a boldness and confidence I hadn't anticipated, smothering my mouth until I wanted to do nothing but give in to him.

"I've known some great kissers, including a few women," I told him later, "but you're in a class by yourself."

We lay naked at perpendicular angles on my big bed, his head cushioned on my hairy stomach.

He smiled a little at my remark and took another slow drag on his cigarette. He was the kind of man who made smoking look almost elegant.

I shifted the pillows behind my head to get a better view of him, and felt myself getting hard again.

His body was long and slender, marked only by a tattooed dagger that decorated one skinny bicep. He was pale and largely smooth, with a few coils of wiry, dark hair sprouting around each nipple. A sparse path of softer hair descended from his navel, disappearing into the canyon below his belly, where the hair became thick and silken and his penis lay limp against a curve of milky thigh, free of the condom I'd removed before washing him clean.

I ran a finger over his chin whiskers, then traced a line up his hairless cheek. He turned his head away.

"What's wrong? You don't like that?"

"It not seem right, men touch like that."

He took a long, uneasy pull on his cigarette.

"Jim, we just spent the last two hours all over each other. My mouth was on every inch of your body, and you tasted most of mine. Or have you already forgotten?"

"That sex. The way you touch now different. It not feel right."

"It's just affection. Physical attraction."

"This new for me." He stubbed out his cigarette in a saucer. "L.A. guys, they move pretty fast."

"Where are you from?"

He hesitated, and when he finally said "Fresno," it sounded like a lie. I didn't believe his true name was Jim Lee, either.

"My family has business there," he said. "I am in Los Angeles only a few months."

"Practically a native."

I desperately wanted to touch him again, to put my hands on every part of him. But I also knew it wouldn't happen.

He'd consumed most of a fifth of Crown Royal, on top of the earlier beer, before finding the courage for our initial embrace. Once started, he'd been wild in bed, half-crazy as he put me on my back and took charge. But now, almost sober again, he was the Jim Lee I'd first met playing pool at The Out Crowd. Reserved, suspicious, afraid of something.

"For someone with so little experience at making love," I said, "you certainly seem to know what you're doing."

"I not say I have no experience making love. Only with the man."

Someone tapped on my door. Jim sat up abruptly.

"Who that?"

"Probably one of the landlords."

I worked my way out from under him.

"They know about you?"

I slipped into sweatpants.

"They're both gay, and they've been together forty years." He looked at me incredulously. "Yes, they know about me."

As I approached the door, I heard footsteps on the stairs outside, going down. I opened the door and found a note from Maurice tucked under an edge of the doormat; Templeton wanted me to call.

I slipped on shoes, told Jim Lee that I'd be gone only a minute or two, then trotted down to the house and tapped on the back door. One of the cats rubbed against my legs, darting in the moment Maurice opened up.

The air inside was heavy with the musky smell of incense. I heard an aria from *La Bohème* playing in the living room, which meant that Fred was probably locked in another room down the hall, watching a boxing match.

Maurice showed me to the phone in the kitchen and withdrew discreetly.

"You asked me to check some facts," Templeton said curtly, when we connected on the phone.

"First, the police won't discuss the matter of powder burns on the suspect's hands, but I'm trying to get some information through department sources.

"Second, Gonzalo Albundo refused to name the gang he belongs to. I have a call out to a priest who works with gangs in the Echo Park area to see if he knows anything, and a couple sources with the LAPD's gang task force unit.

"Third, Albundo has no criminal record of any kind, not even jaywalking. He's totally clean. I also called his school. No truancy. Excellent grades, until they began slipping about a year ago."

"Nice work, Templeton."

"You expected less?"

"Not for a moment."

I asked her to have a librarian at the *Sun* run the name Jefferson Bellworthy through the database research system to see if it turned up in any news stories in recent years. I suggested she connect it with *football* as a subject to narrow the search.

"Anything else, Justice?" Her voice suddenly shifted from businesslike to playful. "Because if there isn't, I have someone waiting in bed."

"So do I," I said.

I heard the receiver click sharply at her end.

When I got back up to the apartment, Jim was dressed. His shirt was again perfectly tucked, his necktie knotted, his black hair slicked neatly down.

I went up behind him and kissed him lightly on the neck, careful not to put my hands on him. As I looked over his shoulder, I saw that he was holding the framed photograph of Jacques.

He glanced back at me without quite meeting my eyes.

"Your lover?"

"He was."

"How long . . ."

"A few years, off and on."

"And where he now?"

"He died, six years ago this Sunday."

I anticipated the questions I was certain he was too discreet to ask.

"Yes, it was AIDS. Yes, I've been tested. No, I'm not infected."

"I sorry, I no have right to ask about him. Or even look at his picture."

He placed it back on the shelf, arranging it exactly as he'd found it.

"You have every right to ask, if only to protect yourself. Although you should never believe the answers. Some people lie, even when they know their lies can kill."

He glanced my way just enough to acknowledge me, without our eyes connecting. It seemed to be a habit of his.

He said, "You not trust people much, I guess."

"Do you?"

He slipped away from me and into his jacket.

"He was Spanish?"

"His father was Caucasian. His mother was Chicana, born and raised here. They were both American."

He glanced back at the photo: the eyes, wide and bright, the mouth shaped by a laugh. I remembered the day Jacques had returned from the clinic, where he'd gone for his test results. "It looks like I've got that Rock Hudson flu that's going around," he'd said, and laughed just before the tears.

"He look like he was nice person," Jim said.

"He was."

Jim went into the bathroom and checked his clothes in the mirror. Then he faced me and shook my hand.

"I go now."

"I'll give you a lift home."

"I take taxi, thank you."

"Where do you live?"

Again, the hesitation. "Koreatown."

"It's late. I'll drive you."

"I be fine, thank you."

I slipped the Crown Royal bottle back into its wrinkled bag and held it out.

"Don't forget your whiskey."

"You keep it, please."

I pushed the bag into his hands.

"If you leave it, I'll drink it. And that wouldn't be good."

We stepped out onto the landing.

The blue-gray leaves of a nearby eucalyptus tree trembled in the warm breeze and gave off their heavy camphor smell. From the house, we could hear the sound of an old Percy Faith LP, complete with needle scratches. I recognized it as "The Theme from *A Summer Place,*" a favorite of Fred's from the early Sixties.

"Can I call you?"

"I sorry," Jim said. "No phone."

He was looking at me again in his peculiar way, with his eyes just off my line of vision.

"How about at work?"

"They no allow personal call."

"Maybe I'll catch you at The Out Crowd," I said, getting the message.

Below, on the candlelit patio, Maurice and Fred danced cheek-to-cheek to the lilting strings of the Percy Faith Orchestra. Jim stared at them a moment, transfixed.

Then he moved down the stairs, holding his head high and his eyes resolutely ahead, as if he found the notion of two men moving so intimately together to be a troubling aberration.

The music suddenly swelled. Sensing motion, I looked away to the patio.

Fred swept Maurice up in his beefy trucker's arms, whirling him around and around in the flickering light. Maurice threw his head back in blissful surrender, his long white hair falling free, a look of pure rapture on his candlelit face.

When I glanced back at the stairway, the man who called himself Jim Lee had crossed the last step and disappeared into the shadows beyond.

Fourteen

THE WINDS STOPPED sometime during the night, and the heat broke before dawn.

I slept fitfully for a few hours, twisting in the single sheet that half-covered me, gripped in a feverish dream filled with flying horses that crashed screaming to earth, desperately flapping wings that no longer worked.

When I woke suddenly, bathed in perspiration, I reached for Jacques until I remembered once again that he was gone. As I settled back down, staring at the ceiling, I could still smell Jim Lee in the sheets and feel the dampness we'd made. But as the minutes passed, it was the image of Paul Masterman, Jr., that fixed itself in my mind.

I wondered if his lovely, well-veined arms were wrapped around his pregnant wife, as their bedroom filled with the same early morning light that was now insinuating itself into mine. I wondered if they made love frequently, and how. I envisioned his body, lean and hard, naked and straining, as he did with his formless, faceless wife what I wished I might do with him.

I finally rolled over on my belly, pressing myself against the mattress in longing that I knew was as foolish and futile as it was aching and intense.

I must have drifted back to sleep, because the next thing I heard was Maurice, tapping lightly outside, then his nimble footsteps on the stairs.

From the window, I saw him hurry down the end of the driveway, where Fred waited with the Jeep running. Then they drove off to their weekly stint as volunteers at the Chris Brownlie AIDS Hospice, where Maurice tended to the needs of the dying, and Fred to the leaky plumbing.

I opened the door to find a tray of coffee, bagels, cream cheese, and fruit, just the way Maurice had so often left one for Jacques after he'd gotten sick. There was even the same little packet of vitamins and a yellow rose, the flower of hope, rising on a thorny stem from a thrift store crystal vase.

I placed the rose between the photographs of Jacques and Elizabeth Jane, then ate, showered, and shaved.

It was almost ten when I drove to the nearest telephone company office, where I used most of Harry's remaining cash to order a phone installed.

I also made two calls. One was to the home of Billy Lusk's mother and stepfather, where I reached their answering machine and hung up without leaving a message. The other was to Derek Brunheim, Billy's former roommate, who told me I was welcome to drop by that morning.

I spent the rest of Harry's money to fill the Mustang's tank, then drove southeast into the mid-Wilshire district, where Brunheim rented an apartment in an elegant older building near the museums.

At the entrance, I ran into a finely dressed, white-haired woman juggling groceries and a set of keys. I held the door open for her and she thanked me, smiling sweetly.

I told her I was there to visit Derek Brunheim, and wondered if she knew him.

"Oh, yes, he's just two units down from me."

She asked if Brunheim and I were friends. I told her I was from the *Sun.*

She frowned, shaking her head.

"It's terrible, just terrible what happened to his friend. Mr. Brunheim was so devoted to that boy."

I offered to carry her bags, and she continued talking as she transferred them to my outstretched arms.

"William liked to sun himself down by the pool—he was very careful about his tan, you know. Mr. Brunheim would bring magazines down, or a cold drink, without even being asked. Sometimes, he'd rub lotion all up and down William's back and legs; he did it with such care."

She pressed knobby, arthritic fingers lightly to my forearm.

"Not that I pry, mind you. It's just that I can see the pool area from my kitchen window, and there are certain things one can't help noticing."

We crossed a flagstone courtyard shaded by towering bird of paradise trees and colorful climbing bougainvillea so thick you could no longer see the trellises. From around a corner came the reverberating hum of a diving board in motion, then the sharp splash of a body parting water. It was all very Southern California, very David Hockneyish, and not at all difficult to picture Billy Lusk lying poolside, sleek in bikini Speedos and languid with thoughts of his own beauty.

"William was under the weather now and then," the old woman went on, as we entered an elevator. "Mr. Brunheim would put aside his work for days on end to tend to him. Nasal problems, for one thing, and not the normal kind."

She lowered her voice to a whisper, even though we were alone.

"We think it was *D-R-U-G-S.* You know, cocaine. But, of course, you hear all kinds of things, so I simply pay no attention to any of it."

We reached her apartment. She turned her key in the lock, opened the door, and took the bags.

"I've also heard that Mr. Brunheim has some health problems of his own, if you know what I mean. But please, not a word about it."

I promised to keep it to myself.

She told me Brunheim's apartment was two doors farther down, and asked me to pass along her sympathies.

"Mrs. Ashburn," she said. "Unit 216."

Fifteen

I PRESSED THE BUZZER outside apartment 220 and heard the yip of a small dog within.

Moments later, Derek Brunheim opened the door. Under one of his corpulent arms was tucked a squirming ball of fluffy white fur with just enough meat on it for a good sandwich.

I told him who I was. He looked me over.

"You'll do just fine, dear," he said, and showed me in.

Brunheim was even bigger in person than he'd appeared during his TV interview, roughly the same height and heft as Jefferson Bellworthy, but without the muscle tone.

A pair of unpressed Bermuda shorts and a faded "Queer Nation" T-shirt barely covered the bulkiest sections of his furry body. His feet were tucked into a pair of blue bunny slippers, and I noticed several purple lesions on his hairy shins. Thick dark curls massed in uncombed tangles around the widening bald spot atop his large head. A dense carpet of beard, probably only one or two day's growth, helped camouflage the craters of his pockmarked face.

As he led me into the apartment, it was with the uninhibited manner of a man who had long ago accepted the effeminacy he was born with, and had no intention of apologizing for it to anyone.

"Forgive the mess," he said, with a wave of one hand across a room that was cluttered but carefully arranged.

He gathered up a stack of bills from the dining room table, along with a set of personal checks designed in pastel floral print.

"I haven't tidied up since Monday," he said, tucking the checks quickly away. "Ordinarily, I'm quite the little housekeeper. But tragedy tends to interrupt one's routine."

We stepped into a musty living room crammed with antique furniture. Crystal or china bric-a-brac filled every nook and cranny. Where there weren't oil paintings and mirrors in grandiose frames, the walls were covered with gay lib posters stretching back to the early Seventies and more recent placards bearing references to ACT UP, the Minority AIDS Project, and the AIDS Healthcare Foundation.

I felt like I'd entered a gay-owned collectibles store on a low-rent stretch of Melrose Avenue; the only thing missing was the Marilyn Monroe memorabilia.

"Those are from my formative years as a flaming firebrand," Brunheim said, when he saw me looking over the posters from the early seventies. "Kicking down the barricades before it became fun and fashionable."

"You don't look old enough to have been involved in the early days of gay lib."

"Bless you, darling."

He threw me a kiss and led me deeper into the apartment. Heavy curtains were drawn closed over the windows, and dim bulbs in ornate lamps cast the room in funeral parlor light.

"In fact," he said, "I was marching in the streets before I turned seventeen. Maybe it was the sight of those hunky cops in those sexy uniforms, as they pummeled us so passionately with their phallic batons."

He motioned me toward a floral print sofa that reminded me of the personal checks I'd glimpsed a moment ago. Hand-embroidered doilies covered both arms, and dainty satin pillows were laid out diagonally against the back like slices of buffet cheese.

"Please, have a seat. Something to drink?"

"Thanks, I'm fine."

He lowered his big body into a hand-carved teak chair that creaked beneath his weight, and placed the dog in a cushioned basket on the floor near his feet, where it stared at me with eyes like shiny black beads.

Brunheim hooked one hairy leg primly over the other, then laid his two hands delicately, one under the other, atop the highest knee.

"I've heard that many people go into a paroxysm of housecleaning when they lose a loved one," he said. "A defensive reaction against grief, something to keep them busy. I used to do that in the early days of AIDS, when friends began to drop like flies. But Tuesday morning, when they called me about Billy, I didn't react that way at all."

Tears brimmed in his puffy eyes, and his voice quavered.

"I went quietly into his room, sat on his bed, and looked at his things. I wanted to see them all one last time, before his mother came and took everything away."

"Margaret Devonshire."

"Yes, Margaret Devonshire." He etched her name with acid. "She was here before noon, the same morning he died. Can you imagine? You learn that your only child is dead and all you think about is raiding the home of the person who put him up rent-free for three years and paid half his bills!"

I'd hoped to look through Billy Lusk's personal belongings; hearing that they were gone was a serious disappointment.

"She took everything?"

"All but a few photos," he said, "and I had to fight for those. Every stitch of his clothes, the stuffed toys I gave him, his electric razor, which was actually mine. The sheets off his bed, come stains and all."

Then, seething: "She even got the picture of Billy and Sam."

"Sam?"

"Samantha Eliason. Billy's best friend. At least, until recently."

"Samantha Eliason, the tennis player?"

"The closet queen of the courts."

Reporters are invariably better off revealing as little as possible about how much they already know, at least until the questioning gets deeper and tougher. I saw no need to tell Brunheim of my tenuous connection to Samantha Eliason through my freelance work at Queenie Cochran's public relations agency.

Instead, I lobbed Brunheim a softball.

"How did Billy happen to be best friends with an internationally ranked tennis star like Samantha Eliason?"

"They met almost ten years ago," Brunheim said, "during the first of Billy's several ill-fated enrollments as a Trojan. I'm referring to the university, not the condom, though, God knows, he's gone through his share of those. Sam was a senior, captain of the women's tennis team. Billy was an eager-beaver freshman, out to meet people and have a good time. I believe they met through a lesbian friend of hers, and I guess they just hit it off.

"Over the years, they spent more and more time together. Billy could play it straight when he had to, and there are those times when a dyke in the public eye needs a male escort to keep the right people fooled. If it had become public knowledge that Sam was a muff diver, she would have lost millions in endorsements."

Brunheim rolled his eyes theatrically.

"Look what happened to Martina! She made millions on the court, but where were all the major endorsement deals? That girl paid dearly for being honest, but at least she has her pride."

I mentioned the photo Brunheim had referred to a minute ago.

"It's a cute shot of Sam and Billy together," he said. "I would have liked to have one, now that he's gone. But they only made two copies, and Billy's mother snatched his off his nightstand when she was here. Sam's got the other one. So that's one keepsake I won't have.

"But at least I salvaged the pictures Billy wanted me to have. They're what really matter."

I followed Brunheim's eyes to a corner Queen Anne tea table, basking like a shrine in the illumination of a Tiffany lamp. Arranged carefully at the lamp's base were a dozen framed photographs of Billy Lusk, posing in dress that ranged from a string bikini to a formal tuxedo. His hair was styled differently for each photo, and tinted varying shades of blonde, but the pretty face was unmistakable, particularly the distinct, upturned nose. It wasn't a face I particularly liked or would have trusted. His eyes seemed earnest but false; they reminded me of billboard blue sky, all surface, with nothing behind them but old advertising.

Each shot was of professional quality, framed in finely crafted silver plate or well-cut crystal that must have cost Brunheim plenty. Yet Brunheim appeared in none of them. In each Billy Lusk was alone, transfixed by the camera's loving eye.

"His mother tried to take those, too," Brunheim said, anger edging back into his voice. "I said, 'Excuse me, Mrs. Devonshire, but Billy gave those pictures to me!' She was gathering them up when I grabbed them away. It got very nasty. We both ended up in tears, screaming terrible things."

"I take it you two weren't fond of each other."

"She hates me. Hated all Billy's queer friends. Couldn't stand the idea that her son was a fag. As if children are born into this world to be exactly what their parents want them to be, instead of the unique creatures God intended."

"There's nothing else of his I might look through? Nothing at all?"

Brunheim smiled mischievously.

"Well, there is another set of photos that I hid away. Billy's 'personal' collection."

He glanced pointedly at my notebook.

"This can't be for the paper," he said.

I folded my notebook away, and he resumed.

"As you know, Billy wanted to be a model. Or an actor, he didn't know which. You know what they're like, those kind. Incredibly vain, but paralyzed with insecurity at the same time. So he went through men the way I go through cherry-filled chocolates.

"The more he had, the better he felt about himself, especially if he was able to seduce a breeder. Of course, it lasted only until the man of the moment was gone. Then Billy needed someone new for reassurance. With Billy's looks, he had no trouble finding willing partners."

"That didn't bother you?"

"My only rule was, never bring them home when I'm here. At least have the courtesy to call ahead, so I can go out."

"There were quite a few, then?"

"He did it with anyone and everyone, dear." The smile that formed on Brunheim's lips seemed shaped by decades of loneliness. "Except, of course, with *moi.*" He reached down for the dog and pulled it into his lap. "Even before I tested positive, when disease wasn't such an easy excuse."

He looked away, fighting his emotions.

"He told me he loved me, of course. Especially when I gave him things. But he said I just wasn't his type."

He found a tissue and dabbed his eyes.

"I'm sorry, Derek."

His head whipped back in my direction.

"Don't feel sorry for me, Mr. Justice! I grew up being an effeminate sissy. I got beat up and called every name there was. I heard the whispers and the giggles behind my back. I was shunned and ridiculed as far back as I can remember—even my parents did cruel things, even if it was unintentionally. And when I got to high school, I had the double curse: a fem with a raging case of acne, a regular Clearasil Queen.

"At that point, you either kill yourself or you get stronger. And, obviously, I'm still here."

I shook my head with admiration.

"You certainly are."

My remark caused him to smile grandly, and his hands fluttered upward.

"Don't pay any attention to me. I go off like that every now and then. I'm just a diva without a stage. Babs without her key light. Bette without the baths."

I glanced at a clock on the wall behind him. It was a few minutes past noon. I needed to hurry him along.

"A moment ago, you mentioned Billy's collection of personal photos."

"Just between us girls?"

"Absolutely."

"Billy had this thing about taking a Polaroid snapshot after every new sexual encounter. Shots of each vanquished lover lying naked on the field of conquest. He's done it for years, and showed me a few of the early ones."

"And these men allowed it?"

"Some wouldn't, especially the straight ones Billy prized so highly. But Billy was nothing if not charming. He told me he made a joke of the whole thing, got them laughing, then snapped a picture off quickly. Or else took a shot of them as they slept in postcoital bliss, totally unaware."

"And where are these photos now?"

"In my storage cabinet in the garage, where his mother can't get at them."

"The spoils of war?"

Brunheim hauled himself up out of the chair and went to the tea table to look down at the framed photos, clutching the dog under one arm.

"You may not believe this, Mr. Justice, but I didn't keep Billy's dirty pictures for myself. Looking at his numerous sex partners causes me no great joy, I can assure you."

He swept his hand like a wand across the photos in front of him.

"I'd rather remember Billy like this. Look at that face, that smile. What an angel. He reminds me so much of the first boy I ever fell in love with, back in the third grade. Back when everything was so . . . different."

"If you didn't keep the other photos for yourself, why did you hide them away?"

Brunheim laughed distantly and stroked the dog.

"To spare his mother the pain of seeing them."

He glanced my way.

"Crazy, isn't it? I can't stand the bitch. For three years, she did her best to insult me, even when Billy had terrible sinus damage from all the cocaine he put up his nose, and I was tending him day and night.

"But as much as I detest her, I still share her grief. And I wouldn't want a mother to have to find photographs like those among her son's things, particularly not at a time like this."

He pressed his face into the dog's fleecy fur.

"I may have a sharp tongue, Mr. Justice. But I'm not an unkind person."

Sixteen

THE CLOCK in Derek Brunheim's living room chimed once.

I'd hoped to be at the *Sun* before the afternoon was gone, but Brunheim was loquacious and highly emotional, and controlling the interview was proving difficult.

I opened my notebook and asked him to tell me how he and Billy had met. I hoped to direct him back to the subject of Billy's private photo collection, without seeming too anxious about it.

Brunheim eased his bulky body into the chair opposite me. The little dog hunkered down in his lap like a pile of white feathers settling, and followed my every move with its beady eyes.

"It was three years ago, a Sunday afternoon tea dance in Newport Beach," Brunheim said. "One of those twinkie conventions where they raise a little money for AIDS and the gym boys parade around, secretly studying each other's pectorals. After awhile, I got tired of all the chatter and took some air on the patio. Billy happened to be out there, and we just started talking. He was adorable beyond description. I would have kept talking to him if the place were burning down."

"Infatuation at first sight?"

"It wasn't just his looks, Mr. Justice. Billy loved to talk and had a wonderful sense of humor. He also had a vulnerable quality, this deep need to be taken care of. I felt close to him right from the start. And before I knew it, he was living with me."

"Considering your feelings, it must have been frustrating, never being intimate with him."

"My relationship with Billy may have been platonic, but it lasted. To me, that's far more gratifying in the long run than enjoying him carnally for a night or two of passing pleasure. Contrary to popular opinion, not every homosexual man behaves like a dog in heat."

He bent to kiss the dog's fluffy white head.

"No offense, Sugar."

"I take it Billy was between jobs."

Brunheim laughed. "Yes, for several years."

"Was he dealing cocaine?"

"If he had been, would you really expect me to tell you?"

"How did he get by?"

"His mother gave him money. And Billy was always able to find someone like myself who was looking for a needy young man to take care of. I just happened to be the last person in his life to fill that role."

He added quickly, "I know what you're thinking. That Billy used me. And maybe that's true. But I used him, too."

He glanced again at my notebook.

"I'd rather you not write this down."

I folded it up, and he continued.

"When we'd be out together, in a club, a restaurant, the opera, people would stare at us. First at Billy, of course, and then at me. Wondering why someone as gorgeous as Billy would be out with such an ugly old queen. But Billy never cared about that. He even held hands with me in public. For all his vanity, he didn't mind that people thought we might be lovers.

"That's what Billy gave me, Mr. Justice. A moment in the spotlight, when I could pretend I was desirable too."

He held his head high and looked at me down the bridge of his long bumpy nose. His voice trembled.

"I'll remember to my dying day what that felt like, Mr. Justice. And I owe it to Billy."

He reached for a tissue, wiped away tears, and blew his nose.

"Now, ask your other questions, and I'll try to be more succinct in my replies. I'm sure you didn't come here to listen to my life story."

I glanced at the clock, then at the list of questions I'd prioritized in my notebook.

''Do you recall anything unusual about Monday night, particularly in the hours leading up to Billy's death?''

''Nothing special. I cooked a nice dinner for us, as I often did. Then did the dishes while Billy napped before going out. He got a phone call around eleven, when I was getting ready for bed. We slept in separate bedrooms, of course.''

''Do you recall who it was?''

''They didn't give a name.''

''Man or woman?''

''It's funny, but I can't really say. Deep enough for a man, but it could certainly have been a woman with a few extra hormones.''

''Samantha Eliason?''

''Possibly. She's rather deep-voiced. But it's difficult to be sure. The voice was indistinct. A bad connection, perhaps.''

''Muffled?''

''Yes, I guess that would describe it. Why?''

''No special reason. Just trying to piece together Billy's last night.''

''If you could, try to put in your story . . .''

''I won't be writing it. I'm just gathering background.''

''Whoever does write it, if they could mention that Billy and I had a nice dinner that night, and spent a quiet final evening together. If they could do that, it would mean a lot to me.''

''I can't promise anything, but I'll try.''

''I'd appreciate it.''

I glanced at my watch. ''Well, I should get going.''

I stood and he did the same.

''Oh, one other thing. Would it be possible for me to see Billy's photo collection—the Polaroids?''

''I don't know, Mr. Justice . . .''

''At the very least, they would indicate the type of man he was attracted to. It might help me know him a little better.''

''I suppose it can't hurt. As long as they aren't published.''

''Even the *Sun* wouldn't print photos of naked men, Derek.''

''I'll look for them after lunch.'' He kissed the dog between its ears. ''Right after Sugar and I take our afternoon walk.''

As I heard Brunheim lock his door behind me, I caught the sound of another door being unlatched down the hall.

Mrs. Ashburn peered out from Number 216.

"Apparently you and Mr. Brunheim enjoyed a nice visit. Nearly two hours, isn't it?"

"He's rather talkative," I said.

She glanced in the direction of Brunheim's door, then lowered her voice.

"I don't suppose he mentioned the arguments."

"Only in passing," I lied.

"It's not something one would want to remember at a time like this. And it's no one else's business, anyway."

"I suppose not."

"They fought all the time, you know. They could really raise their voices, those two. Especially Mr. Brunheim."

"I don't imagine you could make out the nature of their arguments, not from two doors away."

"A time or two, I put my ear to their door. Just to be sure William was safe, of course."

"It's the neighborly thing to do."

"Mr. Brunheim had quite a jealous streak. He couldn't understand why William spent so much time with all those other men, doing whatever it is he did with them, which I certainly wouldn't know about. And not give more of himself, so to speak, to Mr. Brunheim."

She leaned toward my ear.

"I believe the issue was *S-E-X.*"

"How would you characterize these arguments, Mrs. Ashburn? On a scale from irritated to violent?"

"I'll put it this way. There was a time or two when I considered calling 911. Especially that last one. Now, that was a terrible row."

"When was that, exactly?"

"Why, late Monday night, just an hour or two before William was murdered by that gang of Mexicans. That's what makes it so awfully tragic, don't you think?"

"I'm not sure I follow."

"I doubt Mr. Brunheim even had a chance to apologize and make up. Can you imagine the guilt he must feel?"

I rode down in the elevator jotting notes and paused in the courtyard to complete them.

As I scribbled, I sensed movement in a second-floor window, and looked up to see a figure quickly draw back and a curtain fall closed.

I assumed at first that it was Mrs. Ashburn, but when I counted windows from the left, the one with the watcher turned out to be in the apartment of Derek Brunheim.

Out on the street, I climbed into the Mustang and headed toward Wilshire Boulevard.

At the end of the long block, a flashy Celica sedan passed me going the other way. It was new enough that its temporary registration was still affixed to a corner of the windshield.

Behind the wheel, Jefferson Bellworthy drove with such concentration that he didn't notice me.

I swung the Mustang around and followed, stopping at a distance when he parked.

Bellworthy set the car's locks and alarm, then crossed to Derek Brunheim's building.

Moments after he spoke into the intercom, someone buzzed him in.

I had a feeling it wasn't Mrs. Ashburn.

Seventeen

I ARRIVED at the *Sun* at half past two.

Billy Lusk had been dead for roughly sixty-two hours, and Gonzalo Albundo had already been arraigned in superior court, and a trial date set.

Funny, I thought, as I passed the usual cluster of nicotine addicts outside the *Sun,* how the authorities never seem to arrest and arraign wealthy suspects with quite such expediency.

Harry was in the basement composing room, checking early pasteups for tomorrow's pages, but he'd cleared me with the guard. I caught an elevator to the third floor, where I took a seat behind his desk to make phone calls.

In front of me, that morning's *Sun* was open to the story Templeton had knocked out quickly the previous day while I'd begun gathering background on the Billy Lusk case. It was a routine account of a heist in the downtown jewelry district, running twelve inches on page three. Her lead could have been tighter and more to the point; otherwise, it was another solid piece of work.

As I punched in a phone number, I noticed a reporter staring at me from his computer pod through the glass wall of Harry's office.

Apparently, word had gotten around that Harry had me doing some freelance work, because a passing copy messenger sneaked a glance at me as well, before moving on to make her deliveries.

I hung up the phone and stared back at the reporter hard enough and long enough to give him a case of nervous eyes before he looked away. Then I redialed Billy Lusk's mother, Margaret Devonshire.

Once again, I got the Devonshires' answering machine, with a message instructing me to leave my name and number. I didn't want to leave Harry's number, and my new home number was useless until my phone was installed. I hung up again without leaving a message.

My next call was to Southland News Service, which supplied breaking news leads to every significant media outlet in Southern California, both print and electronic. SNS covered the police beat around the clock from the Parker Center press room and had been the first news organization to look into the Billy Lusk murder.

Using Harry's name, I connected with a helpful SNS assistant editor and learned the following: One of their cop shop reporters had arrived for the graveyard shift Monday night at 10 P.M., as scheduled. He'd first learned of the murder around 12:30 A.M., when he'd heard the police radio call come over his squawk box, which had channels for the police, sheriff's and city and county fire departments. Much bigger stories had broken that night, including a major drug bust in the Valley and a four-alarm fire in the downtown garment district, taking most of the reporter's time and attention. He'd gotten back to the Billy Lusk case just before 6 A.M., when his replacement had come on for the morning shift.

She'd checked further with detectives upstairs shortly after seven, but details had still been sketchy; the investigating officers hadn't yet released the identity of the victim or identified The Out Crowd as a gay bar. At 8 A.M., with little more information available, she'd filed a news brief with the SNS main office stating only that a man who appeared to be in his twenties had been fatally shot outside a Silver Lake bar shortly after midnight, and that a suspect was in custody.

The SNS desk editor had put the news tip on the wire a few minutes after that.

At that point, with so few solid details, it had still appeared to be nothing special in terms of news value, just another tawdry murder in a city that averaged two or three a day. Its ethnic, working-class location—"cheap" was the term some editors used—had rendered it even less important. It wouldn't be until hours later, when the victim was identified as white and from an affluent background, that it would be considered worthy of serious coverage.

When I hung up, I found Alexandra Templeton leaning casually against the doorway to Harry's office, watching and listening. A little too casually, to my eye.

She held a big handbag in one hand and a tape recorder in the other, and the odd tension in her face and posture suggested a scene to follow that she'd probably rehearsed.

"Is all this research really necessary, Justice?"

The edge I'd heard in her voice yesterday, and again last night, was gone. She sounded almost playful.

"The story's always in the details, Templeton."

"I think I heard that from Harry. About a hundred times."

"I'm sure you'll hear it a hundred more."

She threw me a smile, which also felt planned.

"Perhaps," I said, "you can tell me how the Billy Lusk story evolved here at the *Sun.*"

"I have to write up the Albundo arraignment. But I guess I can give you a minute or two."

She set her handbag and tape recorder on the floor beside the visitor's chair, and slipped into it.

"From what I understand, the first mention of a gay connection came across the SNS wire just before noon. Harry called me in right after lunch, cleared my schedule for the afternoon, and put me on it."

"Before or after he knew that Billy Lusk had a famous stepfather?"

"Before."

"Good for Harry."

"I made a call to the Rampart Division for some background and was on the crime scene within the hour. Talked with a detective, got a couple leads."

"Bellworthy?"

"He had the day off. I tried calling him at home, but he was out."

"And after that?"

"I did a couple of phoners from my car, got a statement from Phil Devonshire's publicist. When he realized I was writing the story, he wanted me to mention a new line of golf clubs Devonshire's endorsing."

"The tragedy obviously touched him deeply."

"I filed my first draft some time after six, about the time Harry got back from visiting you. We went over my copy, I got a bite to eat, did a rewrite, then gave my revision to the copy desk a few minutes before eight."

"Is that early or late here?"

"Our general deadline for the morning edition is eleven-thirty, but we don't have out-of-state deliveries like the *Times*, so we can do makeovers as late as one or two on breaking news, if we have to."

"Nice to have that extra cushion."

"When you need it."

"Harry tells me you haven't leaned hard on a deadline yet."

The hint of a smile appeared on her lips, hiding more than it showed, and when she spoke again, it was almost a purr.

"What else did Harry tell you about me?"

"Not a lot."

She draped one of her shapely brown legs over the other and adjusted her skirt only slightly.

"Did he tell you that I'm single, unattached, and extremely adventurous in the area of relationships?"

"Harry doesn't talk much about the personal lives of his reporters," I said.

"I guess I'll have to speak for myself, then."

"I'd say you already have."

"Is there anything more you'd like to know?"

She was apparently too new to Los Angeles journalism circles to have heard much scuttlebutt about my private life. Or maybe she really was adventurous and didn't give much weight to sexual preferences.

"Just one thing," I said.

"And what would that be?"

"Can you get me an intern in the next five minutes, cleared for assignment?"

The coy smile disappeared; she uncrossed her legs.

"An intern," she said.

"The best you can find."

She sat up straight, very businesslike, though clearly not happy about it.

"To do what?"

"Make a few dozen phone calls," I said.

"For the feature we're doing? I'm not sure it's warranted."

"Harry said he plans in-depth coverage on the Billy Lusk case."

"Yes, but . . ."

"Is there some reason this story deserves less than our best effort, Templeton?"

"A *limited* effort. There's a difference."

"And why is that?"

"Phil Devonshire's not *that* big a name. Billy Lusk was his stepson, not blood kin. And the victim wasn't noteworthy in his own right."

"I don't see celebrity as the angle."

She frosted over, right before my eyes.

"I'm not sure it's your place to decide what the angle is."

"Tell me, Templeton. If this assignment were about a bunch of racist white kids killing a black man outside a bar in the Crenshaw district, would you dismiss it so lightly?"

She squared her shoulders and folded her fingers primly in her lap, the way she had the first time we'd met.

"I don't think that's fair. Making a comparison between . . ."

"One brutal hate crime and another?"

"Let me rephrase myself." She looked uncomfortable now, trapped. "I don't know that Harry will give us an intern for that much work on this particular assignment. Not with all the election campaigning that's going on."

"Don't worry about Harry. I'll handle Harry."

She rose quickly.

"You're all business, aren't you, Justice?"

"When it feels necessary."

A few uncomfortable seconds passed. Then, she said, "I'll get you your intern."

She pivoted furiously and disappeared back into the newsroom. I punched in another phone number, working down my list.

Harry entered with a cup of coffee while I was on the phone to the campaign headquarters of Senator Masterman.

"Java time," he said, as he had in the old days, and set the coffee near my elbow.

The senator was out campaigning, I was told, and his schedule could not be given out over the phone to just anyone.

"You understand," said an assistant in the publicity office. "Security concerns."

I explained that I was calling on behalf of Harry Brofsky at the

Sun. I gave her Harry's number, asked her to call him directly, and hung up.

"What the hell's going on?" Harry asked.

The phone rang as I pried the lid off my coffee.

"Tell her we're looking for a photo op, but we only have a photographer available for the next two hours."

Harry gave me a look as the phone rang again.

"Please, Harry, just do it."

I picked up the phone and held it out. He muttered under his breath, took the phone, spoke to the assistant, and jotted down information in the narrow pages of an Eastman Reporter's Notebook.

A minute later he hung up.

"Coffee to your liking?"

"Fine."

"I could get you more sugar."

"It's perfect, Harry. You were always very good with coffee."

"That's what I'm here for, Benjamin. To serve your every need."

"You want to tell me what you found out?"

He pinned me with eyes that reminded me his patience had limits, but he opened his notebook.

"Masterman's giving speeches in Orange County through the afternoon. Then he's shooting one of his TV spots in Little Tokyo, at a store that got burglarized last week. They're still setting up equipment but figure to shoot late afternoon, early evening."

He looked up from his notes.

"Now, you want to tell me what's going on?"

I held out my hand, open palm up.

He ripped the page from his notebook and handed it to me. On it was an address in Little Tokyo.

I redialed Masterman's headquarters and turned the phone over to Harry again.

"Now tell her you've changed your mind, that you're not sending a photographer after all. Before she contacts anyone higher up."

He looked at me like I'd lost my mind.

"It's ringing, Harry."

He put the receiver to his ear, got the publicity assistant, asked her to ignore their previous conversation, and hung up again.

"Now that we've finished that little exercise," Harry said, "perhaps you'd like to fill me in."

I sipped some coffee and asked him what he was doing for dinner.

"The same thing I always do for dinner. Grabbing some Wendy's and watching CNN."

Templeton entered the office with an intern in tow.

"Not tonight," I told Harry. "Tonight you're taking Templeton and me to dinner at the Mandarin Deli in Little Tokyo."

"I have a date tonight," Templeton said.

"Cancel it."

She glanced at Harry for help.

Before he could say anything, I said, "Harry, you look like you need a smoke."

"I'll decide when I need a fucking smoke!"

He immediately muttered an apology to the intern for his language. She was a plump, bespectacled college student who'd arrived in Harry's office with a yellow legal pad and a pen already in hand. It was a good sign.

"Katie Nakamura, this is Benjamin Justice," Templeton said.

Nakamura pumped my hand enthusiastically.

"One of your articles was in a textbook we used at Northwestern. It was really good."

"That's nice, Katie," I said. "Katie, here's what I'd like you to do."

She raised the notepad and poised her pen for dictation.

"I want you to contact every TV and radio station in Southern California."

"Now hold on a minute," Harry said.

I stepped in front of him, blocking his way, and talked fast.

"The library can provide you with a media directory, if you don't already have one. Find out which stations covered the Billy Lusk murder. And if they did, exactly when they identified The Out Crowd as a gay bar and when they first aired the story. Exact times are very important. Got it?"

She nodded confidently but tried to look past me for a sign from Harry.

"Go!" I shouted.

She turned and dashed out.

I could hear Harry hyperventilating behind me.

When I turned to face him, he said, with forced calm, "I know there's a good reason for all this, Ben. I just don't know what it is, do I?"

"Templeton can tell you. This is her story, not mine."

Templeton looked at me questioningly.

"I'm just doing some support work," I added. "She's in charge."

"All right," Harry said, turning toward her. "Why all the research, Templeton?"

She searched my eyes. I nodded, just enough to tell her she already knew the answer.

Then she smiled a little, and her face relaxed. I even thought I saw respect in it.

She laid a hand on Harry's shoulder.

"It's like you always told me, Harry. The story's in the details."

Perhaps Harry was pleased to see Templeton and me finally working as a team. Or maybe he was just tired from a long day's labor that wasn't over. Whatever the reason, he decided not to probe any deeper, at least not yet.

He said to Templeton, "I think you have a news brief to file."

She grabbed her handbag and tape recorder, and winked at me on her way out.

Harry found a cigarette and wet the filter with his lips. Then he narrowed his eyes at me and poked my chest with a stubby finger.

"Watch yourself," he said, and went out for a smoke.

Eighteen

TEMPLETON'S CAR was in the shop, so we rode together in the Mustang across the city's central district to Little Tokyo. Harry was still checking galley proofs and planned to meet us there later.

As I dodged potholes and intersections paralyzed by rush-hour gridlock, I tried to untangle the curious facts and conflicting statements surrounding Billy Lusk's murder and arrange them in my mind so I could see some kind of order, some kind of pattern.

I was fairly sure, from what Mrs. Ashburn had told me, that Derek Brunheim was lying about his relationship with Billy Lusk and what had happened the last night they'd been together. Jefferson Bellworthy had conveniently failed to mention that he was friendly with Brunheim, leaving me to wonder how their relationship figured in all this. Jim Lee was another mysterious element; he'd been uneasy when I'd questioned him about where he was the night of the murder, and admitted that he'd at least been acquainted with the victim.

Then there was Luis Albundo, the suspect's older brother, who obviously had a violent hatred of homosexuals. Was it possible that he'd committed the murder and Gonzalo was willing to take the rap, hoping his youth and clean record would get him a light sentence? Did family ties run that deep in the Albundo family?

"Anything's possible," I said.

Templeton glanced over.

"Were you talking to me?"

"To myself."

"Do you do that often?"

"Frequently."

I slowed for a homeless woman rattling across the street with a shopping cart full of deposit bottles.

"It comes with living alone," I said.

"I live alone," Templeton said. "I don't talk to myself."

"Maybe you do, and you just don't know it."

She shook her head, bemused, and looked out her open window.

The high-pitched sound of *ranchera* music blared from a store along Broadway, where vendors hawked fresh fruit ices to swarms of brown-skinned shoppers. Marquees on what had once been the city's grandest movie theaters advertised church services and swap meets, and there seemed to be a bridal shop on every other corner. Across the street, pedestrians parted as a young man fled through the crowd, while two others chased him, screaming in Spanish.

We soon became trapped behind a line of gaseous buses, pinned in by renegade taxis whose battered fenders testified to the speed with which their drivers raced to pick up fares. I swung right onto Seventh Street, heading east into a section known as The Pit, where a ragged collection of street people slept and vomited and scrounged for drugs and ranted wild-eyed outside firetrap hotels. Each time we passed an alley entrance, we were hit by the stench of stale urine.

I glanced at the handbag resting in Templeton's lap, within easy reach of anyone outside the car.

"It might be wise to roll up your window," I said.

She rolled it up halfway, and asked me what I was thinking about.

"What we talked about before."

"Masterman?"

"And the others."

Back at the *Sun,* I'd given Templeton a thumbnail sketch of the various characters I'd come across in my research, and mentioned my encounter with Senator Masterman and his son at The Out Crowd the previous day. I'd suggested we look as deeply as possible into anyone with a link to Billy Lusk, if only to enrich her background material for the follow-up pieces Harry had promised her she could write. She'd agreed to wrangle a feature story on Masterman's campaign, for purposes of snooping.

After our last meeting in Harry's office, and the rapport Templeton and I had finally hammered out, she'd stopped resisting me. She seemed willing now to follow my lead, or at least to work with me side by side, which included a plan we'd discussed to get her closer to the Masterman camp.

I turned left onto Los Angeles Street, where cardboard boxes lined the sidewalk, serving as nighttime shelters for the homeless. Outside the rescue missions, a few hundred men and women queued up, hoping for a meal and a bed. As I looked them over, it occurred to me how closely I had been to becoming one of them, before Maurice and Fred pulled me back from the brink.

I also realized how radically my life had changed again in the two days since Harry's visit. I was sitting beside one of the city's more promising reporters, on my way to do more digging on a story loaded with possibilities. That it was a story others had written off as finished made it all the more intriguing, and I could feel the old exhilaration building.

Or maybe I was kidding myself.

Maybe I was just experiencing the giddiness and confusion of a puerile crush, as I took advantage of the opportunity I'd created to see Paul Masterman, Jr., one more time.

He stood on the curb outside a Japanese import store as we pulled up on First Street, consulting his clipboard while grips positioned decorative pagodas and hanging Japanese lanterns behind him. A Japanese-American family, presumably the one whose store had recently been burglarized, stood nearby, being prepped by the director.

Templeton and I made our way across between the bumpers of idling cars, catching the attention of the senator's son as we approached.

"Ben," he said, looking up with a gorgeous smile that made me wonder if he could possibly be that pleased to see me.

His eyes were clear and bright under tousled hair, radiating the kind of enthusiasm I'd felt when I'd started out as a cub reporter, the kind I could see in Templeton now, and in the intern, Katie Nakamura.

Maybe that was what drew me to Paul Masterman, Jr., so strongly: a chance to rub up against the idealism and hope that had died in me long ago, in what seemed another lifetime. Or maybe it was my sense that he had been involved in a dark struggle with his father, as I had once been with mine, and had somehow emerged with their relationship, and his own soul, intact, as mine could never be.

Or maybe it was the simple, overpowering pull of lust.

As Templeton and I approached, I looked him over from behind my dark glasses, hungry for the physical details of his body. His belt was buckled at his narrow waist on the third notch, snug against his flat stomach. His necktie was loosened in a preppy way, as it had been when I'd first met him, with the collar open just enough to expose the alluring tendrils of golden hair at his throat. His sleeves were turned up halfway to his elbows, revealing bluish veins that intersected at his wrists so boldly they looked like beautiful scars. I would have given up a week's pay just to touch him, if I'd had a week's pay, and thrown in the Mustang for good measure.

"Hello, Paul."

I shook his hand and introduced him to Templeton, explaining that we were on our way to dinner and had just happened by.

His father came over, as a makeup woman scurried to stay beside him, dabbing at the senator's face with a powder puff.

"Dad, this is Alex Templeton. From the *Sun.*"

The senator's eyes devoured her quickly, the way mine were eating up his son, two predatory men with similar appetites but distinctly different tastes.

"Forgive my chauvinism," he said. "But I always assumed from your byline that you were a man."

He took Templeton's hand.

"Obviously, you're not a man."

He lifted her hand toward his lips. Before it got there, she gently withdrew it.

"Actually, I'm neither." She spoke amiably, almost teasingly, with a smile that was exactly right. "I'm just a reporter, Senator Masterman."

"Touché," Paul, Jr., said.

"Touché, indeed," said the senator.

His eyes roved Templeton's face as he spoke, while sneaking forays to the shaplier territory below.

"Ordinarily, Miss Templeton, I don't enjoy being put in my place. Somehow, you make it a pleasure."

"Believe me, Senator, the pleasure's all mine."

She met his eyes with hers and kept them there.

I waved my hand toward the import store and the props being arranged in front of it.

"I see you've found fertile ground for another TV spot."

Senator Masterman turned his eyes from Templeton to me as if I were a bug that needed swatting.

"As long as crime continues to strike all sectors of the community," he said, "we'll continue to talk about it."

"Any niche voting groups you've missed?"

"I don't see victims as members of target voting groups," the senator said. "I see them as human beings, whose stories deserve to be told."

"And who deserve more protection than they're getting for their tax dollars?" Templeton asked.

"Exactly."

The senator turned back to her, clearly pleased.

"It's an imaginative campaign," Templeton said. "You must be shooting a new spot each week."

"That about right, Paul?"

"Close to that," his son said. "With this one, we'll have half a dozen in the can."

She glanced around at the video equipment and crew members, who scurried about like worker bees.

"In the midst of a campaign, the logistics must be formidable."

"Again, I defer to my son," the senator said.

Paul, Jr., offered us his trademark shrug.

"It's a matter of organization. Having a good crew on call. Then moving fast enough to get the proper clearances and permits from the city."

"It might make an interesting feature," Templeton said. "The anatomy of a unique TV campaign, framed by a single week. Gives us a nice hook."

The senator and his son exchanged a glance, raising their eyebrows.

"What exactly did you have in mind?" the senator asked.

"A behind-the-scenes piece. Lots of color, human interest. Nothing too heavy."

"The *Sun* isn't known for doing anything too heavy," the senator said, grinning. "Hell of a sports page, though."

Everyone laughed but me, and Templeton most of all.

"Why don't we set it up?" She demurely dropped her eyes. "I've never actually interviewed a U.S. senator."

"Forget anything you may have heard," the senator said. He slipped an arm around her shoulders. "I'm a pussycat."

She glanced at his arm but allowed it to stay, as if her submission to his overpowering charms had finally begun.

"There's just one condition," the senator said.

He put his free arm around his son, joining the three of them together.

"I want to be sure you give Paul his due. He's the one who makes all this happen."

Crimson flooded his son's face, and I felt the deep tug of envy again.

"We'll make it a father-and-son story, then," Templeton said. "A story with real heart."

The senator beamed, and with good reason. After his nasty divorce a decade earlier, and a history of escapades with much younger women, his family-values image desperately needed enhancement. Who knew how many votes a story in the *Sun* might turn his way in a close election, particularly a puff job written by a starstruck young reporter?

"I'll have to run it by our campaign manager," his son said. He and Templeton exchanged business cards. "But I'm sure it can be arranged. I'll have a publicist get in touch with you. Now, if you'll excuse us, we have a spot to shoot."

Suddenly, everyone was shaking hands. My precious minutes with Paul Masterman, Jr., so carefully arranged and nervously anticipated, were gone.

"It was nice running into you again." I clasped his hand as long as possible, savoring the contact. "I wish we'd had more time to chat."

"Let's be sure to make time."

My eyes felt locked on his like radar. We must have stood like that longer that I realized, because I suddenly became aware of the silence, and of Templeton and the senator watching us.

I turned to Templeton quickly, trying not to sound flustered.

"By the way, Paul and his wife are expecting a baby soon."

"How nice," Templeton said, and everyone smiled uneasily.

Nineteen

THE MANDARIN DELI was an inconspicuous restaurant on the southern edge of Little Tokyo, located on a narrow side street crowded with sushi and dim sum bars.

During the day, it served as a favorite retreat for editorial staffers from the nearby *L.A. Times* who chose not to drink their lunch at a popular watering hole closer to the office. In the evenings, it was patronized largely by Chinese-speaking customers, who came for the authentic spicy food and modest prices. There were other branches, including one a mile north in Chinatown, but the Little Tokyo location had always been my favorite.

During our years at the *Times,* Harry and I had probably lunched together there a few hundred times. I missed the steamy garlic smell that hit you when you stepped in the door, and the reporters laughing in the booths, and the way the waitresses asked shyly if they were pronouncing English words correctly.

Most of all, I missed those moments with Harry, as we went over stories I was working on, or I threw out ideas for new ones. When we conspired about investigative projects that might have some impact, expose the scoundrels, get the rules changed. When we felt like we were doing something that had some value beyond just filling another news hole, getting out another edition, taking home another paycheck.

That was why I wanted to have dinner that night at the Mandarin

Deli, though I wouldn't have admitted it to Harry, and probably not to myself.

By the time Harry called to say he wasn't going to make it, Templeton and I had already consumed a plate of scallion pancakes and were attacking the main course.

She handled chopsticks as skillfully as she handled horny senators with something more on their minds than media relations.

"I'm not a dainty eater," she warned, digging into a platter of moo shu chicken. "You'll have to fight for your share."

I passed a plate of cold noodles with sesame sauce and told her I thought she'd managed the Masterman situation extremely well.

"Just the way we planned," she said, referring to our scheme to slip her into the campaign, where she could dig around.

She handed across the sautéed spinach, heavy with garlic cloves, and we ate for a few minutes in silence. Once or twice she glanced over surreptitiously. It wasn't difficult to tell she had something on her mind more personal than the Billy Lusk matter.

Finally, she set her chopsticks on the edge of her plate and reached into her big purse.

"I had a research librarian run Jefferson Bellworthy's name through Nexus, like you asked."

She pulled out a computer printout, folded into perforated pages, and glanced through it for the sections she'd highlighted.

"Running back for the University of Tennessee in the early Eighties. Played three years of college ball, one on academic probation. Suspended twice for fighting, once with a teammate, once with a coach. Left school early to sign with the Pittsburgh Steelers."

She turned a page.

"Here's the kicker. Arrested in his rookie year for attacking another man with a knife."

"What was the disposition?"

She scanned the page.

"Never went to trial. Bellworthy pled guilty to attempted murder, spent six years in prison. Never played football again."

She handed the printouts across the table, and I glanced over them.

The news reports were brief, offering scanty details. They alluded vaguely to an "argument that escalated into violence" and resulted in "serious injuries to the victim, who nearly died." According to one article, Bellworthy refused to talk to the press about the matter and was just as taciturn in court, giving no explanation and expressing no remorse for what he'd done.

Then I came to the name of his victim, which meant nothing to me except for its ethnicity: Jorge Sandoval.

Bellworthy had assured me he had no special animosity toward Hispanics. Perhaps not, but he obviously had enough hostility toward at least one Hispanic to nearly kill him. I wondered if he had enough left over to send Gonzalo Albundo to prison for the rest of his life, or even to death row, by fingering him for a crime he may not have committed.

Templeton reached for my cup and filled it with steaming green tea.

"Do you think Bellworthy had something to do with Billy Lusk's murder?"

"I have no idea." I folded the printout and handed it back to her. "But we know he's violent, with a criminal record. He and Derek Brunheim are connected in some way. And Brunheim got into a nasty argument with Billy only hours before he was killed."

"You think Brunheim might have hired Bellworthy to do it?"

"Bellworthy's been working double shifts to make ends meet, so we know he needs the cash. He claims he was in the rest room, alone, when Billy was killed. No alibi there. And he's the only witness to nail Gonzalo Albundo."

"Opportunity, possible motive, violent past," Templeton said.

"At the very least, it raises more questions."

"But if Gonzalo Albundo confessed, I don't see how . . ."

"Neither do I," I said. "But I think I should pay Mr. Bellworthy another visit."

"For God's sake, be careful."

She sounded as if she was genuinely concerned.

"Thanks," I said. "I will."

I raised my tea in a toast to nothing in particular. She raised hers in return, and we exchanged smiles across our tiny porcelain cups.

Then we scraped the remaining food onto our plates, and resumed eating in silence. When I glanced over, I caught Templeton studying my face.

"What's wrong? Grease on my chin?"

I swiped around my mouth with my napkin.

"No, your chin's fine." She smiled oddly. "In fact, you've got a very nice chin."

Her words reminded me that she'd been playing the seductress only a few hours earlier. But there was something more going on now.

"What is it, Templeton?"

She laid her chopsticks aside.

"While I was in the library, I also did some research on you."

"Is that so?"

"I warned you that I was curious." She rummaged in the handbag. "I found some interesting clips."

"Six years ago, it wasn't hard to find my name on the newswire."

"Not just the Pulitzer fallout, Justice. I found something that goes much farther back."

I felt the tension coiling up inside. It made me angry, which made the tension worse.

"How far back would that be?"

"Twenty-one years."

I pushed my plate away and sipped tea, forcing myself to look at her.

"You were seventeen," she said. "And your name then was Benjamin Osborne."

I reached for the teapot, drew it over, but didn't pour. I just stared at it stupidly for awhile. When I finally looked over, she had an Eastman Reporter's Notebook open, the same kind Harry used.

"The article came from the *News* in Buffalo, New York. Your hometown. A reporter there wrote a follow-up piece last year on the twentieth anniversary of your father's death. He traced the seventeen-year-old Benjamin Osborne to the Benjamin Justice who wrote a Pulitzer prize–winning series six years ago at the age of thirty-two."

"How enterprising of him."

"He discovered through court records in New York City that you legally changed your name shortly after your eighteenth birthday."

"I took my mother's maiden name," I said. "I thought it would look good on a byline."

"The reporter also wrote a detailed account of what happened twenty-one years ago, on a Saturday afternoon in late November, in the three-bedroom house where you grew up."

The waitress cleared our plates and disappeared. Templeton continued scanning her notes.

"Your father was a police detective. Homicide. Quite a good one, when he wasn't drinking."

"So people said."

"Some of your neighbors and teachers thought you might become a cop yourself. If only to please him, to win his admiration."

I glanced at a booth across the way, where a little Chinese girl sat on her father's lap, eating chow mein with chopsticks. He was grinning and coaxing her, even when she let the noodles slip back into the bowl.

"They characterized him as a cold, hard man," Templeton said.

"How tactful."

"He was also violent. Mostly at home."

I turned my eyes back to her.

"You're stirring up some warm memories, Templeton."

"I can stop now, if you want."

"No. You did your research. Let's see if you got it right."

She drew in a deep breath.

"Your mother was also an alcoholic. But she was a decent person, from all accounts. She tried courageously to keep the family together, took a lot of abuse."

"She believed in keeping up appearances," I said. "That's not necessarily decency, or courage. Especially when kids are being hurt."

"No, I guess not."

Templeton flipped the page, glancing over the next one.

"As you got into your teens, you started fighting back. You were getting bigger, and when you began wrestling in high school, your father couldn't beat you up so easily."

"No, it took him a little longer."

"Then, one afternoon, a Saturday, you and your mother went to the store. Your father stayed behind with your little sister, watching football and drinking bourbon while she did her homework. According to the article, she was eleven at the time."

"She'd just turned eleven. We'd had a party for her the Saturday before. I've still got a photo."

"On the way to the store, your mother realized she'd forgotten her checkbook. She drove back. As you entered the house, you heard your little sister crying in a rear bedroom."

"So far, so good."

"When you went to check, you found your father molesting her."

"He'd penetrated her. He was halfway in, and still pushing." I saw Templeton wince. "I think that's called rape."

She swallowed hard, turned a page in her notebook, and kept going.

"You attacked him instantly, pulling him off. Your mother went for the phone, to call the police. He grabbed the phone from her hands, started beating her. Worse than he ever had. He said he'd kill her if she told anyone, kill all of you."

"Correct."

"You tried to get him off her, but it was impossible. He kept hitting her, while your little sister cowered in a corner, sobbing."

She looked up from her notes.

"Don't stop now, Templeton. You're almost at the best part. The payoff every reporter lives for."

"You ran into the next room." She recited now from memory, keeping her eyes on mine. "You grabbed your father's police revolver, went back, and killed him. You were never charged. It was ruled justifiable homicide."

"Don't you just love a happy ending?"

"Four years later, your mother died of cirrhosis. You were in college then, studying journalism."

"The University of Missouri, to be specific."

"When she was nineteen, your sister died of a drug overdose. According to the article, she was a promising painter."

"Her name was Elizabeth. Elizabeth Jane. Yes, she was quite a good painter, though she never quite believed it herself."

Templeton slipped her notebook back into her bag.

"I'm sorry, Benjamin."

It was the first time she'd addressed me by my first name.

"Don't be sorry for discovering the truth," I said. "That's what you're trained for, isn't it?"

"That's what we're both trained for."

The waitress inquired politely in broken English if we wanted anything more. Templeton asked for the check, and the waitress went away again.

"I'm surprised there wasn't more written about it at the time," Templeton said.

"Buffalo wasn't exactly the media capital of the country. And child molestation, especially incest, was a taboo subject then. So messy, so upsetting. Not considered fit for conversation or for print.''

I laughed a little. ''Today, they'd make a TV movie out of it.''

''Maybe they downplayed it to spare your sister.''

''Maybe. Or maybe because my father was a cop.''

The check came. Templeton handed over her credit card and the waitress took it away.

Templeton reached across the table and touched my wrist. Aside from a formal handshake, it was the first physical contact we'd made.

''You have no reason to feel any shame about what you did,'' she said. ''You shouldn't have to carry that kind of pain around with you anymore.''

She meant well, but I was tempted to laugh; she was so young and saw things so simply.

She leaned closer, and I felt her hand cover mine. I drew it away.

''He raped your little sister, Benjamin. He almost killed your mother. You had every right to shoot him.''

I smiled, which was unfortunate.

''I didn't shoot my father, Templeton.''

She gave me an odd look.

''I emptied his revolver into him. Then I beat him with the butt end of it until his face was a bloody pulp and I couldn't stand to hear my mother screaming anymore.''

Twenty

I DROVE Templeton home, straight out First Street, watching the pillars of skyscraper light recede in my rearview mirror.

We heard the lonely sound of cars rushing by above us as we passed beneath the freeway, just before First Street merged into Beverly Boulevard and an outbreak of graffiti that lasted for several blocks.

The street dipped and rose and dipped again as it took us through the well-kept neighborhoods of Filipinotown. We passed Tommy's Original Hamburgers with the usual line out front, then crime-ridden Western Avenue, then the quaint Larchmont district near Paramount Studios. Then we were gliding past CBS and the kosher shops in the Fairfax district and the Hard Rock Cafe and angling through the monied elegance of Beverly Hills and over to Santa Monica Boulevard for a straight ride almost all the way to the beach.

We rode with the top down, without speaking.

I tuned the radio to 88.1 and picked up KLON-FM. Miles Davis was blowing an easygoing version of "Bye Bye Blackbird" from the Fifties, with Thelonius Monk on piano.

Templeton tapped time on the cracked dashboard with her long nails, maybe out of feeling for the music, maybe out of nerves over what I'd told her back at the Mandarin Deli.

There was a lot more I could have told her, details she wasn't likely to find in faded press clippings: how I'd tried to stop the police department from giving my father a cop's funeral and when I couldn't, how I'd shown up at the cemetery drunk and cursed my mother for being there, and urinated on my father's coffin until my high school coach and some teammates pulled me away. How I'd finished the wrestling season undefeated, all the way through the state tournament to the final round, tearing through opponents with insane rage; how I'd suddenly walked off the mat, just before my last match was to begin, flipping my finger at the jeering crowd, forfeiting my chance to be state champion. How I'd kept walking, through freezing winds all the way to the Greyhound station, and disappeared on a south-bound bus, finishing my senior year in another state where no one knew my real name. How I'd never gone back to Buffalo, not even for Elizabeth Jane's funeral eight years later, after she'd plunged a hotshot of brown heroin into her veins one lonely Christmas Eve on the roof of a seedy hotel in New York's East Village, where they'd found her body shrouded in snow.

I should have been with Elizabeth Jane that Christmas. I should have been with her instead of putting together another story and dreaming of another byline, as I tried to hide behind a blizzard of facts and figures and other people's clever, quotable words.

I should have been with her every holiday, just as I should have stayed with her after my wrestling season ended so self-destructively, protecting her as she grew up, instead of running away forever. But I was a kid then, and when you're a kid you do things sometimes not because they're logical or proper but because you feel overwhelmed and confused, and most of all afraid, and nothing else seems possible, even if you can't explain why to anyone, even to yourself.

Maybe that's why I understood what Gonzalo Albundo was doing by falsely confessing to the murder of Billy Lusk when no one else understood, or wanted to.

But I didn't tell Templeton any of that, either.

I'd never talked about personal matters with anyone but Jacques, and then only after knowing him for years, and forcing him to suffer the kind of cold, confusing distance to which my father had subjected all of us. But Jacques had been a patient and forgiving man, most of all in matters of the heart; he had waited for me to find the courage to open up to him and risk feeling again, the bad with the good, and when he'd died, four days before his thirtieth birthday, he'd taken all my darkest secrets with him.

As we neared the beach, I turned right off Santa Monica Boulevard at Fourth Street, and left again onto Montana Avenue.

The real money in Santa Monica was north of Montana, with mere affluence and comfy yuppiedom confined largely to the south. Templeton straddled both by living directly on the street of demarcation, though on the north side, which put her just a little closer to the kind of wealth she was accustomed to.

She kept a three-bedroom condominium in the Montana Towers, with a view from her sixth-floor balcony of Palisades Park and the ocean beyond. It was worth roughly half a million, even after the real estate crash of 1990, well beyond the financial reach of newspaper reporters, particularly those at the impoverished *Sun*. Templeton's father, who'd started his career with civil rights cases but was now a corporate attorney, had presented the condo to his daughter as a college graduation gift, with the stipulation that she go on to earn a master's degree from a graduate school meeting his approval. She'd chosen Columbia University, which had been at the top of his list, and become a well-endowed property owner the moment she'd been accepted.

I learned all this in the last few blocks of the trip, as Templeton hastily tried to reveal some of her own personal background, perhaps in an attempt to level things between us.

She went on and on, sounding nervous and defensive, until I grew tired of it.

"Don't blame yourself for having a rich father, Templeton. It can happen even in the best of families."

She stopped jabbering after that and directed me to the Montana Towers. It was a ten-story building that looked like the kind of cushy hotel I'd stayed in only when I was on an expense account. Lush ferns were bathed by amber outdoor lights, and the street was lined with manicured palm trees that stretched several stories high. Even the sidewalks looked freshly scrubbed.

As I pulled to the curb, we could smell the salt air. She told me that her favorite time was winter, at high tide.

"In the middle of the night," she said, "when it's really quiet, you can hear the waves break."

"That's nice, Templeton."

I was weary of being with her, wary of more prying. I wanted to get away as quickly as I could. I wanted a drink.

"Would you like to come in for awhile? I could make some coffee."

Then, as if she'd read my thoughts: "Or pour you something stronger."

"Thanks. I'm kinda tired."

She reached for the door handle but didn't open it right away.

"Tell me, Justice. Do you ever date black women?"

"Never."

Her eyes flared.

"I see."

She opened the door quickly and climbed out.

"No, Templeton, I don't think you do."

She shut the door hard and peered down at me.

"And what does that mean?"

"I've never dated a black woman," I said, "but I have been involved with a black man or two."

Alexandra Templeton was not the kind of person to be easily caught off guard, but that night she looked it.

"You've never been involved with a woman?"

"I didn't say that."

"But you have no romantic interest in me."

"It would complicate things unnecessarily. In a lot of ways."

An older couple strolled past, walking a poodle on a pink leash studded with rhinestones.

"You're really quite beautiful, Templeton. Interesting as hell. Sharp as a tack. The whole package."

"But."

"But there's something I need from a man that I just don't get from a woman. Please don't take it personally."

Given her beauty, as well as her numerous other assets, Templeton probably wasn't accustomed to being rejected. My frankness didn't seem to sit well with her.

"Obviously, I overreached." Her smile was as brittle as her voice. "Thanks for the lift."

She sauntered away rather than hurrying, putting her composure on display.

A uniformed security guard opened the door to the Montana

Towers, tipping his cap. She disappeared inside without looking back.

"Wonderful," I said. "Just wonderful."

The time was 8:45, well past my usual drinking hour but early enough to have a chat with Jefferson Bellworthy, if I could find him.

I drove over to Santa Monica Boulevard through a stream of complacent-looking yuppies headed for chic stores and trendy clubs on the Promenade, and found a pay phone. I called The Out Crowd and got Randy, the night bartender. It was Bellworthy's day off, but I learned that he worked Thursday evenings as a private trainer, and where.

As I climbed back behind the wheel, Peggy Lee was on the radio, singing "Is That All There Is?," so perfect a match between performer and material that it begged to be listened to.

But it was Templeton's warning over dinner that echoed in my head: *For God's sake, be careful.*

I pulled back onto Santa Monica Boulevard, which seemed to run like a thread through my life, and pointed the Mustang toward West Hollywood.

Twenty-one

LE GYM was probably the only fitness emporium in Southern California that featured fresh-cut flowers in the espresso bar, Donna Summer disco classics piped into the jacuzzi and, in the men's locker room, side-by-side cologne and condom dispensing machines.

The sign above the check-in desk read: 2-FOR-1 BUDDY SPECIAL NOW THROUGH AUGUST.

A man and a woman, both young and blandly attractive, checked membership cards as hard-bodied men passed through with gym bags, some in pairs and holding hands. A few women came in as well, but they comprised a distinct minority.

I told the woman behind the desk that I was there to see Jefferson Bellworthy. She checked, told me he was working with a client upstairs, and asked me to wait in the lobby.

I took a spot next to a well-fed Kentia palm, surrounded by wall-to-wall mirrors and bombarded by disco music from an adjacent aerobics room. From time to time, men with forty-dollar haircuts and hundred-dollar gym shoes stopped to appraise their body definition in the spotless glass.

"You decide to tone up?"

I turned to find Jefferson Bellworthy standing over me, his powerful body packed into a skintight spandex gym suit that revealed every curve and bulge.

I told him I had a few more questions. He quickly glanced

around, then asked me to bring my questions to a downstairs locker room while he changed.

He led me down carpeted steps, past a few dozen naked men in the main shower and sauna area, where there appeared to be less body fat than on Mount Rushmore. He stopped at the door of the executive locker room and punched a code for entrance.

I knew the executive section in a gym was more private and more costly than the general facilities, especially at a place like Le Gym, and wondered how he paid for it. Or, for that matter, how he could afford the sharp-looking new Celica I'd seen him driving that afternoon on his way to visit Derek Brunheim.

We went inside, passing a towel-wrapped man on his way out. I settled on to a bench while Bellworthy kicked off his shoes.

"For someone working double shifts to make ends meet," I said, "you seem to be living pretty well."

"My membership here's free," he said, spinning his combination lock, "long as I bring in payin' clients."

As he opened his locker, his book on anger management toppled out, along with several loose checks already made out. He ignored the book to hastily gather up the checks, but not before I recognized the pastel floral print from the checkbook I'd seen in Derek Brunheim's apartment. One check landed near enough my feet that I could make out Brunheim's signature at the bottom and a notation above for a hundred dollars.

There were two other men in the room, both middle-aged but with the tight, defined bodies of athletes twenty years younger. They drifted off with towels toward the showers as Bellworthy peeled off his one-piece gym suit.

"I did some checking, Jefferson."

"Checkin' on what?"

"Your background."

He dropped the gym suit to his ankles and stepped out of it, then did the same with his support brief. I did my best to keep my eyes on his face.

"I found out you have a criminal record, Jefferson."

He turned and straddled the bench, his pumped-up arms hanging at his sides like slabs of beef.

I found myself at eye level with the rippled muscles of his furry abdomen, and glanced up into his unhappy face.

When he spoke, his voice suggested a man fighting hard to control himself, and close to losing.

"What reason you got checkin' on me?"

"Routine research."

"Billy Lusk?"

I nodded.

"Don't seem so routine to me."

"You did six years in prison, Jefferson. For attempted murder."

He glanced around, saw that we were alone, then pointed a finger an inch or two from my nose.

"That's right, man. I did my time. And I stayed outta trouble since."

"Stayed out of trouble? Or avoided getting caught?"

"I got me a new life, man. You wanna fuck it up? Is that what you want?"

"Not at all."

"If anybody at The Out Crowd finds out about what I done, I got no more job, man. They won't keep no ex-con on the door or handlin' money back of the bar. Anybody finds out around here, I'm gone. I don't know why you got to hurt a man that tried to help you out."

"I'm just trying to find out the truth."

"Find out what truth, motherfucker?"

"You told me you don't hate Hispanics."

"That's right."

"But the man you nearly killed was Latino."

His eyes shifted uneasily.

"There was no hate."

"It must take a lot of hate to hurt someone as badly as you hurt Jorge Sandoval."

His eyes drifted away from mine and stayed there awhile.

"I didn't hurt him 'cause I hated him." His voice went soft, and there was shame in it. "I hurt him 'cause I loved him."

He stepped back over the bench and faced his locker, stuffing workout gear into his gym bag while he talked.

"He was the first dude I ever got it on with. You know what it's like, the first time? You go a little crazy, man. You think it's love. You think it's forever, that there'll never be nobody else, like he's your whole world."

"Only, he didn't feel that way about you?"

"I caught him goin' down on another dude. Right in the same bed where he'd done me. And I just went off, you know? There was a blade there, kitchen knife. I grabbed it and used it on him."

"You tried to kill him," I said.

"I didn't want him dead. But I was blood crazy over what he done to me. That, plus I guess I didn't want nobody else to have him."

He shook his head again and again, as if trying to shake away the memory.

"I loved that dude so much, man, I can feel it even now."

He resumed stuffing the gym bag, and it occurred to me that there might be a weapon inside. He looked over at me.

"Hate Hispanics, man? That may be how it is with some brothers, but it ain't that way with me."

"Why didn't you explain some of this in court? It might have gotten you a lighter sentence."

"I was in pro football! I was carryin' the ball for the motherfuckin' Pittsburgh Steelers! Most of the dudes I hung out with was either jocks or from the neighborhood. You don't all of a sudden go sayin' to the world that you suck dick, man. You don't go tellin' everybody you take it up the ass."

"You'd rather spend an extra year or two in prison than admit you're gay?"

"Back then, yeah. It woulda been in all the papers and on all the TV shows. That ain't so easy. Not when you just been findin' out about yourself and can't even say no word like *gay,* or any of that shit. You just keep it inside, man, and take what you gotta take."

The thought struck me: *Just like Gonzalo Albundo.*

A laugh escaped from Bellworthy. It sounded bitter.

"If I'd killed a woman, 'stead of a man, I mighta done a year or two for attempted manslaughter and been back playin' in the pros. Ain't that rich?"

He grabbed a towel, then went through his gym bag until he found shampoo.

"Jefferson, why didn't you tell me you knew Derek Brunheim?"

"What the fuck business is it of yours?"

"What do you have to hide?"

He stood there breathing hard and fast, as if deciding whether to talk to me or kill me. Then he slowed and deepened his breathing, relaxing a little.

"Every now and then, Derek come to The Out Crowd with Billy. I'd talk to him while Billy flirted with other guys. I liked Derek, I thought he was a funny dude. He was real fem, yeah, but he was OK."

"You went to his apartment this afternoon."

"Law against that?"

"Did you know that he had a violent argument with Billy the night he was murdered?"

Bellworthy's eyes began moving restlessly again.

"Yeah, I knew it."

"How?"

"Because he told me, motherfucker! He felt real bad about it, remorseful and shit. That's why I went to see him today. Just to tell him it was OK, he had a friend. He was hurtin', man."

"Jefferson, did Derek Brunheim pay you to kill Billy Lusk?"

He dropped his towel and clenched his right hand into a fist as big and hard as a softball; the muscles of his upper body tightened like steel bands beneath his dark skin. If he had a weapon in his gym bag, he didn't need it; he could have killed me with just his fist, probably with one blow.

He opened his hand, turned, and slammed the flat of his palm hard enough against his locker door that the other lockers rattled all the way to the end.

"Damn!"

He whirled back around so fast that his thick penis swung with him, slapping against his thigh.

Then he sank to the bench, bent his head, and cried; he didn't make much sound but the tears rolled unchecked, splashing into the cradle of his thighs and onto his private parts.

After a while, he picked up the towel and wiped the snot running from his nose. We were at eye level now as he looked at me.

"You think 'cause I'm a brother, I can't have no soft feelings for another man? Can't go to him when he's hurtin' and needs somebody strong to hold him? You think I ain't got feelins as human as you?"

We both heard a door swing open. Bellworthy quickly wiped his tears away.

One of the middle-aged men returned from his shower, rubbing body oil into his Mount Rushmore chest. He nodded at Bellworthy like he might be a client.

There was fear in Bellworthy's eyes now as he waited to see if I'd say something that could tear down the life he'd just started to rebuild.

''No,'' I said.

I stood up.

''I don't think that, Jefferson. I don't think that at all.''

I still had questions about the checks from Derek Brunheim, but they could wait.

I went out remembering why, too many times, I'd hated being a reporter.

Twenty-two

EARLY FRIDAY MORNING, I was jolted awake by someone pounding on my door.

At first, half asleep, I thought it might be Jefferson Bellworthy, back to get me after all. Or Luis Albundo, ready to finish what he'd started on the street in Echo Park. Whoever it was banged again, harder.

"Open the fucking door, Benjamin!"

It was Harry.

I nudged an empty wine bottle under the bed with my foot, slipped into some pants, and opened the door to the shock of sunlight and the sound of Harry's raspy cough.

He barged in past me.

"Where the fuck do you get off giving Templeton an assignment?"

"If you're going to visit so early, Harry, the least you could do is bring coffee."

He followed me to the kitchen, where I turned on the tap and flooded my face with cold water.

"Paul Masterman is a U.S. senator!"

"You woke me up to tell me that?"

"Don't get cute, Benjamin. I'm not in the mood."

I dried my face with a dish towel that was borderline filthy. I was flat broke, and my dirty laundry was piling up. I made a mental note to call Kevin at the agency and ask about my sixty dollars.

"First of all, Harry, I didn't give an assignment to anyone, least of all Alexandra Templeton."

"That's not the way she tells it."

"Templeton doesn't take orders from me. We work together. We mutually agreed that hanging out with Masterman's campaign for a couple days might be a good idea."

"Did you, now?"

Harry fumbled for a cigarette, found an empty package in a pocket, crumpled it, and threw it angrily in the direction of an overflowing trash can.

I went back into the other room to find a shirt, searching through a pile of soiled clothes.

"Masterman used the scene of Billy Lusk's murder as a location in one of his TV spots."

"Tell me something I don't know," Harry said.

"We figured a story on Masterman, framed around that particular TV ad, might make an interesting follow-up piece in Templeton's series on Billy Lusk, or at least give us a hook for one."

"I'd say that's reaching for material," Harry said.

"At the very least, Harry, you'll get a timely feature out of it on the Masterman campaign."

"Templeton's a crime reporter. I'll catch hell on this from the guys on the political beat."

"You can tough it out, Harry."

"Don't tell me what I can or cannot fucking do. That's not how this works."

I found a T-shirt that didn't look too bad, and sniffed the armpits.

"You wanted me to get involved, Harry. It was your idea, not mine."

"I wanted you to write a sidebar. Work with Templeton on the Billy Lusk story. Not go after a U.S. senator for reasons that seem to be known only to yourself."

"Give me some leash on this, Harry. I'd like to pursue some leads."

"The Albundo kid signed a confession, Ben. It's been three days since Lusk was murdered. I should have had a story from Templeton by now."

"A couple more days, that's all we need." I slipped into the

T-shirt, tucked it into my faded jeans. "I promise we'll make it worth the wait."

"I want to know what you're after, Ben."

"I'm fishing, Harry."

I went into the bathroom to pee, talking to him over my shoulder.

"Remember how you used to encourage us to go fishing?"

"We could get away with it then," Harry said.

"Meaning you work for a paper now that doesn't have any guts?"

"Meaning you're damaged goods, Ben. Meaning I'm taking a chance on someone who'd be lucky to get a job writing classified ads at a suburban weekly."

I flushed the toilet and watched the water swirl down.

"Then why did you ask me to come back?"

"You know why."

I glanced in the mirror, where our eyes met.

"But it's got to be done slowly, Ben. Nothing too big. I made that clear when we first discussed it."

"You used to have balls, Harry."

"If I lost 'em, the scalpel was in your hand."

I brushed past him, sat down on the bed, and pulled on sweat socks. He followed and sat down beside me.

"I'm just asking you to take it a little easier, Ben. Don't call too much attention to yourself. I'm risking a lot here."

Three days ago, Harry had come to this apartment and stuck the knife of guilt into me. He'd twisted it until I'd agreed to work with him on the Billy Lusk story. Now, he was losing his nerve. It made me sick.

"Risking what? An editor's slot at a rag that's not worth the recycled paper it's printed on? I thought you wanted to shake things up, Harry. Give the *Sun* some credibility."

"Down the road, when you've settled in, you'll be a part of all that."

"Or when I've groomed Templeton to replace me, in case bringing me back doesn't work out?"

"I thought that was how you wanted it, Ben."

I leaned down to look for a pair of running shoes, and to avoid Harry's eyes.

"I'm not sure what I want anymore."

I retrieved the shoes from under the bed and shoved my feet into them.

"I take that back. I know exactly what I want." I tied one shoe, then the other, careful not to break the frayed laces. "I want to find out who killed Billy Lusk so an innocent kid doesn't spend his life in jail for something he didn't do."

"I don't get it, Ben. What is it you see that the rest of us don't?"

I stood up and paced the room, craving caffeine, wanting to get out.

"Loose ends. Pieces that don't fit. Dark motives. Suspicious timing. Troubling questions. Lies."

"Things the cops don't see but you do," Harry said.

"Things the cops aren't interested in because they've got a kid from a poor part of town whose family can't afford a high-powered defense team. Which means the D.A. can get a quick plea and the cops can close the file and everybody can move on to more important matters."

I turned toward the door.

"You want me to walk away from it, Harry? Because if you do, just say the word, and I'm gone."

He stared at the floor, elbows on knees, fingers pressed together.

He knew that if I disappeared again, it might be for good. He knew that I was his only lifeline back to something he desperately wanted but was too weak to reach on his own.

"Just be sure you're on solid ground, Ben. I know you like to take risks. I know you need that excitement."

He looked up with plaintive eyes. He'd grown so old in six years, and so scared.

"You've got nothing to lose," he said. "But this job is all I have. At my age, you don't get another chance. Don't screw it up for me. Help me make it work."

"I need some coffee, Harry. You want to spring for a cup?"

"You can be a cold bastard, Ben."

"Tell me something I don't know."

He got slowly to his feet, letting out a sigh like a punctured tire. "I have to get downtown."

He reached inside his coat and pulled out an envelope.

"Here."

I listened until I heard the last of his heavy footsteps on the stairs. Then I ripped open the envelope.

Inside was a check for $400 from the *Sun*'s payroll department, an advance for my work on the Billy Lusk case.

Harry's way of giving me a little leash.

Twenty-three

I CASHED MY CHECK at a bank down on the boulevard where I'd kept my account open, then used a pay phone to call the home of Margaret Devonshire.

When I got the answering machine again, I decided Billy Lusk's mother simply wasn't picking up, and that calling again would be futile.

Down the block was a coffee bar run by a former priest who'd counseled young parishioners about sin until he'd been caught committing one with a teenaged acolyte. West Hollywood had more than its share—both coffee bars and former priests. I stopped in, grabbed a muffin with more grain in it than a walnut table, and washed it down with two cups of Vienna Roast strong enough to wake the dead.

Then I decided some exercise was in order, specifically a hike in the hills above Sunset Boulevard, just west of Doheny Drive.

By the time I passed the sign marking the southern entrance to Trousdale Estates, I was panting from the climb, and my legs were getting heavy. I passed lushly landscaped homes with circular driveways and tennis courts that covered more square footage than the average apartment. There wasn't a piece of litter or even a trash can visible at the curb, and no children to be seen in the yards, not even toys.

A private guard passed in a patrol car, looking me over in his rearview mirror before disappearing up the hill. Somewhere in the distance, I could hear the rattle of a gardener's gasoline-powered leaf blower. Otherwise, the neighborhood was quiet and the streets vacant, carefully sealed off from the untidy world below.

According to Templeton's notes, the Devonshires lived on Sky Vista Drive, a half mile up the hill. I found the street sign and turned, climbing for a short distance as Sky Vista curved west, opening up to city and ocean views that were now obscured by choking yellow smog.

The Devonshire home spread out across a plateau on the left side of the street. It was a one-story modular place that showed a touch of Streamline Moderne from the Thirties, with a white stucco exterior and the most verdant lawns chemical fertilizer could produce. Along the north-facing walls, the lace-covered stems of Australian tree ferns stretched imploringly for sunlight. At their feet, beds of obedient impatiens spilled over with blossoms of red, pink, and white.

For all its thriving vegetation, the Devonshire house had an antiseptic look, all the rough edges manicured away as if the people who lived there were afraid of life happening on its own.

I slipped into the shade of a ficus tree across the street and watched the windows. For several minutes, there was no visible movement in the house.

Then a woman in a white dress passed behind a bank of windows.

As I crossed to the house, she reappeared and began washing the glass, holding a bottle of window cleaner in one hand and a rag in the other. From the edge of the drive, I could see that she was young, short, and brown, and that the white dress was the standard uniform of a housekeeper.

Her hand moved the rag in circular motions on the glass until she saw me, when it stopped in mid-motion, upraised as if she were waving.

Behind her, the silhouette of another woman, thin and taller, passed like a shadow against the glare of the windows on the south side of the house. As I approached the front steps and rang the bell, the housekeeper kept watch. So did an electronic eye mounted above the door.

Moments later, the housekeeper opened it a crack, keeping the chain hooked. I asked to speak to Mrs. Devonshire.

"She not home, sir."

I heard the soft crunch of tires rolling to a slow stop on the street. The patrol guard sat behind the wheel of his car, peering at me across the wide, cobbled driveway.

"I believe she is home," I said.

Then: *"Por favor. Quiero hablar con la Señora Devonshire. Es muy importante."*

"She not home, sir."

A car door slammed like a warning. I looked again toward the street.

The private guard stood with his arms folded across his unimpressive chest, eyeing me from behind his dark glasses and trying to look tough. He wore a gray uniform with yellow patches and had the unmistakable air of a police academy reject.

By the time I turned back, the door of the house was closed. The housekeeper reappeared at the window and started cleaning another pane, pretending not to watch me.

I sauntered down the driveway and turned back up Sky Vista Drive. The security guard stood rigidly with one hand on the baton hanging from his belt. He looked stiff and uneasy, like a figure at the Hollywood Wax Museum, except that he wasn't famous.

"Going someplace special?"

"Out walking," I said.

"You live up here?"

"Unless I'm mistaken, these are public streets."

"They're public."

"And so well maintained."

I continued hiking, knowing his eyes were on me every step of the way.

When I reached the sharpest part of the roadway's curve, I took off in a sprint and was out of his sight within seconds.

I heard the car door slam and then peeling rubber as he smoked his tires. I ducked behind a thick stand of pink-flowered oleander that rose up from a carpet of ivy. Another second or two passed before the guard sped by, shooting up the hill just the way real cops do but without the siren.

When he was around the bend, I dashed back down to the Devonshire house, slipping up on the west edge of the property, where the housekeeper wouldn't see me from the front windows.

A path of stepping stones led to a gate no more than four feet high. I was over it and hidden before the patrol car came speeding back.

The guard climbed out, looking around the property from the roadway, then up and down the hill. After awhile, he got back in, wheeled the car around, and disappeared up the street again on squealing tires. It was probably the most excitement he'd had in a long time.

I found myself in a small area of several large recycling bins. Beyond that was a potting table, where the carcasses of dead plants withered in plastic containers from lack of water, as if purchased on a whim and then forgotten.

I worked my way through to a small gate that opened into the rear yard.

On an expansive patio of polished terra-cotta tile, a woman I took to be Margaret Devonshire sat alone staring out vacantly at a sea of pollution. She clutched a photo album in her lap and, beneath a broad-brimmed straw hat, appeared as tastefully dressed and carefully manicured as her home.

"Mrs. Devonshire?"

She turned her head slowly, as though she no longer had the energy to be startled.

"My name is Benjamin Justice. I'm from the *Los Angeles Sun.* We're doing a story about Billy's death."

She removed the hat to see me better, exposing herself to the cruel light.

It revealed a painfully thin, once-beautiful woman with a face pulled grotesquely taut from too many facelifts. Her nose, upturned and petite, reminded me of the photos I'd seen of Billy Lusk. Apparently, that much of her face was natural.

"You're trespassing," she said, her voice less fearful than weary. "And I have no wish to speak with you."

"I called several times, Mrs. Devonshire, but only got your machine."

"You left no message."

"I wasn't where I could be reached." I took a step closer and removed my dark glasses. "I realize this is a difficult time. I just have a few questions."

She glanced over my outfit, which looked more suitable for collecting garbage than reporting, although I'm not sure she appreciated the difference.

"Do you have credentials, Mr. Justice?"

"I'm afraid not. I'm freelance."

Her weariness finally gave way to reality: She was alone with a strange man who was in her yard without invitation, and who did not appear to be what he said he was.

"I don't think your coming here like this is at all appropriate."

The haughty displeasure in her voice was at odds with the fear that had crept into her rheumy eyes. She turned her head toward the house, keeping an eye on me at the same time.

"Francesca!"

The housekeeper scurried out, reacting with alarm when she saw me.

"*Francesca, por favor quédate conmigo.*"

Francesca, please stay with me.

Mrs. Devonshire apparently expected her housekeeper to lay down her life for her employer for five dollars an hour, the kind of thinking that would make sense only to the very rich and the very poor.

The older woman picked up a portable phone on the table beside her, pulled up the antenna, and punched in numbers.

"You can call the patrol or the police if you wish," I said. "But I think you'll only hurt yourself in the long run."

She put the phone to her ear and refused to look at me.

"I've already spoken with Derek Brunheim," I said.

When she heard his name, she dug her frosted nails into the armrest of her chair so hard I thought they might snap.

"I think it only fair that I get your side of things, Mrs. Devonshire. It would be a shame to quote Derek Brunheim at length, with nothing from you but a 'no comment.' "

She looked at me as one might a garden slug.

Then, into the phone, she said, "I'm sorry. I must have misdialed."

She pushed the antenna back into the phone and laid it aside.

"Thank you, Francesca, it's all right."

"*¿Sí?*"

"*Sí.* Please bring iced tea. *Dos, por favor.*"

When Francesca had gone, Mrs. Devonshire said, "Please sit down, Mr. Justice. There's no reason both of us should exhibit poor manners."

She slipped on a pair of dark glasses and turned her gaze back out at the smog-shrouded skyscrapers of Century City.

I took a chair next to her, found a pen, and opened my notebook.

''I'll talk to you on one condition,'' Margaret Devonshire said. ''That every word I say is off the record, unless I signify otherwise. Then you may write it down.''

''Fair enough.''

''Also, before the article is printed, you will submit it to me for my approval.''

''I'm afraid that's not possible.''

She stiffened, peering sharply at me over her surgically shaped cheekbones.

''And why is that not possible, Mr. Justice?''

''Someone else will write the article, so it's not my call. But I can tell you that no self-respecting journalist would ever submit their copy for a subject's approval.''

''Are you sure you work for the *Sun,* Mr. Justice? I didn't think it had standards.''

''I'll be happy to check quotes with you, Mrs. Devonshire. But that's as far as I'll go.''

She sighed like someone who was still adjusting to the insubordination of a rudely changing world.

Francesca appeared and served us iced tea in goblets of Waterford crystal, with wedges of fresh lime on the side.

''Drink your iced tea while it's cold, Mr. Justice.''

I did as I was told. When Mrs. Devonshire spoke again, much of the superiority was gone from her voice.

''First, you need to know that Billy was my only child. Do you have children, Mr. Justice?''

''No.''

''Then you wouldn't understand. Especially for a mother, I think, losing a child goes beyond common grief. But to lose your *only* child . . . you feel that your entire world is gone. That every support, every prop that's held you up has suddenly been pulled away.''

She glanced around at the house and the expansive grounds, then at the costly crystal in her hands.

''You also take sum of your life, and realize it doesn't add up to an awful lot.''

"I think I can understand that."

"You've lost someone who meant that much?"

I nodded.

"Then perhaps," she said, "we share something in common after all."

She smiled artificially, without a trace of sincerity, the way she'd probably smiled thousands of times during her life.

"Billy's father died when he was eight. I remarried much too quickly, within the year. I'm not the kind of person who's comfortable on her own. I like a life that's predictable from day to day, moment to moment. Instability unsettles me to a serious degree."

"You and Phil Devonshire have been together close to twenty years, then."

"Yes. It's been a good arrangement. Phillip is much like myself. Orderly, disciplined, very much in control. Although a more—how shall I put it—commanding person."

She stopped, as if she'd just realized how much she was telling me. She took another sip of tea, then put her drink aside.

"What exactly did Derek Brunheim tell you?"

"He told me that Billy was charming and a loyal friend in many ways."

"Go on."

"That you and he didn't get along."

"That much is certainly true."

"He also said that Billy hadn't worked for some time. That he had a serious cocaine habit. And that, sexually, he was rather promiscuous."

She gripped the chair's armrests again, and a bit of color seeped into her ghostly face.

"I suppose he offered details."

"Some."

"Are you going to put any of that in your paper?"

"Possibly."

"My God."

She rested her forehead on her hand, rubbing at the worry lines.

"Would you care to go on the record, Mrs. Devonshire? The more substantial the information I have from you, the less likely I'm going to need to rely on Derek Brunheim."

"I don't seem to have much choice, do I? Thanks to Derek Brunheim and his pathetic fantasies."

I opened my notebook, jotting notes while she talked.

"When my first husband died he left Billy a modest trust fund. It was closed to Billy until his thirtieth birthday, as an incentive for him to make something of himself. About two years ago, we realized that Billy was using cocaine on a regular basis. That's when Phillip stepped in. He was adamant that Billy enroll in a treatment program and submit to regular drug tests. Billy flatly refused, insisted he didn't have a problem. So Phillip cut off his allowance. They had some terrible fights over that."

"Was cocaine the only issue?"

"If you thought it was, I doubt you would have asked the question."

I waited. The silence loomed larger until it forced her to say something.

"All right, you may as well know. We also demanded that Billy end his friendship with that awful man. Derek Brunheim."

She closed her eyes for a moment in apparent revulsion.

"I doubt you've told me everything he said, Mr. Justice. I can imagine that most of it was lies."

"That's why I'm here, Mrs. Devonshire. To try to sort things out."

"Trust me, he's a sick man. He was the one who introduced Billy to drugs."

"Do you have proof of that?"

"He wanted to make Billy dependent on him, to take him away from me. What better way?"

She wrung her hands together as if they were cold. Her chin trembled as she spoke again.

"He succeeded quite well, wouldn't you say?"

"Did it bother you that your son was homosexual, Mrs. Devonshire?"

She regarded me critically for a long moment, as if deciding exactly how to respond.

"Billy was not homosexual, Mr. Justice. He was *rebellious.* And that's where I take much of the blame."

She stood and wandered to the edge of the patio, carrying the photo album with her. I followed, standing beside her as she looked out across the city.

"I think Billy always wanted to hurt me, for remarrying so soon. For sharing myself with another man, so to speak. Through the years, he acted out in certain ways. Moving in with that perverted man was one of them. But it had nothing to do with his sexuality. It was just a phase."

She glanced over.

"I know that sounds naive and unenlightened in this day and age. But in Billy's case, it happens to be the truth. A mother knows."

"Billy died outside a gay bar, Mrs. Devonshire. He was a regular customer there."

"I spend much of my time and a good deal of my money helping the disadvantaged, Mr. Justice. That doesn't make me poor."

The phone rang in the background. There was a click, and the answering machine picked up the call.

She opened the album to a photo of her son at about age two, all big blue eyes and golden curls, clutching a toy airplane in his tiny plump hand.

"Frankly, I wish that Billy had been homosexual," she said, studying the photo. "It would make his death much easier to accept."

"Because you would have loved him less?"

"Grandchildren, Mr. Justice. If there was anything I was looking forward to, it was Billy settling down and having children."

"Did your husband share that sentiment?"

"Phillip wouldn't have liked it much, I don't suppose. It would have brought not only Billy back into our lives, but a wife and grandchild, and it would have disrupted our routine. But that was a sacrifice I'd happily make to hold a grandchild in my arms."

She flipped to the next page and to more photographs of her only child.

"At least if I'd been certain Billy was homosexual, I wouldn't have expected that and been so disappointed. Would I?"

It was a long way to get to the kind of logic Margaret Devonshire needed to make her pain tolerable. Viewed through her narrow prism, I supposed it made some kind of sense.

She turned the page again, to a shot of her son splashing in a backyard play pool, dated twenty-five years earlier.

"You probably think I'm a very selfish woman, don't you, Mr. Justice?"

"You seem lonely, Mrs. Devonshire."

She tried to laugh but it didn't quite get out.

"Since his passing, I've probably talked more about Billy with you than with anyone else. Most of the time, it's just myself and Francesca here. I haven't welcomed visitors."

"And Mr. Devonshire?"

She continued turning the pages, almost in rhythm with her speech, which had slowed considerably, as though her emotion was winding down.

"Naturally, he feels badly about what happened. But he was never close to Billy. He has grown children of his own from his first marriage, and several grandchildren. So it's not the same for him."

The laugh finally came, sharp with bitterness.

"The day Billy died, Phillip played eighteen holes. He shot par."

I remembered from Templeton's notes that the police had called in Margaret Devonshire to identify her son's body early that afternoon. She'd probably gone alone, while her husband golfed.

She glanced at my notebook, realizing again just how much she'd been saying.

"Please, nothing in your story about Phillip, or the part about grandchildren."

"I see no reason for it."

I looked over her shoulder to a picture of Billy in a Cub Scout uniform, his cap tilted to one side.

"Your son was a beautiful child," I said.

"Wasn't he? Look at that darling little nose. That's the one thing everyone always commented on. Today, people pay fortunes for a nose like that. Billy was born with his."

"I believe he got it from you."

"Thank you for noticing, Mr. Justice."

"Mrs. Devonshire, I'm going to ask you a difficult question."

She braced herself with another false smile.

"Can you think of anyone who might have had a reason to kill your son? Someone other than the boy who was arrested?"

"That's not a difficult question at all. From the beginning, I assumed Derek Brunheim was involved."

"Why would Brunheim kill your son, when he was so fond of him?"

"That's just it. Billy was ending their friendship."

"Are you sure?"

"He told us so himself, two days before he was taken from us. He was tired of the way he was living. We told him that if he changed his ways, we'd set him up in his own apartment and help him finish his education. He planned to go back to film school for the spring term."

"And you believed he'd follow through?"

"Phillip warned Billy that this was absolutely his last chance. That if he failed to meet certain expectations, we'd cut him off completely, including any future inheritance. All he would have would be the trust fund, which wasn't much. We worked it all out, and Billy promised to tell Derek the next day that he was moving out."

Her face became strained, but I also thought I saw a glint of satisfaction in her eyes.

"I can only imagine that man's reaction," she said, "when he realized we'd finally beaten him."

I reminded her of Gonzalo Albundo's confession.

"I believe he comes from a poor background," she said.

"Meaning Derek Brunheim may have hired him to commit murder?"

"Your words, Mr. Justice. Not mine."

I asked to look through her son's personal belongings, but she flatly refused. She did, however, agree to loan me a recent photo of him to accompany any article the *Sun* might run, and removed one from the album's last page.

I asked to use the bathroom before leaving, and she led me inside. With the bathroom door locked behind me, I quickly surveyed the contents of the drawers and medicine cabinet. The latter held a pharmacopoeia of prescription drugs, including pills for nerves and chronic depression; most of them were prescribed to Margaret Devonshire and dated long before the death of her son.

On my way out, I glanced into her husband's trophy room, where he'd mounted an impressive collection of handguns and rifles in a glass cabinet.

"For some reason, Phillip enjoys collecting them," Margaret Devonshire said. "I suppose he thinks it's a manly kind of thing. Personally, I never liked having them around."

She opened the front door, exposing her gaunt face again to the unkind light.

"But Phillip's like most men, I'm afraid. He likes to have his way."

Twenty-four

I HIKED BACK DOWN the hill with the patrol car following slowly behind until I was past the stone gates and out of Trousdale Estates.

In one hand, I carried the photo of Billy Lusk inside an envelope, on loan from his mother. I didn't like the feeling of his dead face pressed between my fingers, but at first I wasn't sure why.

Then I realized that meeting Margaret Devonshire had shaken me up a little.

There was a lot about her and her lofty world I didn't care for, including her condescending attitude toward much of the human race. She'd raised a son who'd been spoiled, manipulative, and ridiculously vain. But for all there'd been to dislike about him, he'd been flesh and blood, and the most important person in her life. Her grief was real, and I knew what that felt like.

I left Beverly Hills and crossed back into West Hollywood, where I called Derek Brunheim from a pay phone on the Sunset Strip.

I made some small talk, then mentioned Billy Lusk's personal photographs as casually as possible. Brunheim said he had them for me and agreed to meet me for an early dinner at a cafe in Boy's Town. I had no idea what I might find, but I wanted a look.

As I hung up, a young woman was kneeling on the sidewalk outside the Viper Room. She placed a flower on the spot where River Phoenix had died a year or two before, thrashing with convulsions from a drug overdose. The campfire scene from *My Own*

Private Idaho flashed in my mind, and I didn't know if it signified glorious immortality, tragic waste, or maybe just plain stupidity—or if I was merely troubled by my meeting with a grieving mother.

I didn't want to think about young men dying anymore, and tried not to as I headed back down to the apartment. But when I got there, I walked in to see the *East of Eden* poster hanging crooked on the wall, with James Dean's message scrawled near the bottom: *To my buddy Maurice, a beautiful guy. Love always, Jimmy.* And then Jacques's face smiling at me from the shelf, looking more alive in that one photograph than I'd felt in years.

I wanted a drink in the worst way.

Not wine but something hard, straight from the bottle, *right now.* When you want that and it's barely past noon and you have four hundred dollars in your pocket, it might as well be 6 A.M. and the end of your life.

I did my laundry instead.

I concentrated on putting just the right amount of detergent in each washer and just the right amount of money in each dryer and meticulously sorting and folding my clothes afterward. When I got home, I even put everything in the proper drawers, something I hadn't done since I'd moved in three months earlier.

As I was making up the bed, I saw the envelope.

It leaned against the vase that held the yellow rose, and bore the return address of the *Los Angeles Sun.* My last name was scrawled across the front in graceful handwriting that I immediately recognized as Templeton's.

Inside was a newspaper clipping from the *Los Angeles Times,* dated Father's Day the previous year. A note was paper-clipped to the corner: *Justice—I came across this in the files and thought it might interest you. Templeton.*

The clipping was a first-person piece from the *Times*'s Life & Style section, accompanied by a three-column photograph of Senator Paul Masterman and his son; their arms were around each other's shoulders as they beamed for the camera, two handsome, healthy men for whom life seemed to have fallen nicely into place.

Below the photo was a headline, A FATHER AND SON REUNION, followed by the deck: A SENATOR'S SON WAGES A DETERMINED BATTLE TO OVERCOME FAMILY TROUBLES AND WIN HIS DAD'S LOVE.

Beneath the deck was the byline of Paul Masterman, Jr., and then his story.

> Before this year, picking out a Father's Day card was one of the most frustrating experiences of my life.
>
> Most of the cards carried messages like "To the World's Greatest Dad." Or "To My Old Man, Who's Always Been There for Me." Or "I Love You, Dad, More Than I Can Ever Say."
>
> The problem was, I didn't feel any of those things. Buying a card that expressed my love for my father, or acknowledged his love for me, would have been dishonest. When my father read it, its falseness would have embarrassed us both, underscoring how alienated we really were, and how little genuine affection had ever been expressed between us.
>
> So I always ended up buying one of those joke cards that uses humor to avoid the awful truth so many sons face: The emotional distance that separates them from their fathers makes Father's Day the most awkward and painful day of the year, when it should be one of the happiest.

The next several paragraphs recounted his parents' bitter divorce, the years of infidelity and family turmoil that had preceded it, and the pain of seeing the details publicly aired in the press.

Then the piece jumped to an inside page, recounting Paul Jr.'s single-handed campaign to break through his father's emotional armor.

> First, I had to come to terms with my own anger and find the courage to express it fully and frankly, no easy task when your father is Senator Paul Masterman. I laid it all out in a letter, with nothing held back, and mailed it to him. Next, I sat down with Dad face to face, and forced him to deal with old issues between us, dredging up all the guilt and pain so that we might get past it. Finally, I accepted him as someone less than perfect, as we all are, and forgave him, knowing that he loves me, but that he just didn't know how to express it until we sat down and learned how together.

> It was the beginning of the healing process we both needed, and the building of a new relationship between us, based on communication and trust.

It was a nicely written story, sappy but touching, with an ending that must have hit a nerve with many male readers.

> This year, for the first time, I looked forward to picking out a Father's Day card. The one I chose opened with these words: "I'm So Lucky to Have You for a Dad."
>
> Today, I'll give my dad his card. The two of us will spend some time together. We'll laugh, exchange hugs, share our thoughts and feelings. The way all fathers and sons were meant to do, every day of the year.
>
> Happy Father's Day, Dad. I love you.

I folded the clipping so that just the photograph showed, then folded it again so the senator was out of the picture. I smoothed it out and used the paper clip to hold it together, and propped it up against the bud vase, between the photos of Jacques and Elizabeth Jane.

Then I sat on the edge of the bed and thought about what was happening to me.

I was getting involved in other people's lives. I knew that the more involved I got the more I would care. And if I cared, there would be inevitable disappointment and loss, inevitable pain.

Yet I also felt I deserved the pain, more than anyone.

Paul Masterman, Jr.

He'd found the courage to act decisively, to do the one thing that could set things straight, get his life on track.

It occurred to me that if I could get Gonzalo Albundo out of jail, *save him,* it might straighten things out a little for me.

It was the right thing to do. A matter of simple justice. I needed to do the right thing.

Paul Masterman, Jr.

I wanted to be able to put things right the way he was able to do, to summon up whatever was good inside me and do something with it, to carry on with strength and belief.

I wanted him to be my friend, my advisor, my lover. I wanted him to hold me, to save me before I lost whatever was left of myself, before I lost my mind.

Paul Masterman, Jr.

I'd never wanted anyone so much, this completely, this obsessively, this hopelessly. It was crazy, but it also felt as real as the bed I was sitting on.

I dozed off staring at his picture and slept stuporously in the afternoon heat, feverish and sweaty. I dreamed about the falling horses again, and then he was in the dream somehow, naked, and I was touching him, and the horses disappeared and I realized it was Jacques I was clutching, and I felt everything swell up aching below my belly and then hot semen pumping out of me, bringing me back, reminding me of who and where I was.

As I slowly woke, it was like coming out of a coma that I didn't want to leave.

Shadows slanted in, the way they often had in this room when Jacques and I had fallen asleep after making love. It was one of those moments when you feel like someone who is gone is back with you again. Then you gradually realize it's only an illusion, slipping away as consciousness returns. Sadness engulfs you and then an overwhelming feeling of emptiness, like a bottomless dark hole you could fall into forever.

For a moment, I heard Jacques's voice somewhere in my head, and the words he'd spoken as I drove him to County Hospital the final time.

I'm more worried about you than me.

Then he was gone, leaving me on a lumpy bed in a lonely room, haunted by what I needed most and knew I could never have.

I wanted something concrete to grab onto. I rolled over and found my watch. It was nearly five.

I crawled off the bed and shook off sleep with a shower and a shave.

Then I put on fresh clothes and headed down to the boulevard to meet Derek Brunheim.

Twenty-five

AS I TURNED the corner at Hilldale onto Santa Monica Boulevard, a wave of strolling men swept me along, and the sexual energy felt electric.

Traffic was backed up for blocks as hundreds of men flowed into the neighborhood to see what the warm Friday evening might have to offer. By midnight, the number would be in the thousands.

Not that many years ago, before AIDS and the political reawakening that came with it, Boy's Town had been an enclave primarily of attractive young white males. Now, the range of ethnic beauty on the street was finally beginning to reflect the change in Southern California itself. There were even some women in the crowd, ranging from booted, short-haired dykes to more conventional lipstick lesbians, mostly in pairs and holding hands.

Folding tables lined the sidewalk near the curb, where volunteers registered passersby to vote in the November election or sought donations for lesbian or gay candidates. In front of the cafes and coffeehouses, friends gathered around small tables, drinking and carrying on, including a deaf group that communicated excitedly in sign language. One table erupted with appreciative catcalls as a crewcut muscular man in cutoffs and combat boots passed by, moving with the sturdy cadence of a Marine on leave, which he may very well have been. He gave his admirers a wink, but kept marching with a sense of purpose that could only mean a favorite bar in the next block.

A sleek black car slipped into a yellow zone at the curb, and an actor whom I recognized from the film *Amadeus* jumped out. He scurried into A Different Light, the gay bookstore, with his shoulders hunched and his head down. Seconds later, he emerged carrying an order of books that must have been waiting for him, darting back to his car and pulling into traffic without ever looking anyone in the eye.

Outside a coffeehouse, a fifteen-year-old, well known in the neighborhood for his budding political militancy, sat on the lap of a bare-chested, well-built man with a gold ring through each distended nipple. The boy waved a delicate hand at two sheriff's deputies as they rolled slowly past in their black-and-white cruiser, and when they failed to respond, blew them a kiss.

For all the numbers and the revelry, it was a peaceful crowd. In the years I'd lived in and around the neighborhood, I'd seen only two fistfights, and those were between hard-swinging women outside the lesbian bar farther down the boulevard. The primary danger on the streets of Boy's Town wasn't its inhabitants but the occasional carful of gay bashers who piled out with pipes and baseball bats to knock a lesbian or gay man senseless, or beat them to death.

The scene carried hidden dangers, of course, HIV foremost among them, if you chose to take certain risks. And the sexual objectification could be every bit as severe and dehumanizing as the kind practiced in the straight clubs on the Santa Monica Promenade, or anywhere else. But Boy's Town was where many men felt safe from a hostile world, free to be themselves, if only for a few hours, and if only in a fleeting, superficial way. Jacques had always said it was both the most liberating and the most oppressive place he'd ever known.

I found Derek Brunheim sitting alone at Boy Meets Grill, tucked in a corner just inside the open doors.

He was dressed all in black, despite the summer weather, looking distant and not particularly happy. Patsy Cline's "Crazy" was playing on the sound system while sleek Hispanic busboys moved between the tables and certain customers eyed them intently, trying to figure out if they were homo or hetero.

"I've never cared much for the Gay Ghetto," Brunheim said, surveying the street as I took the chair across the table. "I always get the impression that these airheads feel gay liberation extends no further than their erections."

"It definitely has its shallow side," I said.

With one hand, he swirled white wine in a glass. In the other, he clasped a cardboard carton the size of a telephone book, which I assumed contained the photos.

"I've been thinking about you since our last visit," he said. "About your line of questions. Now you've chosen to meet me here. Am I correct when I assume that you're one of us?"

I nodded.

"Married?"

"Widowed, you might say."

"The plague?"

I nodded again.

He sighed, rolling the stem of his wineglass between his fingers.

"So many men, so little time," he said. "My, how the meaning of that line has changed."

His eyes strayed back to the party on the street outside.

"Look at them. They couldn't care less about Stonewall, or any of the queers and dykes who risked their lives marching in the streets twenty-five years ago. The fact that people are dying, getting bashed, thrown out of their apartments, losing their jobs means nothing to them. Just as long as they have a clean, well-lighted place to cruise and a cock to suck at the end of the night."

He drained the wine from his glass and set it sharply on the table.

"They're just having fun," I said. I felt defensive for Jacques's sake, because West Hollywood, for all its snobbery and illusions, had been his only real home. "There's a sense of community here. A place to belong."

"For some."

Brunheim's mouth curled venomously, drawing in his pitted face.

"Billy called it a gay paradise. And, of course, for someone like Billy, it was." The tone of his voice turned nasty. "But trust me, honey. If you're old or fat or ugly or female, Boy's Town can be the loneliest place on earth."

A waiter arrived with menus. His head was shaved clean and three tiny gold rings pierced one of his nostrils. I ordered a carafe of Pinot Grigio, and he went to get it.

"I had a talk with Jefferson Bellworthy," I said. "You two are closer than I realized."

"He's a dear, sweet man."

"I also spoke with Margaret Devonshire."

"The Wicked Witch of the North."

"After talking with her, I admire you even more for shielding her from the photographs." I glanced pointedly at the carton in his hands. "I could certainly understand the temptation to hurt her, to strike back."

"Don't think I haven't considered opening this little Pandora's box and flinging her son's lurid sexual history in her face."

The waiter arrived with the carafe of wine and two fresh glasses, which he filled. We ordered food, and as the waiter hurried off, I reached for the box in Brunheim's hand.

"May I?"

He clutched it tightly, drawing it away.

"You seem awfully anxious to have this, Mr. Justice."

"Do I?"

"Yes, you do."

I sat back in my chair and drank some wine. I'd obviously taken Brunheim, or at least the foulness of his mood, too lightly.

"Jefferson called me," Brunheim said. "He warned me to be careful."

"About what?"

"You."

"Is there something you're afraid I'll find out?"

"Why should I trust you with these photographs? Why do you want them so badly?"

"They may tell me something about Billy I won't learn elsewhere."

"What exactly is it you're looking for?"

"I won't know until I see it."

"I didn't come here to play chess, Mr. Justice."

I leaned forward on my elbows to close the distance between us.

"Reporters don't always know what they're looking for, Derek. They go exploring, not always sure where they'll end up."

"And where would you like to end up?"

"At the truth." I paused for effect. "Is that a problem for you?"

My eyes were as direct as my language. To my surprise, Brunheim met them straight on and didn't waver.

Finally, he shoved the box across the table.

"Take them. I'm happy to have them out of my life. I just hope you won't use them to hurt Billy."

I placed them on the chair next to me, under the table, out of his reach.

I finished my wine and refilled both our glasses. Brunheim asked if I'd gleaned anything from Margaret Devonshire that was worth repeating. I mentioned her allegation that he'd deliberately addicted her son to cocaine.

"That doesn't surprise me," he said. "What other vicious little scenarios did she concoct?"

"She said that Billy was moving out, ending his friendship with you."

"In her dreams."

When I said nothing, he looked at me incredulously.

"Surely, you don't believe that cunt!"

"You haven't been entirely honest with me, Derek."

He reached for a basket of rolls, took one, and lathered it thickly with butter.

"Perhaps you'd like to elaborate." He tried to maintain a cool supremacy, but the confidence was gone from his voice.

"You told me that you and Billy spent a quiet last evening together."

He ate the roll in two bites and washed it down with wine. Then he twirled the glass again, glaring at me over the rim.

"Isn't it true," I said, "that you and Billy actually had a violent argument that night?"

He gripped the stem of his glass so tightly I thought it might break.

"Where did you hear that?"

"I'm a reporter, Derek. People talk to me."

"If you're even remotely suggesting that I wanted Billy dead . . ." His nostrils flared, revealing dense thickets of dark hair within. "I could smash your face in, Mr. Justice. Don't ever underestimate the fury of a radical fem."

"Do you have an alibi for that night? Roughly from eleven-thirty through the following hour?"

"I was home asleep. I already told you that."

"Not exactly. You told me that when Billy got the phone call before he went out, you were getting ready for bed."

"I slept alone, as usual. I suppose that leaves me without an alibi, doesn't it? Tough titties."

"What exactly is your relationship with Jefferson Bellworthy?"

"I don't sleep with him, if that's what you mean."

"You've been paying him money."

Brunheim swallowed hard with surprise.

"The other night at the gym," I said, "I saw several of your personal checks made out to him."

"If I want to give him money, that's my business."

"How many more have you written?"

"A few. So what?"

"Maybe you paid him to commit an act of violence you didn't have the stomach for yourself."

Brunheim's hand flashed, and before I could duck, cold wine splashed across my face.

At that moment, the waiter arrived with the food, waiting awkwardly while I mopped my face with my napkin.

"Don't mind us," Brunheim told the waiter. "We're just reenacting a scene from a favorite Forties movie. Naturally, I'm taking the Joan Crawford role."

When the waiter had gone, Brunheim handed me a fresh napkin.

"I should have ground my glass into your fucking face, you piece of insensitive shit."

His words were as harsh as his tone was incongruously light. He spread his napkin neatly on his lap and picked up his fork, as if nothing unpleasant had transpired between us.

"No point in letting good food go to waste," he said.

He shoved the fork into a pile of pasta, pushed it into his mouth, and followed it with several more.

"If you must know," he said, "Jefferson gives me massages."

"At a hundred dollars a session?"

"It's the going rate for good-looking men who treat you nicely. And worth every penny, I might add. Jefferson has incredibly strong hands, and he knows how to touch a man in just the right way. I get ninety minutes of heaven, then a quick jackoff at the end. I'd much prefer to spend my hundred dollars on that than a new pair of Kenneth Coles."

He spooned grated Parmesan onto his pasta and wolfed down a few more bites.

"It's the only sex I've had in three years," he went on. "If you can call it sex. You probably don't know what it's like to be without that kind of human contact, Mr. Justice. But I can assure you, it's not natural."

He shot me a sharper glance.

"And don't get the idea that I'm ashamed of paying for it. Whatever discretion I have is for Jefferson's sake. He's a proud man, he doesn't want people to know. Please, promise me you won't tell him that I told you. Or anyone else."

"You've got my word, Derek."

I reached for the wine and refilled his glass. We ate for a minute or two in silence, enough time for him to clear half his plate.

"Tell me, Mr. Justice, are arrogance and callousness prerequisites for being a journalist?"

"I suppose they help."

He offered me the basket of rolls. I took one, split it, and dipped a section into a saucer of olive oil.

"I'm sorry about my little outburst," he said.

"I probably deserved it."

He paused, holding a pat of butter on the end of his knife, as if balancing a thought.

"If you're looking for someone with a motive for murdering Billy, I suggest you look elsewhere. Someone you may not have thought of."

"A name would help."

"You already know it." He molded butter on his roll. "Samantha."

"Samantha Eliason?"

I'd nearly forgotten about the famous tennis player. Given how close she'd been to Billy Lusk, it was a serious oversight.

"Billy's best friend until last year." The insinuation in Brunheim's voice was impossible to miss. "Then she suddenly wasn't around anymore."

"Do you know why?"

He shook his head and crammed half the roll into his mouth, leaving his lips greasy with butter.

"But in the last few weeks, I heard Billy on the phone with her a few times. Not enough to make out what they were saying, but enough to know it was ugly."

"Interesting," I said.

"Isn't it?"

He raised his joined eyebrows.

"I also know that she was giving him money."

"How much money?"

"Large amounts," he said. "Thousands. In cash."

Then he popped the rest of the roll into his mouth, looking quite content, as if he'd just told me everything I needed to know.

Twenty-six

I USED THE PAY PHONE outside Boy Meets Grill to call Queenie Cochran's PR agency.

On the fourth ring, I caught Kevin as he was leaving to meet his boyfriend at the Nuart Theater for a James Dean retrospective.

The Nuart was out by UCLA, for most people only a few minutes from Queenie's Century City office. But Kevin needed extra time to get his wheelchair in and out of his van, and he didn't want to miss a frame of the first movie.

"Better make it quick, Ben."

The agency had just signed a new contract with Samantha Eliason for continuing representation, so her file was current, but when I asked for her unlisted phone number, Kevin refused.

"Anyway, she's out of town for the weekend. Check back Monday, and maybe we can help you."

"Where out of town?"

"You know I can't tell you that, Ben."

"It's important, Kevin."

"So's my job. What's this about, anyway?"

"Kev, how would you like a framed, unfolded one-sheet from *East of Eden?*"

"I've got one at home. They're not that hard to find."

"Autographed by James Dean?"

This time, there was a pause. A long pause.

"You do not," Kevin said.

"It's yours if you tell me where I can find Samantha."

"This is really dirty, Ben."

"It's in mint condition, Kev. His handwriting is almost, how do I put it . . . childlike, vulnerable."

"Really rotten."

"Yet with a strong masculinity struggling to get out. Or maybe it's the other way around. I can't be sure."

"Not funny, Benjamin."

"It's yours if you want it, Kev. But it's now or never."

He lowered his voice and said quickly, "She's at a private hotel in Laguna Beach." He followed with the address and phone number. "You didn't hear this from me. If Queenie finds out, she'll string me up by the you-know-whats and turn me into a castrato."

"You're a peach, Kevin."

My next call was to Katie Nakamura at the *Sun.* Not surprisingly, the well-disciplined intern was working late, even on a Friday.

I asked her about the media survey she'd undertaken for me related to Billy Lusk's murder.

"I finished it this morning. Mr. Brofsky told me to put a hard copy in your box."

"What box?"

"You have a box now with your name on it, for mail and messages. Mr. Brofsky's talking like you're going to be on staff. Congratulations, Mr. Justice!"

I cursed under my breath, asked her to fax Templeton a copy at home, and thanked her for her fast work.

Then I went home to take James Dean off the wall, and to go through the photographs Billy Lusk had taken of every man he'd seduced in the past several years.

Back on Norma Place, Maurice and Fred sat on their front porch, sipping cocktails and chatting with a young straight couple pushing a baby stroller.

Maurice informed me that a visitor was waiting by my apartment door, and that he appeared to be rather drunk.

I headed up the driveway, clutching the carton of photographs.

Jim Lee sat on the landing, leaning against the wall with his eyes closed and a cigarette that was all ash dangling from his lips. An empty pint of Crown Royal was beside him, and the alcohol had turned his sharp Asian features soft and puffy. Even so, he was a handsome man, ripe with the promise of sex, and I was hard before I reached the top step.

His sleepy eyes fluttered open at the sound of my footsteps. He lurched to his feet, and I caught him just before he fell.

He was drunk enough that he let me kiss him right there, where someone might see. Then he pulled me inside, flopped on the bed, and ordered me to take off my clothes.

When I was naked, he stared at me with the look drunks get that's equal parts dopiness and fearless candor.

''Why your dick so big,'' he said, slurring his words so badly they ran together into one.

I unknotted and slipped off his tie, unbuttoned his shirt, then pushed him back on the bed and ran my tongue over every inch of his chest. I nibbled at his nipples until they became as hard as pebbles, rolling them between my teeth and biting deeper until he cursed me and yanked me away by my hair.

I pulled away the rest of his clothes and fell onto him. We thrashed around, feeling blind and feverish and crazy, finding the hardest and hairiest places on each other with our hands and mouths. There were moments when he was tender, brushing my body with his lips, and times when he pulled bunches of hair from my chest with his teeth, causing me to cry out before I forced his mouth back to mine, where I wanted it.

Then he suddenly rolled away from me, facedown, with his tattooed left arm thrown out to one side. He lay there passively, his posture an unmistakable invitation.

I ran a finger down the bony track of his spine, along the curve of his waist and hip, over smooth buttocks that were barely bigger than my hands. I delicately pried them apart to reveal a crevice sparsely lined with fine, dark hairs and so clean he must have prepared himself carefully for this moment.

He reached back and grabbed the hardest part of me, and pulled me to him; but the moment he felt the probing tip of my erection, he shoved me roughly away.

I massaged the insides of his thighs, reached up between them to caress his loose testicles, gently stroked his slender, rigid cock. He squirmed, buried his face in a pillow, moaned softly.

When I touched him again in the place where I most wanted to be, he reached back as he had before and pulled me toward him, as if he wanted me inside him just as much. But the moment I made contact, he shoved me off again, even more rudely than before.

"Don't worry," I said. "I'll put on a condom."

"Nobody fuck me," he said, spitting the words at me.

"That's not the signal I'm getting."

I ran a hand over his backside again, but this time he rolled over and kicked me away.

"Anybody fuck me," he said, "I get a knife and kill them."

I grabbed his feet by the ankles and held them still.

"Then stop playing games with me, Jim."

"Fuck you, too."

He pulled his legs free, turned over on his belly, and covered his head with an arm. Within a minute, his breathing grew rhythmic and heavy.

I shook one of his shoulders gently and spoke his name, but he didn't respond. His breathing grew deep and guttural, then gave way to snores.

I slipped quietly from the bed and picked his clothes up from the floor. As I draped his pants over the chair, his wallet fell from a rear pocket. Inside, I found some cash, a few credit cards, a picture of a pretty little girl with Korean features, and a California driver's license with a Koreatown address. The photograph on the license was clearly that of Jim Lee, but the name was different: Jin Jai-Sik.

I wrote it down in my notebook, along with the license number, address, and his birth date, which told me he'd just turned thirty. Then I slipped the wallet back into his pants and laid them neatly across the chair with his other clothes.

Jin Jai-Sik snorted, and his snoring stopped, but he remained asleep.

I sat on the bed and opened the box of Billy Lusk's photographs. Inside were two or three hundred Polaroid snapshots of naked men on his bed, most attempting to cover themselves, others laughing with their legs wide open, a few blissfully asleep and unaware of the prying camera.

Most of the subjects appeared to be in their twenties and thirties, but a few were older, and one or two may have been teenagers. If there had been a pattern to Billy Lusk's sexual tastes, all I could discern was trim, male, and fair-skinned.

In many of the photos the nightstand beside his bed was visible, and on it a framed photo of Billy with his arm around the tanned and sturdy shoulders of Samantha Eliason. It was the photograph Derek Brunheim had mentioned the first time I'd spoken with him, the one Margaret Devonshire had taken with her the day her son was murdered.

After looking through several dozen snapshots that meant nothing to me, I grew distracted by the sleeping form of Jin Jai-Sik.

I pushed the box of photos under the bed and stretched out beside him, propping my head on one hand to study him.

Half his face was buried in the pillow. Now and then it twitched in torment, and his jaw muscles tightened furiously as he ground his teeth, so hard it sounded like walnuts cracking.

The first time we'd spoken in The Out Crowd, he'd lied to me about his name and been evasive when I asked him where he'd been when Billy Lusk was murdered. Now I wondered if he'd done more with Billy Lusk than just play a game or two of pool.

Perhaps he'd been one of Billy's sexual conquests, I thought. Perhaps Billy had tried to force Jin Jai-Sik into submitting to anal sex, maybe even succeeded, and Jin had killed Billy out of anger and shame, just as he'd threatened to kill me.

I placed one hand on his shoulder, another on his hip, and gently turned him over on his back. He mumbled in his sleep and swatted weakly at me once or twice, but didn't wake.

Of all the people I'd encountered who were connected to Billy Lusk, Jin Jai-Sik seemed the most cryptic. It made his sexual allure even darker and more compelling. But I wondered if, deep beneath, he and I were all that different. I knew what it was like to kill a man who had hurt and humiliated me. I remembered even now, twenty-one years later, how good total retribution could feel, along with the horror.

As I ran my hands over Jin Jai-Sik's slender body, touching him wherever I pleased, I wondered if he shared a similar violent memory, a more recent one, in the nightmares he was having now.

I brushed the thick black hair from his forehead, then kissed his anguished face.

Until he woke, Jin Jai-Sik was mine.

Twenty-seven

I GRADUALLY came awake Saturday morning to an insistent thumping on the door.

I slept on my side, with my head on Jin Jai-Sik's shoulder and one arm flung across his chest. His body gave off rancid vapors from last night's whiskey, and his breath stank of cigarettes. He stirred but didn't wake.

Outside, an unfamiliar voice called my name.

I rolled away from Jin and out of bed, cursing as I stepped on his shoes. I kicked them under the bed and hopped into sweatpants on my way to open the door.

Kevin's boyfriend stood outside, looking sheepish. I recognized his round Chinese face from a chance meeting at the agency, where he programmed the computers.

"Sorry to wake you," he said. "Kev couldn't wait for the poster. You know how he is."

Kevin sat in his Electric Wilshire at the bottom of the stairs, holding his hands up in a gesture of apology.

"I would have called first," he said, "but you don't have a phone. When are you going to get one?"

"This morning," I said, and went inside to get the poster.

Jin was awake, covering himself with the sheet.

"The Chinese guy, he one of your lovers?"

"No, he's not one of my lovers."

I carried the poster, frame and all, to the door, where I handed it over to the boyfriend.

He glanced past me at Jin Jai-Sik, threw me a knowing smile, and went down the stairs, where Kevin grabbed the poster and looked it over.

"This is great!"

"I thought you might like it," I said.

"Not a word to Queenie," Kevin said.

"On my honor, Kev."

He turned his wheelchair back down the driveway, passing a telephone installation man as he approached.

"Benjamin Justice?"

"That's me."

"Got your phone for you."

I invited him up, showed him the phone jack, and left him to his work.

"What you do, bring him in here?" Jin whispered, drawing the sheet up higher around him.

"It's West Hollywood. He understands."

"You make me feel dirty." He kept his voice low and a little tough. "Like you do last night."

"We were equal partners last night." I put an edge in my voice to let him know I didn't feel intimidated. "In case you were too drunk to remember."

He inched off the bed, wrapping himself in the sheet, and slipped into the bathroom, locking the door behind him. Moments later, I heard the water running.

By the time he finished showering, the telephone was installed and the service man was on his way out.

I wrote my new number on a piece of paper and shoved it into Jin's coat pocket.

He peeked from the bathroom to make sure we were alone, then emerged with a towel tucked around his waist. He brushed past me to the chair, where I'd placed his clothes the night before.

"I'm sorry if I was rude," I said.

He kept his back to me and stepped into his shorts, pulling them up under the towel before he let it fall away. Droplets of water glistened on his back, which bore the marks of my frenzied passion from the night before.

I picked up the towel and patted away the moisture. The

scratches were jagged and pink against his pale skin. As I gently touched each one, I felt blood pumping into my cock, raising it like a flag.

"You sure you don't want to come back to bed for a while?"

"I sure."

"I put my phone number in your jacket pocket."

He slipped wordlessly into his shirt, still facing away from me. I decided to let him dress in privacy and went into the bathroom for a quick shower.

I was rinsing off when I remembered stepping on his shoes that morning as I rolled out of bed, and kicking them irritably from underfoot.

"Christ."

I jumped from the shower and darted out dripping wet, scanning the room. Jin Jai-Sik was no longer there.

Then I fell to my knees and looked beneath the bed. The box of photos was gone.

Twenty-eight

THE NEW TELEPHONE felt strange in the apartment, and not entirely welcome.

Yet within minutes of discovering the photos missing, I used it to call Templeton.

I reached her at home, and the conversation was brisk and businesslike.

I gave her Jin Jai-Sik's name, birth date, and the only address I had for him. She promised to run them through criminal records before we met later that day to attend the memorial service for Billy Lusk.

I also gave her my new phone number, and before we hung up, she offered a quick rundown of her progress on the Masterman story.

She told me she was getting excellent access to the senator's campaign staff, piecing together a detailed anatomy of one week's well-organized effort to generate votes. Masterman's schedule had included a late-night speech on Monday before the local machinists union, launched about the time Billy Lusk was ordering his whiskey sour at The Out Crowd.

Templeton expected to finish up her background research by early afternoon and conduct her core interviews Sunday or Monday. I suggested she assign a *Sun* photographer to get pictures of all the principals, and she told me she'd already taken care of that.

Neither of us mentioned the personal exchanges we'd shared the previous night.

My next call was to Paca Albundo. Her father picked up, speaking accented English in a tight, troubled voice.

When he left the phone to get his daughter, I could hear a woman wailing in the background. It didn't stop when Paca came to the phone, so I assumed the hysterical woman was her mother.

"You seem to have good timing, Mr. Justice."

She sounded numb, her emotions remote.

"What's going on?"

"Gonzalo was raped last night. They called us from the jail hospital this morning. Our priest is here, mainly for my mother. We still haven't told the old ones."

"Can you tell me what happened?"

"A guard heard Gonzalo crying. They found him face down on the floor of a dormitory cell. He'd been beaten, and his pants were soaked with blood. He refused medical treatment, tried to fight them off. It took several guards to get him to the hospital ward. They had to hold him down so the doctor could examine him. The doctor told my father Gonzalo was raped by several men."

"Where is he now?"

"In a hospital bed, in restraints. On what they call a suicide watch."

I thought about HIV, but kept it to myself. The Albundo family had enough to deal with for now.

When I tried to offer my sympathy, Paca cut me off, almost coldly.

"There's something else, Mr. Justice. The doctor told us Gonzalo had two tattoos scratched on his right arm. They were very crude, and both were infected. The doctor said they were made in the last day or two."

"Is Gonzalo right- or left-handed?"

"Left."

"You think he made those tattoos himself," I said.

"Yes."

"But if he was in a gang, why didn't they do it for him, cleanly?"

"They know how to do that, Mr. Justice, but Gonzalo doesn't."

"And if he'd had the protection of a gang, no one would have raped him."

"It seems reasonable, doesn't it?"

"Yes, it seems reasonable."

The hardness suddenly went out of her voice.

"He's safe for now, Mr. Justice. But for how long? Please, help us."

I wanted to tell her I couldn't help anyone; I didn't even know how to help myself. I wanted to tell her I'd been running from involvement most of my life, letting people down when they needed me most.

"I remember the kind of stories you used to write . . . before you had your problems," she said. "You were a good reporter. You know how to find things out."

I could hear the tears she was holding back, and the next words she spoke stabbed at my heart.

"I'm begging you, Mr. Justice. For Gonzalo and for our family. Please find out who killed Mr. Lusk before Gonzalo dies in that horrible place."

Twenty-nine

I DROVE to Laguna Beach with the top lowered, shooting down the 405 at eighty with an eye out for the highway patrol.

The heat beat down from a cloudless sky, cut by a pleasant breeze, a perfect summer day I couldn't enjoy.

While certain pornographic images, even sadistic ones, appealed to the nether regions of my psyche, the vision of Gonzalo Albundo being raped on a filthy floor in County Jail wasn't one of them. Yet it was all I could think about as I headed south with the weekend traffic.

That, and what Samantha Eliason might be able to tell me about the murder of Billy Lusk.

I turned off at Laguna Canyon Road and wound my way west toward the ocean.

A stream of visitors stretched out ahead of me for miles, many of them gay men who'd be spending the weekend in the clubs, motels, and hillside party houses that catered to trim men with nice tans and a certain attitude. With weather like this, I thought, the drugstores in Laguna Beach would be selling condoms like penny candy, the way merchants in other resorts move them so briskly to heterosexual college kids during spring break.

I hung a left as soon as arching volleyballs and the glittering Pacific Ocean were in sight, working my way through narrow side streets to avoid the gridlock at the intersection with Pacific Coast Highway.

A few blocks later, I swung back toward the highway and nosed the Mustang into the traffic creeping south, past galleries and cafes spilling over with sunburned tourists who looked grimly determined to have a good time.

The address Kevin had given me was a mile beyond the main business district, on the ocean side of the inclining highway.

As I got close, I encountered two surfers pulling out in their van, and cut off a station wagon filled with kids and beach balls that tried to get to the parking space before I did.

The hotel I was looking for wasn't hard to find.

It was stately and expansive, located on the grounds of a turn-of-the-century French-châteauesque estate. The three-story main house, its corners distinguished by small turrets, was perched near the edge of a rocky cliff a hundred feet above a small cove.

A seven-foot security fence extended around the sides and rear of the property, camouflaged from public view by blooming passion-flower vines. The entrance was located on the north side, near the top of a public stairway that led to the beach. A locked security gate, equipped with an electronic camera and intercom, barred unwanted visitors.

I joined the herd making its way down the steep steps to the white sand beach, where hundreds of others were already spread out, tanning, playing volleyball, or tossing Frisbees down by the water while wet dogs leaped about, barking happily.

Ten stories above, the windows of the resort's main residence faced out to sea. A deck and paths ran the length of the property, and the rooftops of individual cottages could be glimpsed nestled on the grounds in a heavy growth of foliage.

There seemed to be no comfortable way in but through the proper front entrance.

I trudged back up the stairs, rummaged through the back seat of the Mustang, found a large used envelope in the assorted trash, and filled it with junk mail to give it some heft.

Moments later, I stood in front of the inn's security gate. I pushed the intercom button and a friendly male voice crackled through the speaker.

"Welcome to Cliffside. May we help you?"

I held the envelope up for the camera and told him I had a delivery for Samantha Eliason. I mentioned Queenie Cochran's public relations firm and smiled amiably.

He buzzed me in.

I followed a brick path toward the sound of splashing water, past two middle-aged men in matching swimsuits who kissed affectionately but without much passion, in the manner of older couples. A mixed group of men and women splashed each other in the pool. Around it, another dozen guests stretched out in the sun, half of them naked or topless, some sipping champagne with their late brunch.

I surveyed the female faces. Samantha Eliason's was not among them.

"I'll be happy to take that for you."

It was the friendly voice I'd heard over the intercom. It belonged to a wisp of a man in a colorful Hawaiian shirt whose forehead bore the weblike scars of a serious bout with shingles.

"My instructions are to deliver it to Sam personally." With a smile, I added, "We call her Sam at the agency."

"Take the path to your left. You'll find her in the third cottage down."

The door of the first cottage was half open; Streisand show tunes could be heard playing inside. In front of the second cottage, a fortyish man with a powerful torso and Mediterranean looks sat in an Adirondack chair reading a copy of Walter Mosley's *Black Betty* from behind dark glasses. The third cottage was open but protected by a screen door.

I stepped up to the porch and looked in.

I saw a child's playpen in the living room and cuddly toys strewn about, along with enough adult athletic gear to stock a small sporting goods store.

When I'd gotten a good look, I rang the bell.

Samantha Eliason appeared from the kitchen, wearing shorts and a halter top, her dark hair just long enough and just curly enough to qualify as conventionally feminine.

As a tennis player, she'd never been as great a champion as Martina Navratilova, nor as open about her personal life, but they shared the lean, efficient musculature and powerful stride that only comes from years of dedicated training. If Eliason hadn't won as many titles as Navratilova, she certainly had made millions of dollars more in product endorsements by carefully guarding her sexual orientation from public exposure, as Derek

Brunheim had so colorfully pointed out the first time I'd interviewed him.

Queenie Cochran had gone so far as to plant false leads in the press linking her client to heterosexual romances that didn't exist. They always went out to a select list of columnists, some of whom were closeted themselves. Those who cooperated got lavish gifts from Queenie, with the price tags and receipts attached for easy cash exchange.

"Yes?"

Samantha Eliason came to the door with the guarded manner that many celebrities develop like a second skin. I noticed immediately that she'd put on weight and was more full-breasted than she'd looked in any of her televised matches.

"My name is Benjamin Justice. I'm doing some research for the *Los Angeles Sun.*"

"How did you get in here?"

Her voice was deep enough to pass as a man's, with a commanding strength that would serve her well behind a microphone.

"I'm a skillful liar," I said. "Don't blame the man at the desk."

She glanced past me in the direction of the footpath.

"Please leave."

"It's about Billy Lusk. I know you were close friends."

"I haven't seen Billy for some time."

"I just have a few questions."

Her eyes darted back and forth from me to the footpath like a spectator watching one of her fast-paced tennis matches.

"I really don't want to discuss this right now."

"You know he was murdered."

"Of course." Then, as if she needed to explain: "Billy's roommate, Derek Brunheim, called me."

Laughter reached us from two cottages away. Two men emerged sharing a joint, on their way out with towels and beach chairs.

The barrel-chested occupant of the adjacent cottage had risen from his Adirondack chair to watch us intently.

"Could I come in? It might be more private."

"My public relations agency arranges all interviews, Mr. Justice."

"I can't wait for that. There's a boy in jail being held for Billy's murder. He was raped last night by several inmates. He won't survive in there for very long."

"I don't see what that has to do with me."

"You and Billy had a falling out in the past year. Your arguments have escalated recently."

"I'm calling the front desk, Mr. Justice, and asking them to escort you out."

She took a step back and picked up a phone just inside the door.

"I also know that you've been sending him large amounts of cash."

She paused with her finger still on the button.

I thought I saw fear cross her face. She managed to quickly hide it with the considerable skill she'd developed over the years in hiding so much of her life.

"If you'll be honest with me, Samantha, it's possible none of this ever has to get into print. But if you don't deal straight with me, I'll consider any and every aspect of your personal life fair game."

"That sounds like coercion to me."

"Not at all. You've used the media to promote yourself to the public as heterosexual. That leaves your private life open to scrutiny, especially if there's evidence you were deliberately deceptive."

She put the phone back on its cradle and glanced in the direction of a clock.

She said quickly, "I can only talk for a moment."

"I'm all ears."

"Billy had some problems. Specifically, coke. He had debts. I helped him pay them off so that he could get a fresh start. Something any close friend might do."

"And the arguments?"

"Naturally, I tried to get him to stop using. Billy was in total denial about how the drug was affecting his life. You know how cokeheads can be."

"When did you see him last?"

"Months ago. February, I think."

"When you returned from Europe?"

Her husky voice tightened, giving her away.

"How did you know about that?"

"I have sources."

She stiffened, and answered reluctantly.

"Yes. About that time."

"Where were you Tuesday morning, shortly after midnight?"

"At home. In Brentwood."

"Alone?"

"I was with someone."

"Would that person be willing to verify your alibi?"

"I believe that's a question the police should ask, if it comes to that."

"The police have signed off on this case, and I think you know it. But I haven't."

"It's not someone I wish to bring into this."

"I take it it's a woman."

"I didn't say that."

I didn't enjoy watching Samantha Eliason squirm, but I reminded myself that she lived in a prison of her own making. She had weighed the price to be paid for mainstream acceptance and corporate marketing deals, and now she was paying it.

Any other time, I would have left her alone. At the moment, however, Gonzalo Albundo's survival seemed more important than Samantha Eliason's comfortable place in the closet.

"Was Billy Lusk blackmailing you, Samantha?"

"I really can't talk to you any longer."

She reached for the door.

"Just a couple more questions . . ."

She twisted the handle of the screen door, thrust it open, and stepped out right into my face.

"Get away from me!" she screamed. "Leave me alone! Stay out of my life!"

Her fury, fueled by a fear I didn't yet understand, was formidable; she literally trembled with it.

The man next door threw down his book and started toward us. I realized then that he was probably her bodyguard, instructed to keep a low profile unless action was absolutely necessary.

Before he reached us, I said to her, "If you have anything to add, I'd appreciate it if you'd call me."

I pushed a slip of paper into her hand with my name and home number on it.

By then, the bodyguard had me by the arm and was dragging me roughly down the steps. I shook him off, just as roughly. He was professional enough to want to avoid trouble, and allowed me to walk ahead of him on my own.

He followed me back down the brick path and stood watching until I was out the gate, listening to it lock behind me.

I took a minute to think over what had just transpired and why, making mental notes as I worked my way through possible scenarios.

Then I started up the hill toward the highway.

I hadn't climbed more than fifty feet when I faced a young woman pushing a baby stroller in my direction.

She was a fresh-faced redhead with a trim, athletic look and freckles everywhere. I glanced into the stroller and saw a child of five or six months. Soft, golden hair curled from under the baby's blue denim cap.

Then I saw the tiny, upturned nose.

It was an unmistakable copy of the nose in every photograph I'd ever seen of Billy Lusk.

"Beautiful baby," I said.

"Isn't he?"

She paused to let me have a better look, smiling radiantly from an honest, open face.

"What do you call him?"

"William," she said. "After his father."

I asked her if she was staying at Cliffside, and she nodded.

"Isn't it great?"

"We love it," she said.

"You and William?"

"I'm with someone," she said. "William's mom."

She took out her key and unlocked the gate. I held it open for her until she and the stroller were safely inside. She thanked me, bid me a nice day, and went on her way.

I watched her push the stroller down the brick path, taking the left turn toward the three cottages. I stepped quickly back inside and closed the gate quietly behind me.

I kept my distance as I followed. She pushed the stroller past the first cottage, then the second. Samantha Eliason's bodyguard was no longer in sight.

As she approached the third cottage, I ducked into the woodsy landscape for cover. I hunkered down behind a big Scotch broom, parted some yellow-blossomed branches, and watched her turn up the walk to the porch.

Samantha Eliason stepped anxiously out.

She brightened as the baby was lifted into her arms, and rubbed her nose against his, talking baby talk.

Then she and the redheaded woman exchanged a kiss, put their arms around each other, and went inside.

That's when I heard a footstep in the dry leaves behind me, and turned into a hail of blinding pepper spray.

Thirty

"HOW MUCH do you want, Mr. Justice? My bank account has its limits, but we might be able to work something out."

I was stretched out on the sofa in the second cottage, a wet towel over my eyes, having first flooded my face with water at the kitchen sink.

The bodyguard stood over me with his can of pepper spray, ready to nail me again if I made the wrong move.

"I'm not here to get money out of you, Samantha."

"Then why?"

"I told you. The Billy Lusk story."

"I called Queenie Cochran. She told me you do some freelance writing for the agency now and then, which explains how you know certain things. But to use her words, there's no chance in hell that you're on the staff of the *Los Angeles Sun.*"

"I didn't say I was on staff . . ."

"She also reminded me of who you are and why you were run out of the newspaper business six years ago."

"I'm working freelance for the *Sun,*" I said. "Strictly legwork."

The fire that I'd first experienced in my face and eyes had diminished to an unpleasant but tolerable stinging. Each time I tried to open my eyes, it felt like there was ground glass beneath the lids, so I kept them closed.

"Have Queenie call Alexandra Templeton at home," I said. "She works for the *Sun.*"

"Why should I?"

"Templeton's the lead reporter on the Billy Lusk story. She'll tell you I'm working with her. Or you can call her yourself."

Eliason must have figured it was worth a simple phone call, because she asked for Templeton's number. I heard her from across the room, speaking in low tones. I removed the towel from my eyes and opened them just enough to see her with the telephone to her ear.

She hung up, came back, and faced the bodyguard, looking unsure if she were relieved or perplexed.

"He's telling the truth. He's working on a story about Billy."

I asked the bodyguard to point his can of pepper spray in another direction. Eliason nodded, and he put the can away.

"I deeply regret this, Mr. Justice," Eliason said. "But I'm not going to apologize."

I sat up, groaning, and used the towel to wipe away the perspiration that coated my face and neck, despite the air conditioning.

"You were trespassing," she went on, trying to sound forceful rather than defensive, but not succeeding. "Then you were caught spying on me. I have a right to protect myself."

"With preemptive assault?"

"You have no idea what it's like living in the public eye. The strange letters. The threats. The possibility of violence. It's always there."

I glanced at the bodyguard.

"If he holds his hand over a candle for a few hours, maybe I won't press charges." I pinned her with my eyes. "Or file the kind of lawsuit that can smear all this across the papers, not to mention tabloid TV."

I had no intention of doing either, but I needed to regain some leverage as quickly as possible.

"You promised me that what transpired between us would remain confidential."

"If you dealt straight with me," I said. "You didn't."

She dropped her eyes, and I saw the tension coiling itself in her well-developed neck and shoulders.

"You want to start over and try it again, Samantha? It might be your last chance. But you'd better get it right this time."

She found a plastic case of Panter Silhouettes, lit one, took two quick puffs, and said to the bodyguard, "Get Patricia."

He left.

"Look," I said, "I don't want to hurt anybody. I just want to know what's going on."

She took another drag, agitated, and stared at the smoldering cigar.

"Another one of my secret vices." She laughed uneasily. "I quit for the baby, but this whole thing with Billy . . ."

She stubbed out the cigar and moved around the cottage, opening the windows.

The air had cleared by the time the redheaded woman appeared carrying the sleeping baby. She didn't look so radiant now; she looked confused and worried.

Eliason asked the bodyguard to go outside, which he did.

"This is Patricia, Mr. Justice." She hesitated. "My lover."

The word didn't come out of her mouth easily. She offered the other woman an apologetic look.

"That's the first time I've acknowledged that to anyone other than a few close friends."

"You met Mom and Dad," Patricia said.

"That's true." Eliason smiled at the milestone and relaxed a little. "I did, didn't I?"

In short order, Patricia informed me that she was a physical therapist who lived communally with several other women in a big house they'd purchased in Santa Barbara; that she was spending more and more time at Eliason's Brentwood home, helping with the baby; that the two women had met while mountain biking in Arizona; and that she'd introduced Eliason to her parents three weeks ago during a trip to Duluth for their thirtieth wedding anniversary. It was more than I needed to know, but at least it indicated that they'd started to trust me.

Eliason took the baby from Patricia, cradling him in her arms.

"And this is William," she said, sounding very much the proud mother.

"Yes, we met. I saw the resemblance to Billy. That's what led me back."

"As you've probably guessed, I gave birth to him when I was away in Europe. We named him when Billy and I were still getting along."

"At some point, you and Billy must have been doing more than just getting along."

"Billy and I were good friends, Mr. Justice, but we were never intimate. We conceived William using the Thanksgiving method."

"That's one I'm not familiar with."

"Turkey baster," Patricia explained matter-of-factly. "Sam got pregnant on the second try." She laughed, and a pink blush seeped in among her freckles. "We've been giving thanks ever since."

"I've always wanted a family," Eliason said. "A committed partner, which I have in Patricia. And a child to love and cherish, which I have in William."

"Billy's idea or yours?"

"He knew I was looking for a sperm donor, and he volunteered. The genes made him a natural choice. He was bright, good-looking, healthy. He tested HIV-negative. And we really cared about each other. At least before . . ."

"Before the drugs changed him?"

She nodded.

"When I was still carrying, I told Billy that if he'd become drug-free, I'd let him spend as much time with his child as he wanted, without any financial responsibility. I wanted William to know his father, for Billy to be part of our lives."

The baby stirred in his sleep, and she gently jiggled him until he became quiet again.

"I guess that won't be possible now," she said.

"But after he got in deeper with his coke habit," I said, "he started squeezing you for money."

She nodded again.

"His parents had cut him off, and he was getting desperate. He asked for a little at first, then larger and larger amounts."

"And when you resisted, he threatened to expose you as a lesbian."

She chewed a corner of her lower lip. Patricia laid a hand on her dark hair, stroking it gently.

"Ever since we met two years ago, I've encouraged Sam to come out," Patricia said. "I told her it would take so much pressure off her. Meeting my parents was the first step. Coming here, being more open around strangers like us, that was next."

She gave Eliason a supportive smile.

"I think she just needs a little more time."

"If you'd planned to come out," I said, "wouldn't that take the muscle out of Billy's threats?"

The distress deepened on Eliason's face.

"I'm afraid it was more complicated than that." She gnawed seriously at her lip now. "It still is."

Patricia picked up the story.

"Billy told Sam that if she didn't give him what he wanted, he'd tell his mother about the baby. That they'd file for custody, use Sam's sexual orientation against her in court. Talk to the media. Leave her without a career or a child."

"You could have fought it legally," I said.

Eliason pressed her cheek to her son's downy head.

"And I might have lost. The courts take kids away from lesbian mothers all the time. The prospect of losing my child . . . I don't even want to think about it."

"So you decided to keep William a secret? Even from his grandmother?"

"Mrs. Devonshire is extremely possessive," Patricia said. "If she knew about William, she'd do anything to get him for herself."

"And anything," Eliason added, "to keep me away from him."

The baby woke, and his pink mouth puckered into a yawn. He reached for his mother's hair with tiny fingers.

My next question was one the entire conversation had been pointing toward.

"And what would you do to keep him?"

Eliason flushed with anger and turned away, pacing the room with the baby against her shoulder.

"She wouldn't commit murder," Patricia said firmly.

She walked to Samantha and put an arm around her shoulders. "Not this woman. No way."

"I won't pretend I didn't despise Billy for what he was doing to us," Eliason said. "But if someone killed Billy other than that boy in jail, it wasn't me."

"Any ideas?"

The two women exchanged a troubled glance.

"I think you should tell him," Patricia said.

Eliason shifted the baby to her other arm before she spoke.

"Derek Brunheim was obsessed with Billy, Mr. Justice. And every bit as possessive as Mrs. Devonshire."

"That doesn't make him a murderer."

''Billy called Sam on Monday night,'' Patricia said. ''She was nursing the baby, so I answered the phone. It was late. Only an hour or two before Billy was killed.''

''I didn't want to talk to him,'' Eliason said. ''I assumed he wanted more money, and I wasn't in the mood to deal with him. But Patricia said there was trouble.''

''Billy had told Derek he was moving out, and Derek went ballistic,'' Patricia said. ''Billy was really scared. I told Sam I thought she should talk to him.''

''I'll never forget how frightened he sounded,'' Eliason said. ''In fact, I remember his exact words.''

''I'm always interested in exact words,'' I said.

''He told me Derek had murder in his eye.''

Thirty-one

MARGARET DEVONSHIRE had closed the funeral services for her son to everyone but the immediate family, so Billy's closest friends had hastily arranged a Saturday afternoon memorial service of their own, and had the decency to invite the Devonshires.

It was held at a small reform temple on Beverly Boulevard that welcomed members of the gay and lesbian community to its regular worship services, and had special programs for them as well.

During the 1980s, I'd attended more memorial services than I could remember, but Jacques's had been the last. I wouldn't have been at this one except that Templeton had asked me to go with her, pressing me when I'd tried to get out of it.

Because she'd been preoccupied with other assignments, including her Masterman research, she was feeling cut off from the Billy Lusk story. I'd briefed her on the principal characters, but she wanted to see what some of them looked like, as she put it, "up close and personal." At least that was the explanation she gave for wanting to be with me on a weekend evening.

It must have been a slow news day, because we arrived separately to find three TV crews out front. We took seats inconspicuously inside at the back, off to the right. The late afternoon light cast a pleasant glow through a stained glass Star of David formed in blue against an amber background, set high in a west wall.

Templeton wore a tasteful gray dress with a flowing scarf of deep burgundy that complemented her dark skin and willowy stature, but still managed to be appropriately subdued. My nose caught the subtle scent of cologne as she shifted her chair closer to mine.

She filled me in on the Devonshire family background, which she'd looked into with special interest. Margaret Devonshire had converted to the Jewish faith when she'd married her first husband, Billy's father. When she later remarried, Phil Devonshire had belonged to a posh country club that excluded Jews and nonwhites. He'd insisted she renounce her links to Judaism so that he could keep his membership, and she'd complied, further upsetting her already alienated young son.

"Not that Phil Devonshire's racist or anti-Semitic," Templeton added, with a straight face. "He just likes to be with his own kind."

"From what I hear about Phil Devonshire," I said, "he's the ultimate control freak. My way or the highway. And Billy was someone he couldn't easily control."

"Meaning what?"

I told her about Phil Devonshire's fondness for guns, and how he and Billy had been at odds over Billy's drug use and sexual proclivities.

"It sounds like you've put Mr. Devonshire on your list of suspects," Templeton said.

"Or maybe I just don't like him very much."

From our location in the back, we could observe the former golf pro sitting midway down the aisle, looking very much like he wished he were somewhere else. He'd put on considerable weight since his professional playing days, along with a toupee and a drinker's pickled nose. For the service, he'd dressed in a blue blazer and flashy yellow necktie that seemed close to mockery, considering the occasion. He struck me as someone who probably had more sensitivity for his favorite five iron than for other human beings.

Next to him, Margaret Devonshire was dressed in somber black, looking more worn-out than when I'd first met her, and not at all comfortable attending a service she hadn't personally supervised.

All around the Devonshires, younger men and women chatted and embraced, and a few were already dabbing their eyes with hankies. It was a sizable crowd that included both gay and straight couples, which indicated that Billy Lusk must have been more personable throughout his life than his recent history indicated.

There were a few older straight couples as well, who exchanged words with Margaret Devonshire, while her husband nodded mechanically with a tight smile fixed to his silent lips.

I directed Templeton's attention to Derek Brunheim, who was seated in the front row, surrounded by friends and holding court in his customary way.

Then I pointed out Samantha Eliason, sitting alone near the back, across the room, her face hidden behind a veil.

"How do you know it's her?"

"The shoulders," I said. "And the walk, when she first came in."

"From what you've told me, she had as much motive for wanting Billy dead as anyone."

"She admitted that Billy was blackmailing her," I said, "and threatening her with the loss of her child. The question is whether her girlfriend is lying about the phone call they claim they got from Billy the night he was murdered."

"Her girlfriend could also be lying about where Samantha was that night."

"Good point."

To our left, a tall, broad-shouldered shadow fell across the floor beneath the entrance archway.

As it moved forward, Jefferson Bellworthy followed it into the room, dressed in a sharp-looking black suit over a white silk shirt with a Chinese collar. He strode down the aisle to the front, where he and Brunheim embraced.

I identified Bellworthy, and Templeton gave him an appraising look.

"Now that's what I call a fine brown frame."

"You can cool down, Templeton. He's as homosexual as I am."

"I've never shopped for labels," she said coyly, and turned her appraising eyes on me.

I didn't give her the satisfaction of a reaction.

"Bellworthy seems like a nice enough guy," I said. "But he's also got a violent streak. If anyone was in the right place at the right time to murder Billy Lusk and get away with it, it was him."

"Then there's your friend, Jin Jai-Sik. I don't suppose he'll show up for the service."

"Not likely."

"I ran his name through records, like you asked," she said. "Two drunk driving convictions. Nothing else."

Just as the room began to dim with the fading sunlight, as if on cue, a young rabbi took the podium. He spoke briefly about Billy Lusk in a personal way, mentioning in particular his gift for making friends, then centered his remaining remarks on the issues of tolerance and brotherhood.

After that, a succession of Billy's friends, not including Samantha Eliason, rose to remember him; a few recalled colorful events from Billy's social life that must have caused Margaret Devonshire an uneasy moment or two. A young woman took the stage to perform Billy's favorite song; she sang a slow, evocative version of "Last Dance" a cappella, and the room filled with the sound of mourners weeping softly and blowing their noses.

When Derek Brunheim stood to speak, Phil Devonshire put an arm around his wife's shoulders, as if to protect her from the evil that was to follow.

Brunheim talked theatrically and at length, a performance that was both funny and touching, interrupted two or three times when he paused to cry. His words seemed rehearsed but not his tears, and I wondered if Margaret Devonshire felt as much compassion for his grief as he did for hers.

The moment the service ended, Samantha Eliason quickly slipped out a side door, where neither the cameras nor Margaret Devonshire were likely to see her.

Phil Devonshire was on his feet nearly as fast.

He led his wife briskly up the center aisle, a hand at her back to move her along, superiority stamped all over his bloated face. He typified the kind of person for whom I felt a special loathing: rich, powerful, arrogant, bigoted. The type who would smile and make pleasant small talk with Jews and people of color when circumstances required it, but who would do whatever was necessary behind their backs to keep them off his golf course and out of corporate boardrooms.

I had little doubt that he did the same with homosexuals, and I wondered to what lengths he would go to eliminate them from his own family, especially if they vied with him for so much of his wife's attention, the way his stepson had.

Templeton stood, and I followed her toward the crowded aisle.

"Coming here today must have been difficult for you," she said.

I had an idea where this conversation was headed, but wasn't interested in going there, and I kept my silence.

"Isn't tomorrow the sixth anniversary of Jacques's death?"

I resented the familiar way with which she spoke his name, but kept quiet about that as well.

"I talked with one of your landlords," she said. "Maurice. He let me into your apartment yesterday."

"Yes, I found the clipping from the *Times.*"

"He filled me in on some things."

"I'm surprised you've found so much time to look into my personal history," I said. "What with all your pressing assignments."

"I made the time. I like to finish what I start."

She slipped her arm through mine as we shuffled toward the foyer with the other mourners.

"Jacques is an unusual name," she said. "Was he French?"

"He changed his name from Walter to Jacques when he was fourteen. After hearing an old recording by Jacques Brel."

"How interesting."

"At least that's the story he told me. He had different versions for different aspects of his life, as the need arose."

"Sounds like an intriguing man."

"He was an abused kid whose stepfather sodomized him until he grew hair on his ass." I hoped the harsh truth might shock her into leaving the subject alone. "To survive emotionally, Jacques retreated into fantasy a lot of the time. He spent most of his life trying to decide if he wanted a father figure to protect him or abuse him."

"Which one were you?"

"We never quite figured that out."

We stepped into the foyer and the dying sunlight.

"Maurice told me about Jacques's illness," Templeton said. "How you took care of him the last few months of his life."

"Someone had to take over. Maurice and Fred were worn out. It was my turn."

"Maurice said you and Jacques loved each other very much. That you broke up several times but always got back together. Like destiny, Maurice said."

"Maurice has a flair for the romantic," I said. "Maybe that's why he and Jacques got along so well."

"But you did get back together a final time, just before he got sick."

"We were each working through some things. It was looking like it might work out."

"Caring for him those last months must have been very hard."

"It's always hard when someone you care about takes a long time to die."

I thought, *There are times when you want them to die, to just get it over with, and then you hate yourself afterward for wishing it.* But I didn't tell her that.

We moved down the wide steps, where mourners mingled, and toward the street. I saw Phil Devonshire at the wheel of a new Chrysler, driving away fast as the TV cameras panned for a final shot.

"Two weeks after his death," Templeton said, "you filed your AIDS series with the *L.A. Times.*"

We'd reached the sidewalk. I stopped to face her.

"I really don't care to discuss this, Templeton."

"It was the story of two lovers, one caring for the other as he died of AIDS. Was that just a coincidence, Justice? Or was that series about you and Jacques, with the names changed?"

"Are you researching a story of your own?"

"I could be."

"No comment, then."

Her Lexus was at the curb. My Mustang was around the corner. I glanced impatiently in its direction.

"You're angry with me for looking into this, aren't you?"

"I'm not your keeper, Templeton. You can talk to anyone you please. Do all the digging your reporter's heart desires."

She offered a little smile, like a peace pipe.

"How about some dinner? There's a terrific Thai place just down the street."

"Thanks. I've got an errand to run."

She took out her keys but made no move to her car.

I was suddenly aware of how close she was standing. So close that if she moved another inch, her chest would be touching mine.

"Then I guess it's time to say good-night," she said, and closed the inch between us.

I stood my ground, and our bodies made contact.

I looked past her, at two men embracing. Their arms were wrapped around each other, almost desperately tight, as one wept on the shoulder of the other.

I felt Templeton's hand on my chest.

"What are you thinking about right now?"

I looked right into her eyes, tired of all the masks. Especially my own.

"Paul Masterman, Jr.," I said.

"Seriously?"

"Quite."

"Why?"

"Because he turns me on."

I felt her hand drop away and heard the jingle of her keys.

"I'll call you," she said, "if anything new comes my way on Billy Lusk."

She placed a hand on my shoulder and stretched as if to give me a friendly kiss.

When I continued to hold my ground, her mouth moved deliberately toward mine, until our lips touched. She pressed further, and our lips parted just enough so that each of us tasted the moisture in the other's mouth. It was much more than just a parting kiss between friends.

She pulled suddenly away.

"We'll have to talk about that."

She said it in a voice that was part sultry temptress, part scolding mother, and oozing with self-satisfaction.

She drove off, leaving me angry that I'd let her set me up so easily, when I should have seen it coming a mile away.

Thirty-two

THE TEMPLE where Billy Lusk was eulogized was only a few miles from the address I'd copied from Jin Jai-Sik's driver's license.

I turned the Mustang east on Olympic Boulevard and put on the headlights against the dusk. The air was warm and still, "earthquake weather" in L.A. parlance, though the only things rumbling at the moment were the wheels of the Mustang, which needed aligning.

I cruised along an unrelieved stretch of commercial real estate that had been a corridor of flames during the last riots, until I reached the heart of Koreatown.

A tangle of neon signs, formed from the slash mark ideographs of hangul, the Korean word system, loomed brightly above the bustling business district.

The address I was looking for was in the residential section to the north, where most of the faces were Hispanic, but Korean families were part of the mix. I found the house on a broad, clean street of restored Victorians and Craftsmen, which managed to look hospitable despite the cast-iron burglar bars that covered almost every ground-level window.

I left the Mustang at the curb and followed a cleanly edged walkway across a gentle slope of lawn. Three steps led to a broad porch and massive front door of lacquered wood, with a heavy knocker of burnished brass.

Lights were on inside, but dense curtains guarded the interior from prying eyes.

A thin, graying Korean man, tidy and well groomed, answered the bell with a newspaper in his hand. He wore dark pleated slacks and a starched white dress shirt, and examined me dispassionately through wire-rimmed glasses.

I told him my name and that I was looking for Jin Jai-Sik.

"No English," he said. "Sorry."

I glanced at the copy of *The Wall Street Journal* in his hand.

"It's very important that I talk with him."

The man took a quick look back into the big house, where a little girl sat at a dining room table, bent over a book. It was difficult to tell if she was the same child whose photograph I'd seen in Jin Jai-Sik's wallet, but the general resemblance was close.

The man stepped out and quietly shut the door.

"Jin no longer live here."

"Are you his father?"

The pain in his eyes gave away the truth.

"Jin no longer live here," he repeated more firmly.

"He has something that belongs to me. It's important that he return it."

I wrote my name and phone number in a small notebook, tore out the page, and handed it to him.

"If Jin does not return what belongs to me, I may have to inform the police. Please, Mr. Jai-Sik. Have him call me."

"I try."

He turned back into the house but paused at the door.

"If Jin take something not belong to him, I apologize for him and for his family."

He went in, and I heard the door being locked and latched.

Along the porch, window curtains parted, and the little girl peeked out.

Before I could get a good look at her, someone whisked her away, and the heavy curtains fell closed again.

Thirty-three

I MADE MY WAY HOME in the sluggish Saturday evening traffic along Santa Monica Boulevard.

The prostitutes were out in force, wooing potential customers, who drove slowly in the right lane.

On the street corners between Van Ness and Highland avenues, most of the hustlers were black and Hispanic, giving way to more and more young white men after that, with a rash of slinky transvestites in the first block or two on either side of La Brea, displaying themselves in the warm night air like sweet-smelling gardenia blossoms ready to be picked.

A mile farther on, I crossed La Cienega into the heart of Boy's Town, where the traffic slowed to a crawl, and music from the clubs blasted the street. Men were everywhere, bunched on corners waiting for lights to change, streaming by in crosswalks, flowing in and out of the clubs and cafes, their eyes alert to the next striking face, the next impressive body, the next chance at love.

I arrived back on Norma Place to the tinkle of dinnerware and laughter coming from the house. Maurice and Fred held a small AIDS fund-raising party on the third Saturday of each month, during which guests were wined and dined for a twenty-five-dollar donation. Together, Maurice and Fred belonged to half a dozen AIDS organizations, part of an army of men and women committed to battling and coping with the epidemic.

There were times when I wished I had an ounce of their courage to get so close to it. To see it, to touch it, to feel it all around. To acknowledge that in all that life out there, death was quietly, relentlessly at work.

The driveway was filled with cars, so I parked on the street, hanging my residential permit on the rearview mirror to avoid a ticket. I was exhausted from the long day and had a lot on my mind. Otherwise, I might have recognized the '52 Chevy pickup parked at the end of the block, with its engine idling and its sharp yellow paint job begging to be noticed.

I hurried up the drive with my hands in my pockets and my head down, hoping to get to the apartment unseen by anyone inside the house. I didn't make it.

Fred stepped out on the front porch, scratching a plump gray cat behind the ears, and invited me in for dessert. When I demurred, Maurice appeared behind him, gently wheedling.

"Just for a minute," I said, and mounted the steps toward a houseful of people I didn't know and didn't want to meet.

Fred set the cat on the porch railing, and I told him I'd rather have a glass of wine, if it was all the same. I was on the top step when I remembered the yellow pickup and realized, too late, what it meant.

As I turned, I heard five or six shots in rapid succession, their sound more a crack than a pop.

In the same moment, I heard glass shattering as the bullets took out windowpanes across the front of the house.

Maurice and Fred wisely hit the porch floor, with Fred's big body thrown protectively over the smaller Maurice.

My reaction was just the opposite.

I faced the street and braced myself for a bullet, determined to play out my part in the violent little scenario I'd helped create. As frightened as I was, I felt ready for whatever happened. A weary part of me welcomed the quick, clean escape a single bullet could provide, if only the shooter were a halfway decent shot.

I was asking too much of Luis Albundo.

As I waited for the bullet's impact, I stared into his rage-filled eyes a moment before the pickup sped away, its license plates covered over with newspaper and tape.

The sound of its peeling tires gave way to the din of screaming and pandemonium inside the house. I sensed my feet still firmly on the step, my body intact, my heart pounding wildly. I felt a strange disappointment.

Maurice and Fred picked themselves up, amazingly unshaken, and did a quick inventory of injuries. Both had seen action in separate wars, Fred as a soldier and Maurice as a medic, and it showed as they moved among their guests with calm and purpose.

They found only minor cuts, caused by flying glass, and everyone chattered incessantly, pumped up with adrenaline and relief.

Then Maurice discovered the lifeless ball of gray fur behind the porch railing, where a bullet had struck the cat directly in the chest. There was a little blood, but not much, and the cat's eyes were open.

Maurice closed them, then carefully picked the animal up, cradling it in his spindly arms. Fred tried to help, but Maurice pushed him away, disappearing in his delicate way with quick, tiny steps around the side of the house.

Distant sirens added their wail to the general uproar, becoming louder as they got closer.

I found a glass of wine sitting untouched on the porch and drank it down all at once, the way you'd drink a glass of cold water on a hot day.

Patrol cars pulled up out front at dramatic angles, filling the street, while neighbors bunched together on the tree-lined sidewalks.

Fred handed me a fresh glass of wine and asked me if I was all right. I said I was, and as I drank it down, my shaking hands began to settle.

I crossed the yard and approached a sergeant, who stood by her patrol car talking into a radio transmitter.

I told her the shooter was a man named Luis Albundo, spelled it for her, and mentioned that I was the target. I described him for her, along with his vehicle, and suggested he might be heading east, back to Echo Park.

After she'd relayed the information to the sheriff's communication desk, I told her about my involvement in the Billy Lusk murder case, and my confrontation with Luis Albundo three days before.

"Billy Lusk was murdered with a thirty-eight," I said. "The gun tonight sounded like a smaller caliber. But if they find one, and it is a thirty-eight, they'll want to run it through ballistics."

"You sound like you know something about guns," she said.

"My father was a cop."

Within a few minutes, she got a call on her police radio informing her that deputies had apprehended Luis Albundo on the Sunset Strip. The yellow pickup had become hopelessly trapped in a gridlock of limousines in front of The House of Blues.

"No gun," the sergeant said. "He must have tossed it. We'll search all possible routes. You OK?"

I told her I was. A few minutes after that, another patrol car pulled up, and I was asked to identify the man sitting in the backseat in handcuffs.

"That's him," I said, and they drove Luis Albundo away as he shouted obscenities at me in Spanish.

I went up to my apartment and called Paca Albundo to tell her she had another brother in jail.

Thirty-four

"IT'S OVER," Harry said. "You're off the story."

We stood in the parking lot of the sheriff's West Hollywood substation, where Luis Albundo had been booked for attempted murder, among other charges.

Harry had come down to talk with the deputies when they'd learned that I had no press credentials from the *Sun*. Before they'd reached him, he'd also gotten calls from the *Sun*'s publisher and from Queenie Cochran.

"You can't pull me off the story now," I said.

"I just did."

Harry climbed behind the wheel of his Ford Escort. I stood between him and the door so he couldn't get away.

"Why? Because Queenie Cochran's pissed and the *Sun* might not get to do any more puff jobs on her clients? That's stupid, Harry."

"I'll tell you what's stupid. Trespassing on private property and spying on Samantha Eliason, that's stupid. Antagonizing this Albundo guy until he tries to do a drive-by on you, that's stupid. Forcing your way into an interview with Margaret Devonshire, now that's *really* stupid. Her husband plays poker with the publisher, for Christ sake!"

"A disrupted poker game! Oh, Harry, how ever can I make amends?"

"You've put the entire Billy Lusk coverage in jeopardy." He

pushed me aside and pulled the door closed. ''Not to mention my goddamn job.''

''I was doing *my* job, Harry. The one you gave me to do.''

''You're a loose cannon, Ben.''

''I've always been a loose cannon.''

''You don't get it, do you? You can't get away with it anymore. Six years ago, you screwed up big time and everybody's watching you now. I warned you to take it slowly, keep a low profile. But you didn't listen.''

He switched on the ignition. I reached through the open window and turned the key, shutting the engine off.

''Harry, I know Gonzalo Albundo didn't murder Billy Lusk.''

''No, you don't know that. You think it, maybe. For your own personal reasons, whatever they may be.''

''In my gut, I know it.''

''Have you forgotten that he's an admitted gang banger? That a witness puts him at the scene? That blood on his clothes places him with the body? That he *confessed,* for Christ sake! Those are the facts, Ben!''

''You always taught me to look beyond the obvious, Harry. Assume nothing, check everything. Remember?''

''All right,'' Harry said tersely. ''We'll go through this one more time. Tell me exactly what you know.''

''First of all, Gonzalo Albundo is not a member of any gang we can find. Everybody who knows the gangs in that area says he didn't run with one. Everything in his past indicates complete antipathy toward gang-banging. He was raped in jail, no gang protection there. And no tattoos on his body, except for some he crudely scratched on himself, after the fact. He doesn't fit the profile of a gang banger, Harry. Not even close.''

Harry wiped his glasses on a handkerchief, something he often did when he was about to end a discussion.

''So why was he down there, Ben, hanging around a gay bar?'' He said it calmly, and it felt faintly patronizing. ''And why did he confess?''

He slipped his glasses back on and said, ''I'm waiting, Ben.''

I decided to play my hand, while there was still time.

''Because he's gay.''

Harry slumped a little behind the wheel, shaking his head. ''And just how the fuck do you know that?''

"For starters, I found a gay magazine and a package of condoms hidden in his bedroom."

"Which proves nothing."

"He may not be active yet. But he's at least curious, and probably much more than that. His sister told me he's become withdrawn in the past year, no communication. It sounds like he could be in deep conflict about his sexual feelings."

"This is psychobabble, Ben. It's not your field."

"Hear me out, Harry."

He found a cigarette, lit it, and stared out at the brick wall in front of him. Over its top, I could see the baseball field across the street. In between, a stream of men sauntered from their cars to the clubs.

I kneeled down to Harry's level.

"I think that Gonzalo sneaked out late that night, dropping from his bedroom window. When his sister showed me his room, I found the screen unlatched. He probably rolled his car down the hill with the ignition off to avoid waking anyone, then drove to The Out Crowd.

"He got there in a matter of minutes. He hung around outside in the shadows, trying to meet a man or just see what was going on. That's when he heard Billy Lusk arguing with someone, then a gun go off. He might even have seen Billy go down. It's even possible he could identify the real killer."

"What about the blood on his clothes?"

"In his bedroom, I saw Boy Scout merit badges for first aid training. He probably went to Billy's side instinctively, to help. That's when he picked up the blood, and when Jefferson Bellworthy saw him kneeling over the body."

"If he wanted to help, why did he run?"

"He realized that if he stayed and was questioned as a witness, he'd be exposed as a homosexual. When he saw Bellworthy, he panicked and took off."

"That doesn't explain the confession."

"He'd rather confess to murder than admit to his family and friends that he's queer."

"That's nuts." Harry finally looked at me. "You don't choose to rot in jail or die by lethal injection just because you like boys instead of girls."

"You do if you grew up with an older brother who was violently homophobic. If the idea of living a gay life goes against everything within your cultural and family traditions. If your parents are Catholic, and you love and respect them more than you respect yourself."

"Sorry, Ben, I don't buy it."

"Gonzalo Albundo is a frightened, confused teenager, Harry. He feels he has no rightful place in the world. That he's all alone. No hope, no future. It's the reason so many gay kids commit suicide. Gonzalo Albundo is just one more of those suicidal kids, Harry, self-destructing in a different way."

"That's all conjecture, and not terribly convincing."

Harry stubbed the cigarette out in his ashtray.

"Look around, Ben. We're in West Hollywood. If the kid's gay, he comes down here and meets a thousand guys like himself."

"This is the last place some people would ever want to come, Harry. It's a strange world to a lot of guys. It scares away more gay kids than it attracts."

"OK, then he joins a gay church or one of those gay rap groups or gets some counseling at those gay centers they have. But he doesn't take the blame for a murder he didn't commit. You can't sell me on that one, Ben."

"Damn you!"

I stood and pounded the meaty side of my fist hard enough on the Ford's roof to make Harry jump.

"Damn you and your white heterosexual arrogance. Like you know everything. Like the story begins and ends with how Harry Brofsky sees it. Damn you and the rest of the media that's owned and run by men like you!"

I whirled away from the car, frustrated almost to tears, then turned back on him.

"You remember what it was like to be sixteen or seventeen, Harry? How confused you were about some things? How terrified? Now imagine what it's like to be that age and know you're a faggot in a world that hates faggots. Some of those kids would rather die than face the truth about themselves or reveal it to someone else."

At least he was meeting me with his eyes; I was getting that much respect, anyway.

"I know something about this, Harry. I know how desperate it can feel."

"I admire your compassion," Harry said, and I knew right then that I'd lost. He started the engine. "But I think your personal feelings are clouding your objectivity."

"Fuck objectivity! How often have I heard you say that? There's no such thing as objectivity, only fairness."

"You're off the story, Ben."

"Harry, don't."

He was backing out. I held on to the car, moving with it.

"I have to, Ben. You're too close to it. It's making you do crazy things, and neither one of us can afford for that to happen again."

"You got me into this, Harry. You've got to let me finish it."

He shifted gears, out of reverse.

"Go home, Ben. Get some sleep. We'll talk in the morning."

I kicked the side of his car, leaving a dent deep enough to serve soup in.

Harry hit the accelerator and sped to the exit, where his left turn signal blinked at me like an obscene wink.

I watched his taillights disappear down San Vicente Boulevard, becoming small red blurs through my angry tears.

Thirty-five

IT WAS A FEW MINUTES past midnight, technically Sunday and the anniversary of Jacques's death.

I felt more lost than I ever had without him.

With the Billy Lusk story to work on, I'd begun to feel like maybe I was useful for something again. I'd even had the self-deluding notion that I might somehow save Gonzalo Albundo from himself and whatever demons were driving him to self-destruction, the way Jacques had once saved me.

And now, in simple journalistic jargon, I was off the story.

I walked aimlessly along the boulevard, weaving through the Saturday night crowd.

An old Russian immigrant couple trudged along in front of me, worn out from their long day's labor, keeping their eyes straight ahead. Bus drivers in brown uniforms walked home from the nearby depot carrying empty thermoses, or waited to catch buses to other neighborhoods. Restaurant workers, mostly young and Latin, waited with them, their pockets filled with tips and their heads with thoughts of sleep.

For hundreds of others on the street, though, the night was just beginning.

I stopped for a moment in front of the club where Jacques and I had met for the first time ten years earlier. Maurice liked to say that the search for love had been Jacques's religion, the disco his temple, the dancing his sacrament. The first time I laid eyes on him, it had certainly seemed that way. I'd come in out of the rain for a drink, to see him gyrating on the strobe-lit dance floor like a dark spirit, lost in the music, so graceful and gloriously sensual I knew I had to have him.

The name on the club was different now. So were the faces in the line outside. And the dual notions of HIV and the need for protection added an undercurrent of caution that hadn't been there a decade ago. Yet the crackle of sexual energy and the rush of romantic expectation were the same.

I thought seriously about going in, straight to the bar for a double Cuervo Gold and to hell with what happened after that. And I almost did.

Then I saw a man not much older than me standing alone at the bar, surrounded by men close to half his age, hoping one might want him. He'd taken a position near the door, where he could watch the faces and bodies coming in, picking out the ones that met his specifications. He had a drink in one hand, a cigarette in the other, and a thin, false smile that looked propped up by alcohol and desperation.

I knew I was looking at myself a few years from now, or tomorrow, if I walked through that door tonight.

I turned away and made myself keep moving.

I cut up Larrabee Street, past the trendy video bar on the corner, past the upstairs clinic that counseled gay and lesbian couples, past the video store with special sections near the front for Judy Garland, Bette Davis, and Joan Crawford and another near the back for gay porn.

Jacques and I had hiked up this street too many times to count, heading toward Sunset Boulevard, on our way to Book Soup to browse, or to Tower Records, or farther on to Queens Road to wind our way for miles up into the dark hills, where we could watch the city spread out below us like an ocean of lights.

"Look," Jacques had said the first time he'd seen the Queens Road sign, "they named a street for us!"

I passed two men kissing at the next corner, as openly as straight couples elsewhere in the city. Then more couples, mostly male, out walking their dogs.

In the next and steepest block, I stopped to stare into a second-floor apartment, feeling like an intruder but unable to pull myself away.

The curtains were open and the lights were on. A man with a metal walker struggled to cross his living room, trying to reach his kitchen, unconcerned about who might see.

I guessed his age at roughly forty. He was chalk white and deathly thin, a walking cadaver in diapers that clung, just barely, to his emaciated body. Each step was followed by half a minute's rest, during which he sagged against the rails, gasping for air.

Ten minutes passed before he reached the border of his kitchen, and a few more before he managed the several feet to his refrigerator door. He opened it and forced something into his mouth with a spoon, getting down a few swallows. Then he turned the walker around for the long journey back.

So many men, so little time.

"It's better that you went as quickly as you did," I said to Jacques. "It's better that you didn't end up this way."

I headed back down the hill, using the alleyways and side streets to work my way home, free of the crowds.

It seemed like a good time to get out of West Hollywood. A good time to move on, before Harry changed his mind and came around again, trying to draw me back into his life with a lightweight assignment and new rules. Before Paca Albundo called to pressure me for more help getting her little brother out of jail. Before Templeton tried to put her hooks deeper into me, for reasons even she might not understand. Before I figured a way to run into Paul Masterman, Jr., one more time, playing out my silly adolescent fantasies.

I had at least three hundred dollars remaining from the advance Harry had given me. The Mustang was running pretty well. I could throw some clothes together and grab Jacques's photograph, and Elizabeth Jane's, and be driving up the coast or across the desert or down to Mexico before the bars were closed.

The house was dark when I got there. Before going to bed, dependable Fred had swept up the glass and boarded up the broken windows.

I found Maurice sitting in a wicker rocker on the patio out back. He'd bundled his dead cat in a blanket and clutched it like a parent who'd lost a child to starvation or war, but wasn't ready yet to give up the body. The other two cats curled at his feet, as if they sensed what had happened and knew it was their duty to keep him company.

Maurice and Fred had given Jacques more comfort and security than he'd imagined was possible. They'd tried to do the same for me. I felt I should say something to Maurice, some kind of good-bye.

I pulled up a chair and we sat for awhile without speaking, listening to a possum rummage in the trash cans beside the garage. One of the cats jumped into my lap to be scratched. As she curled there peacefully, I wondered why it was that certain animals could coexist with such ease, when human beings found it so difficult to accept each other's differences.

We heard the rattle of a trash can lid and saw the possum waddle down the driveway, dragging its ratty tail.

The cat opened an eye, then closed it again. It nuzzled my hand for more attention and I scratched it under the chin, where it liked it most.

"I miss Jacques," Maurice said. "I miss him so very, very much."

His face bore his sadness plainly, but it was also beatific with age and wisdom. Jacques had always said that if he could be like anyone when he got older, it would be Maurice.

"I'd give everything," I said, "for just one more minute with him."

"Yes, I know."

"I could say so much in just one minute."

Maurice patted my leg with his bony hand.

"He hears you, Benjamin."

I put the cat down and wandered out into the yard, shoving my hands deep in my pockets and listening to the quiet.

I knew I wasn't ready to leave West Hollywood, not yet.

I wasn't ready to leave the streets where Jacques and I had first walked and talked. The streets where he'd reached down and taken my hand as we strolled, unconcerned about who might see. The streets where we'd marched side by side in political rallies, or laughed together over silly things only the two of us could understand, or ducked beneath awnings to get out of the rain and impulsively kissed. The streets where we had made our plans, in the rare and wonderful moments when things had felt right between us.

I sensed that he was still here, in the one place he'd always felt safe, and when I left I wouldn't know him anymore. I wasn't yet prepared to say good-bye.

Through the open upstairs door, I heard my phone ring.

I didn't move, preferring to keep the other world out of this one.

It rang again.

"Better get it," Maurice said. "You never know."

I took the stairs two at a time and caught the phone on the fourth ring. It was Jin Jai-Sik.

He was drunk, but when he told me he had something for me, he sounded clear and determined.

He gave me an address where I could find him in Koreatown.

Thirty-six

THE SIGNS along Vermont Avenue were mostly in hangul, so I followed street numbers.

They led me to a club that was tucked deep into the corner of a mini-mall and looked unimposing from the outside.

Inside, the place was stylish and expansive, opening up to dining rooms on one side and a polished parquet dance floor on the other, with contemporary art on the walls and a tall vase of exotic flowers in almost every corner.

In the middle of the dance floor, a young couple kissed, dancing slowly to a tune heard only in their own hearts. Nearby, a sharply dressed deejay in an elevated glass booth packed up his music for the night. Three more young couples passed me going out, speaking animatedly in Korean. I was the only Caucasian in the place, but no one seemed to care or even notice.

Jin Jai-Sik sat alone at the front bar, mumbling over an empty shot glass, while an attractive female bartender dutifully listened. He was dressed in a dark sport coat and light slacks, and, in his lap, clutched a black shoulder bag large enough to contain the box of photos I'd come for.

When he saw me, he straightened up, his face suddenly ebullient.

"My friend, Benjamin Justice!"

He stood, wobbling, and placed the shoulder bag carefully on the bar stool next to him. He bowed decorously, shook my hand, and glanced at the bartender.

"Teresa, this my friend, Benjamin Justice."

I shook her hand, and he pushed me onto an empty stool.

"Drinks for us," he told her, "and one for you." He laughed. "Because you so beautiful."

She smiled patiently, glanced at her watch, and reached up at the end of the bar. Crown Royal bottles crowded the top shelf, filled to varying levels, each marked with a different name or set of initials. She found one marked "JJS" that was nearly empty, brought it back, and set it on the bar.

Jin spoke to her in Korean, and when she shook her head, he raised his voice.

She hesitated, looking unhappy. Then she reached under the bar and brought out a fresh bottle, which she placed beside the other.

Jin pushed a finger into my shoulder.

"You drink with us," he said.

I asked the bartender for a glass of white wine.

"No pussy drink!" Jin shouted. "If you want me give you something, you drink man's drink!"

I glanced at the shoulder bag on the stool beside him, then at the bartender watching me. I nodded and she skillfully poured three shots, equal levels in the small glasses, finishing off the old bottle.

The liquor was amber, gemlike. I held it up to the light, appreciating the color and the feel of the smooth, solid glass in my fingers.

I hadn't tasted hard liquor in several months, and felt my insides caving in.

I set the drink down and pushed it away.

"You want what I have?" Jin said. "You drink with me."

I looked into his eyes. There was nothing soft in them, nothing yielding.

I picked up the glass. Jin raised his to mine, and the bartender joined us. My hand trembled.

"To my two good friends! Teresa and Benjamin!"

We threw our heads back and emptied the liquor into our throats. As it went down, my body shuddered gratefully and immediately demanded more. I pushed my glass across the bar.

The bartender opened the new bottle and poured. I drank quickly, without bothering to toast.

Jin craned his head toward Teresa.

"She pretty, yes?"

I nodded.

"You single. She single. Maybe she like you."

He turned to her.

"You want to go out with this Caucasian guy? He got big dick."

I put a hand on his wrist.

"Jin, let's go."

He pulled his arm free.

"We go when I say! Not when you say!"

He pointed to the empty shot glasses. She filled two of them, but whisked hers out of sight below the bar.

I could feel the alcohol flowing through me now. Everything was slowing down, feeling good.

"This time you say toast how," Jin commanded.

I lifted my glass.

"To my friend, Jin," I said, looking into his narrow dark eyes. "Whose sorrow I hope to one day understand."

The fierceness suddenly went out of him. His shoulders slumped, and he hung his head, letting it bob drunkenly.

"You make me feel bad. Why you do that to Jin?"

I held my glass upraised until he lifted his head and tapped my glass with his. We downed our drinks, and he put a hand on my shoulder to keep from falling. I felt his warm breath on my face.

"They're closing, Jin. It's almost two."

He peered into my eyes, and the cruelty returned.

"More drinks!"

"I've had enough."

I could hear how weak and unconvincing I sounded. It made me feel ashamed, and I seized on it to help fight the craving that was eating away at me inside.

Jin clutched the shoulder bag with one hand. With the other, he picked up his glass and held it between our noses.

"You have enough when I say."

I put a hand on his leg, high inside his thigh, where the bartender couldn't see. I reached deep and stroked him through the thin material of his pants, until I felt him stiffening.

"I think we should go," I said. "Right now."

He looked at me like he hated me. I kept stroking him, and gradually saw desire overcome the anger in his face.

He nodded dumbly and pulled out his wallet. Inside were three singles, nothing more.

"You got money?"

My wallet was fat with the remainder of Harry's advance. Jin plucked out two twenties and pushed them at the bartender for the bottle. Then he took another, slipping it toward her for a tip.

"Because you so beautiful, and I want marry you," Jin told her. Then, to me: "She beautiful. Yes?"

"Yes, she is."

"He like you," Jin said, getting to his feet. "I think he like to take you out. You want to take her out?"

The bartender and I exchanged an understanding look. I reached for the bag, but Jin grabbed it first.

"This mine. You want it, you do something for me later."

He grabbed the bottle of Crown Royal and shoved it into the bag. "This go with us."

The young couple from the dance floor shuffled toward the door, still necking, and we followed them out.

I turned toward the car in the parking lot, but Jin staggered away toward a side street, disappearing around a corner.

I went after him, catching up as he weaved along the sidewalk, caroming off parking meters.

"It's after two," I said. "The clubs are closed."

"This Koreatown. Never close."

He stumbled on for another block, then turned into an alley. He found an unmarked door imbedded with an electronic eye and pushed a buzzer.

A young woman opened the door, balancing bottles of OB beer and glasses on a tray. When she recognized Jin, a cautious smile appeared on her face, and they spoke in Korean.

We went in, and she locked the door behind us.

Inside it was warm and noisy; the air was heavy with cigarette smoke. Koreans of all ages, from sleeping babies to toothless grandparents, filled the booths and tables and little side rooms. Waitresses scurried about with bottles of beer and orders of food, and customers moved from table to table, greeting friends.

Around the main room, television sets were suspended from the ceiling, all showing the same karaoke video: a young Korean couple walking hand-in-hand on a pristine beach while romantic string music played in the background.

A balding, strongly built man stood at his table gripping a microphone and singing the lyrics that appeared in hangul beneath the scenes.

The waitress led us to an empty booth. Along the way, Jin boisterously greeted old friends. Most were courteous and responsive, but wary.

As we slid into the booth, the song ended, and the crowd rewarded the singer with polite applause.

Jin placed an order. The waitress went away and returned quickly with two small glasses, which he filled with whiskey.

He pushed one at me. The air had sobered me up a little and sharpened my sense of shame, and the booze started to look as poisonous as it did inviting.

"What about the photos, Jin?"

"First, we drink more whiskey. Eat. Drink some beers. Then I go with you and you get what you want."

He drank his whiskey down at once. I held my glass to my lips and waited.

His head fell forward, almost to the tabletop. I dumped my drink into a small vase of plastic flowers and reached across to touch his face.

His head bobbed up.

"We go your place soon." His words slopped together now, and his voice was full of contempt. "I give you back your dirty pictures."

"They're not mine, Jin."

"They yours. I find under your bed."

"Why did you take them?"

"I see them and think maybe my picture there too. That you get my picture when I sleep and put it with all your other lovers."

"I didn't take those photos, Jin. They don't belong to me."

He reached across the table, grabbing at my shirt but missing.

"You lie!"

"They're not my pictures, Jin."

"So why you have them, then?"

"They belonged to Billy Lusk."

"Who that?"

"The man who was killed at the bar."

"Yeah, I know."

"He slept with those men, not me. He took those photos."

He looked at me stupidly, barely able to keep his head up.

"You say the truth?"

"Yes."

"Why you keep them, then?"

"I need to find something."

"Find what?"

"I don't know. Maybe nothing. But I have to look."

"They really not your pictures?"

"Not my pictures."

His head weaved strangely, and his eyes roved the table, fixing on me only fleetingly.

"I sorry, then."

He picked up his glass and managed to find his lips with it. When he discovered it was empty, he shouted in Korean to the waitress, who was nearby. She hurried toward the kitchen.

"Jin."

His eyes had glazed over like those of a dead fish. I thought he might pass out or throw up, or both.

"Are you sure your photo wasn't with the others? And that you didn't remove it?"

"I tell you!" he shouted. He thrust his chest angrily against the table. "I never sleep with that man! Only shoot pool!"

"But you still haven't told me where you were on Monday night, just before he was murdered."

He looked away, growing sullen.

The waitress arrived with beer and sandwiches. As she left, Jin shouted angrily after her, and she hurried off again, returning moments later with a microphone.

Jin chewed at his sandwich and watched the TV monitor closest to us.

A minute later, the video he'd requested appeared on the screen: a young Korean couple with a small child, walking hand-in-hand through the tree-lined streets of Seoul.

As the music came up and the lyrics appeared on the screen, Jin swallowed some beer and raised the microphone to his lips.

When he sang, the slurring seemed magically to disappear. His voice was clear and steady, deep and resonant.

He sang in Korean, with strength and passion, but also unabashed tenderness. Tears welled up in his eyes, but his voice never quavered, and his eyes never left the screen.

I thought at that moment that Jin Jai-Sik was the most beautiful man I'd ever seen. Impossible to know or befriend, perhaps, but immeasurably beautiful.

The room grew quiet, and he sang as if totally unaware of anything around him, lost in the images of a homeland that was still part of him, but only a memory and a dream.

The others seemed to sense what he was feeling, and to share it. As he finished, they erupted into enthusiastic applause. Several men stood and raised their glasses to him, shouting their praise in Korean. A few wiped away tears.

Jin laid the microphone on the table, and looked at me passively, as if everything had been resolved for him.

"We go now. I got no more money. You pay. I sorry."

Thirty-seven

I FINISHED MY SANDWICH on the way to the car, and was only moderately drunk as I climbed into the Mustang for the drive home.

I was still intoxicated enough to kill someone, but we managed to glide through the near-empty streets without mishap or arrest.

Jin sat silently beside me, sipping from the Crown Royal bottle and listening to a succession of innocuous love songs he'd found on the radio, dedicated to girlfriends and boyfriends by heartsick teenage callers.

When we were inside the apartment, and the door was locked behind us, I reached for the light switch.

Jin covered my hand with his.

"No lights."

The dirty window provided shadowy illumination from a half-moon and a distant streetlight, and I could make out the shape of the Crown Royal bottle as he tilted it to his lips.

He handed it to me and I drained the last few ounces, before setting it on the night table, wishing we had another one and thankful we didn't.

Jin tossed his shoulder bag on the bed.

"Fuck me," he said.

I stood there looking at the bag.

"You know you want it," he said.

He unbuttoned his shirt, slipped it off, and laid it over the chair. Then he removed his shoes and peeled off his socks.

"You want pictures, yes?"

"Yes. I want the pictures."

"So you get both."

He stepped out of his trousers, pleated them carefully, and placed them with his shirt.

"You get everything you want from Jin."

He stepped out of his shorts, placed them on the chair, and faced me naked.

"Just give me the photos," I said. "That's all I want."

But it was a lie. Under my clothes, my cock was as swollen and hard as his was soft and unaroused.

He stepped over to me, grabbed my shirt, and ripped it away, popping buttons.

"Stop, Jin!"

I grabbed his wrist.

He reached down with his free hand and pressed it against my erection.

"You ready. You got hard dick. So do it."

I grabbed his head and kissed him forcefully enough to bruise his tender mouth.

He pulled away, went to the bed, and lay facedown, his dead eyes turned to the dim window light.

"No kiss. Just fuck."

I pulled off my clothes, found a condom, rolled it on. I straddled him and lubricated him quickly, feeling him constrict inside.

He reached back and grabbed me by the balls, pulling me toward him so violently it hurt.

I lowered myself over him like a spider and found the opening I wanted. It tightened again as I entered, like a fist closing, and I felt a jolt of pleasure. I moved slowly, and had barely penetrated him when he cried out and tried to push me off.

"No more games, Jin."

I shoved him back down, my big hands on his narrow shoulders. He fought me, but I outweighed him by fifty pounds and was twice as strong.

He cried out again as I pushed deeper, and I almost lost him once as he thrashed wildly to get free, screaming Korean words I didn't understand. I encircled his upper body with my arms, clamped my legs around his, and pressed forward until I was all the way in.

I started slowly, but each stroke came faster than the last until the rhythm was furious and beyond control. I had no sense of myself now, or of him, of where or who I was, only of sensation and rage and the wild narcotic of power. The more he struggled against me, the more he cursed me, the harder I felt driven. I became lost in him, blind to everything but the sweet feeling building uncontrollably where our bodies joined. Then I was consumed by the hot explosion, riding on perfect waves of dark, terrifying sensation, and it was over.

I lay on top of him, panting heavily, growing sick with what I'd done.

I'd never been more aware of how much of my father I carried within me. Of how difficult it was to escape him, no matter how much I tried.

I felt Jin trembling beneath me and realized he was crying. I slipped out of him as gently as I could. Inside, he was slick with his own blood.

"I guess this mean I really gay," he said.

"It doesn't mean you're not a man, any more than when you fucked me."

I laid a hand on his shoulder but he pushed it off and crawled away from me on the bed.

"Korean man not permitted be gay. Only be with woman."

He pulled himself up to his hands and knees, sobbing.

"I want you fuck me so I must be gay."

His body shook convulsively, and when his words came, they were choked with tears.

"I tell you where I go the night when they kill Billy. You want to know, yes?"

"Yes."

"I go to see my little girl. She live with my dad and my mom, because my wife . . ."

Sobs heaved up out of him in waves.

"They take care my little girl. I no allowed to see her. So after my dad sleep, my mom, she call me. I go their house. I watch my little girl when she sleep. So she not know I there."

"Why?"

"If she know I there, she might tell my wife parents. And then they try to take her live with them. And I never see her no more."

"Where's your wife?"

He crawled off the bed, stood, and pressed his face against the wall. He began to cry again, so hard it turned into a wail.

"My wife and I have problem between us. The sex. I finally tell her I like mens, that I am gay man. She try to kill herself and our baby. But only she die. Our daughter OK."

A scream tore out of him, followed by more tears than I thought a man could have inside.

"I put so much shame on my family. Very bad shame."

"I wish you'd told me this before."

"You American. American different. Korean not talk about self, not talk about private thing. We swallow our pain. That our way. That always be our way."

"You and I might not be as different as you think."

I went to him, but he slipped away from me and into the bathroom. Then I heard the shower running. The door was ajar.

I went in, got rid of the condom, and stepped into the shower beside him.

I took the soap from his hands, turned him around, and washed his back and legs. Then I pried him apart and washed the place where I'd hurt him so wrongly.

I turned him back around to face me and washed his front. When I lathered and stroked the part of him that was hard, he clutched me fiercely, and cried out as he erupted.

I rinsed him off, and he let me hold him, our faces touching and our wet bellies pressed together, until the water finally grew cold.

He separated from me to find a towel.

"Please stay," I said.

"No. I go."

"We can sleep late. Get some breakfast."

He resolutely shook his head. I reached out and touched his face.

"Will you be all right?"

He took my hand away.

"Korean mens, they always all right."

He went out. I finished washing and toweled off, then stared into the mirror awhile, trying to figure out who I'd become.

When I went back out, Jin Jai-Sik was gone. I wasn't surprised, or all that disappointed. It made everything easier.

He'd turned on the light, neatly made up the bed, and set the box of photos at the foot.

I went to the window and looked out. To the east, dawn was turning the sky pink.

Jin Jai-Sik strode down the driveway to the street, stopping to look back for a moment. I started to wave, but he'd already turned, angling across Norma Place and out of sight.

I sat on the bed and opened the box.

Atop the pile of snapshots was a note: *Good-bye. I not see you again. Please have good luck. Jin.*

I put the note on the night table, anchoring it with the empty Crown Royal bottle.

I knew that I had to be busy now, to fill the rest of the morning with work and duty, and then the day, and then the night, until I put some distance between myself and the whiskey I'd shared with Jin Jai-Sik. If I didn't, I'd be comfortably drunk again before noon, and probably stay that way for the rest of my short, miserable life.

I dumped several years of Billy Lusk's sexual history onto the blanket and glanced through the Polaroids one by one, counting as I went.

When I reached number 203, I recognized a familiar face. He slept peacefully on Billy's bed, an arm thrown back on the pillow, his naked body fully exposed to Billy's spying camera.

I studied the photo awhile, reached for the phone, and called Alexandra Templeton at home.

"Sorry for the early call, Templeton."

"Justice?"

A yawn worked its way out of her.

"Look," I said, "I know who murdered Billy Lusk."

Thirty-eight

BEFORE WE HUNG UP, I agreed to meet Templeton at her place at one that afternoon.

Her job in the meantime was to convince Harry to join us, help me fix things up with him, then move forward on the Billy Lusk story as quickly as possible.

We didn't talk about the kiss she'd drawn me into the previous evening, and I hoped it wouldn't come up. We had more important matters to resolve, and not a lot of time to do it.

I shaved, put on some decent clothes, and went out for breakfast, hoping to quell the hangover I felt coming over me like a toxic spill.

I ate at a twenty-four-hour coffeeshop east of Fairfax, where the booths swarmed with energetic kids who had danced at after-hours clubs until 4 A.M. A ragged assortment of tired-looking tricks and skinny hustlers with amphetamine eyes sat at the counter like a police lineup, joylessly sipping their coffee.

I sat with them at the far end, picking my way through a plate of pancakes and eggs while I mulled over everything I'd learned about Billy Lusk and the people who knew him in the five days since his death. I jotted it down in a notebook, then endlessly revised and reorganized it to give myself a sense of order and to keep my mind off booze.

I washed the food down with three cups of coffee and some Tylenol, but the hangover came on anyway. I paid the check at the register, and on my way out told a hustler for the third time that I wasn't interested.

Back on Norma Place, I swept the patio and helped Maurice and Fred set up folding tables for the memorial service they held each year for Jacques.

Maurice placed my photograph of Jacques on a small table in the shade of the jacaranda, surrounded by candles, incense, and fresh-cut flowers. Before he'd died, Jacques had compiled a list of music he wanted played at his first service: "Imagine," by John Lennon; "We Can Be Heroes" and "Space Oddity," by David Bowie; "Respect," by Aretha Franklin; "Careless Whisper," by Wham! and Verdi's *Requiem* in its entirety. He'd also left specific instructions for the mourners: "Cry a lot and say wonderful things about me."

Fred queued up the tape and started the music as Jacques's friends and a few relatives filed in from the street. The group had thinned in recent years, a dozen or more gone from AIDS, but I counted about forty women and men, and several small children.

Jacques's mother and sisters showed up, but not his stepfather, whom I'd barred from the first memorial service six years before, following Jacques's express wish that I keep him away. He'd showed up anyway, telling me he'd gotten counseling and needed to be there to cope with his guilt and "facilitate his closure." I'd told him he'd fucked his stepson enough while he was alive without fucking him again now that he was dead, then knocked him down and kicked him until he was off the property.

He hadn't tried to come back. I didn't expect him to show up today, or ever again, but I kept my eye on the street, just in case.

Maurice directed people to coffee and juice on a side table, and there was light chatter while the two cats dodged children who tried to pull their tails. Maurice explained to the gathering what had happened to his other cat, whose ashes would eventually be spread beneath the jacaranda, and said a short Buddhist prayer for its soul.

Then he spoke about Jacques, and how important his family of friends had been to him always, but especially in his final days.

Others followed, repeating anecdotes or recalling new ones about how Jacques had changed their lives and insisting that his spirit lived in everyone he had touched.

I watched and listened from the apartment, standing just inside the doorway, until it was over and everyone had gone.

Then I went down to help Maurice and Fred clean up, before driving out to Santa Monica for my meeting with Alexandra Templeton.

Thirty-nine

I SPOKE to Templeton on her intercom, while the guard eyed me from his lobby desk inside.

She told me that I'd find her front door open and buzzed me in. I didn't like the sound of that, and went up warily.

The interior of the Montana Towers had all the pretensions of elegance one would expect in a westside condominium complex, right down to the artificial plants, which fooled you until you took a closer look.

I rode an elevator to the sixth floor, studying myself in a wall of mirrored glass. I saw a man with ashen skin and foggy eyes who needed sleep and something stronger than Tylenol for his pounding head.

A carpeted corridor led me to Templeton's door, which I found ajar, as she'd promised. I stepped in, and called out to let her know I was there.

At the far end of a hallway to my right a bathroom door opened. Templeton stepped out naked, drops of water catching the light on her almond-colored skin.

She feigned surprise and covered herself with her arms.

"Sorry. I didn't expect you so quickly."

As she reached back for a towel, her upper body arched, fully exposing her breasts and stretching her belly taut above a dark cloud of pubic hair.

She draped her front with the towel, told me to make myself

comfortable, and disappeared into a door halfway down the hall, giving me a glimpse of bare bottom as she went in.

I glanced around the living room while my mind ran through the little charade that had just taken place.

Windows big enough for a Lamborghini showroom opened to a generous balcony and an unobstructed view of Palisades Park, with a silver streak of ocean beyond. An ivory sofa faced the view, soft and deep, with a matching love seat next to it. The plants on the glass-topped coffee table were real. So was the Romare Bearden collage hanging above the fireplace. It was all spotless and in place, and every bit of it looked like money. Daddy's money.

I walked down the hallway and turned into the room that Templeton had entered moments before.

When she saw me, she cried out my name and snatched the towel off the bed to cover herself. It felt about as unscripted as a television soap opera.

"I've had a troubling night, Templeton, and the morning hasn't been much better. I look like shit and feel worse. I'm not sure why you're playing these games, but they need to stop."

She grabbed her robe from the bed, turned her back to me, and slipped into it.

"I have no idea what you're talking about."

"Maybe I'm supposed to play the role of the timid faggot, afraid of women. Is that what the kiss was about yesterday? Is that what's behind your little act this morning? If I squirm and get nervous, will it make you feel superior in some way? Is this your way of putting me down, getting back at me?"

"Getting back at you?"

She laughed, but it was hollow.

"For what?"

"For shattering your fantasy six years ago," I said. "When I wrote a fraudulent newspaper series and broke a college girl's heart."

She turned to face me, pulling the robe tight.

"God, what an ego you have."

She knotted the sash furiously at her waist without taking her eyes off me.

"You're not trying to seduce me, Templeton. You're trying to humiliate me."

Her jaw remained set, but her eyes faltered.

"Whatever your reasons," I said, "they don't matter right now.

You're about to write what could be the biggest story of your career. The fate of Gonzalo Albundo may depend on what we do in the next few hours and how well we do it. It's vital that we work as a team. We can't afford to let anything personal get in the way of that."

Her eyes changed again, becoming steady.

"The way you let your personal life get in the way six years ago?"

"This isn't the time, Templeton."

As she talked, she wound the towel around her damp hair, fixing it like a turban.

"When you wrote that AIDS series, I believe you created the two lovers as a way of idealizing a personal situation that was too painful for you to handle."

"This really isn't the time."

I turned to walk out but she moved around me and blocked the door.

"Jacques's death left you consumed with guilt, didn't it?"

"You didn't know him. Stop using his name as if you did."

"I think that to this day you feel you didn't love him enough, didn't do enough to save him. That you weren't there for him emotionally the way he had always been there for you. Because you didn't know how. Because you were too afraid."

I was worried that I might slap her, and pushed my hands deep into my pants pockets.

"Maurice told me you did your best," she said. "Taking care of Jacques, tending to his physical needs."

"Yes. I took care of his physical needs."

"But you couldn't tell him you loved him, could you?"

Like any good investigative reporter, she had prepared herself well before the final interview; she knew the answers before she asked the questions.

"No," I said. "I couldn't tell him that."

"You couldn't hold him the way he needed to be held. You couldn't be his lover in the truest sense of the word. Not in those final months. Getting that close terrified you, because you knew you were losing him."

Bingo. I said nothing.

"But the worst moment was yet to come, wasn't it, Justice?"

She recounted the last hour of Jacques's life almost minute by minute, when he'd known he was dying of pneumocystis and continually asked a nurse named Amelia Tomayo where I was, until she'd lowered the oxygen mask over his face for the final time.

"You found Amelia Tomayo," I said.

"She still works at County. She spoke to me, off the record."

"Nice work."

"When Jacques died, you were on assignment. At the moment he needed you most, you were in the Hall of Records, digging through documents related to a slumlord case."

I thought of Phil Devonshire, off playing golf while his wife visited the morgue.

"Yes," I said. "I was at the Hall of Records."

"You could have been at the hospital. Harry would have given you time off. All the time you needed."

"Of course."

"But you didn't ask for time off."

"No."

"Why, Justice? Because you couldn't bear to watch Jacques die?"

"I'm not sure any of us really knows why we do what we do."

I felt exhausted, sick. I sat down on the edge of her bed, staring at the spotless Berber carpet.

"You'd planned to write a first-person series about you and Jacques, hadn't you, Justice? About one man caring for his dying partner."

I nodded.

"But the truth was too painful. When the time came, you couldn't do it, could you?"

She'd beaten me down. I didn't want to fight her anymore. I wanted some peace.

"No," I said.

"So you wrote it the way you wished it had been. You created two fictional men, working with the real feelings you never expressed when Jacques was alive. That's where the power of the writing came from. And that's why it won the Pulitzer."

"There are couples like that all over this city, thousands of them," I said. "All over this country. Tens of thousands. Helping each other die."

"They say there's sometimes more truth in fiction than in facts."

"Is that what they say?"

She sat beside me, leaving a few careful inches between us.

"It's time to forgive yourself, Justice."

I turned to look into the large brown pools of her eyes. I saw no animosity, only concern.

"Have you forgiven me, Templeton?"

"Is it important?"

"It wouldn't hurt," I said.

Forty

"SHALL I put on some music?"

Templeton padded into the living room barefoot in a light sheath, carrying an overstuffed file folder and a laptop computer.

I was studying her CD collection, racked in a glass cabinet: Miles, Coltrane, Mingus, Monk. Art Pepper, Sarah Vaughan, Betty Carter, Mose Allison, Joshua Redman. We shared remarkably similar tastes, at least in music.

In a crazy way, I was falling in love with Templeton after all.

I still had no interest in going to bed with her, but there was no longer any doubt that we were attuned to each other in some special way, and becoming friends.

"If it's all the same," I said, "I'd like to get down to work."

I sank into the deep cushions of her sofa while she spread her material on the glass-topped table in front of us: an impressive array of notes, transcribed interviews, photocopied documents, and computer printouts, all efficiently organized, labeled, and indexed.

I compared phone numbers from my own notes with lists she'd obtained, and crucial times related to Billy Lusk's murder to schedules she'd compiled. Her interviews, cleverly framed to glean information many reporters would never have gotten, filled in much of the rest.

She handed me a copy of the media survey put together by the intern, Katie Nakamura, and I looked over the data I'd requested. It all added up pretty much the way I expected.

Harry called on the downstairs intercom. Templeton buzzed him in.

While we waited, I asked her how she'd convinced him to give me another chance.

"I told him that if he didn't, I'd quit the paper."

"I appreciate it."

"I appreciate the opportunity I've had to work with you. I hope I get the chance again."

"I wouldn't count on it," I said.

"Whatever happens, Benjamin, it's your story. You know that."

Harry buzzed, and she let him in.

He was wearing a mustard-yellow sport shirt and plaid Bermuda shorts; sagging nylon socks disappeared into his scuffed brown loafers. Harry never had been much of a fashion plate, least of all on weekends.

"I take it there's been a turn of events," he said, which was the closest to a concession I figured I'd ever hear from Harry Brofsky.

While Templeton got me Tylenol and poured fresh juice for each of us, I showed Harry the photograph I'd found in Billy Lusk's memory chest.

Then, over the next half hour, with Harry sitting between us, Templeton and I went through the data from our files, building our case step by step to its conclusion.

"Jesus fucking Christ," Harry said, when he'd been shown the last piece of the puzzle.

I told him how I thought we might handle the story, and the timing I had in mind.

He had the same worried look I'd seen in my apartment two days earlier, when he'd begged me to back off before I cost him his job. In a few hours, if we followed my plan, there would be no backing off, and Harry knew it.

Templeton saw the fear as well.

"Harry, do you remember what you told me when you hired me?"

His glasses were off, and he glanced at her with conflicted eyes.

"You said not to bother going into the newspaper business unless I wanted to take some chances, make some waves. You told me that if I were the type who liked to play it safe, I should look for work in public relations. Because the newspaper business already had too many cowards and gutless career-climbers, whose main objective was to protect their jobs and collect their pensions."

She took his plump hand and pressed it between her dark, slender fingers.

"I went to work for you, Harry, because you made me believe."

He rose on his white stubby legs and fumbled for a cigarette. Then he went out to the balcony while Templeton and I sweated it out inside.

We watched him strike a match and cup his hand against the breeze. He kept his back to us and stared out at the whites of sailboats scudding through the low chop between Malibu and Redondo Beach. A thin column of smoke drifted above him, where the breeze carried it away.

Finally, he stubbed the butt, flicked it over the railing, and came back in.

He faced us across the low table, jingling coins in the pockets of his Bermuda shorts.

"You know, Ben, if we do this piece, your byline can't be on it."

"I know that."

"The story's gotten too big, it's too touchy. Your name would just . . ."

"Harry, I know."

Templeton asked him what our next step should be.

He glanced down at the photograph we all felt could help convict a killer.

"I think you'd better set up your final interview."

Forty-one

PACA ALBUNDO attended Mass each Sunday morning with her parents at St. Vibiana's Cathedral downtown, then spent the day working at the central public library, less than a mile away.

I called her from Templeton's condominium, and she agreed to meet me at the library after it closed at five.

I arrived a few minutes early, sporting a fresh haircut and a jacket borrowed from Fred. I'd had a nap and a good lunch and the world was pretty much back in focus, although my craving for alcohol nagged at me like unexpended lust.

I killed some time wandering the library gardens in front, following the waterways and staring into the fountains while I tried to shut down my feelings, the way reporters sometimes have to do when they cover stories that make them want to cry or throw up or find another line of work.

I stopped at the grotto fountain on the south side, where the water made its way down stone steps to the main pool. Etched in the arch above were the words of Frederick Douglass, dated 1849: *Power Concedes Nothing Without a Demand. It Never Did. It Never Will.*

I looked at my watch. It was time to go in.

I followed the red-tile corridor to the eight-story atrium in the east wing, where I rode the escalator down to lower level four, watching the skylight and hanging sculptures grow more distant above me and sensing the weight of two million books all around.

Paca was behind a counter in the history section, checking a stack of volumes on Native American culture against a list on a computer screen. Other librarians were at work around her, and she suggested we find a more private place to talk.

She led me to the Cook Rotunda, where we had the big chamber all to ourselves, standing directly beneath the dome. A mural depicting Los Angeles history—priests, peasants, trading ships—covered the upper walls. I felt small standing there, a speck in time, and my personal concerns didn't seem so important anymore.

"I'm not making any promises," I told her, "but I think your brother may be released from jail soon."

"Luis?"

"Gonzalo."

Her small hand seized my arm.

"Are you sure?"

"I think there's a good chance he'll be cleared."

She let go of my arm and turned away. When she faced me again, I could see the distrust.

"Why are you telling me this if you can't be sure? Why not wait until we know for certain?"

"Because if it happens, you need to be ready."

She hesitated, and when she spoke, her voice was weak and insincere.

"I'm not sure what you mean."

I reached into my coat for a brochure I'd picked up that afternoon from the Los Angeles Gay and Lesbian Services Center. I handed it to her and told her she'd find help there.

"They can even put you in touch with special programs for Hispanic kids," I said. "They do a lot of good work, salvage a lot of lives."

She didn't say anything, so I asked her if any of what I was saying made sense.

Her voice picked up some strength.

"Yes."

"He's going to need all the support you can give him, Paca. It may be hard for you. Harder for your parents. But it's a million times worse for him. He's the loneliest kid in the world right now. And the most frightened."

She nodded. "I understand."

I'd promised Templeton I'd meet her at six, a few blocks away.

"I have to go."

Paca grabbed my wrist.

"When will we know?"

"Within a few hours. If things go the way we hope."

"Thank you." She pressed the back of my hand to her lips. "For everything."

"Take care of him, Paca."

I left her standing there, looking tiny but resourceful, with history and knowledge all around her.

I walked outside, into the shadows cast by downtown skyscrapers.

Among them were the five metallic-looking columns of the Bonaventure Hotel, rising in a cluster thirty-five stories above the city, looking like the futuristic spires of a space age metropolis.

I turned in their direction, where Templeton waited.

Forty-two

I'D ASKED TEMPLETON to arrive at the Bonaventure ahead of me so I wouldn't be waiting alone.

I didn't want to be tempted by the tinkling of cocktail glasses in the lounge and the sight of all those gleaming bottles calling to me from behind the bar.

She met me as I stepped out of the elevator at the top floor.

She carried a Gucci briefcase, rather than her usual oversized handbag, and looked mature and serious in high heels and a business suit buttoned all the way to the neck.

"Nice threads," I said.

"Thanks. Feeling better?"

"I could use some coffee."

I knew she must be experiencing some anxiety over the work ahead, as I was. But I also figured she was too professional to mention it, which proved to be the case.

As we made our way to the restaurant, she informed me that deputies had found Luis Albundo's gun. He'd tossed it into the vines around the historic Frank Lloyd Wright House on North Doheny Drive. She'd also been informed that it wasn't the weapon used to murder Billy Lusk, which by then was a surprise to neither of us.

We told the host that a third party would be joining us. He grabbed three menus, led us around the revolving restaurant, and seated us by a window that faced northwest.

With its outer walls of partitioned glass, the circular restaurant resembled a giant spaceship, hovering eerily above the city. As its floor slowly rotated, we could see the Hollywood Sign against the golden hills in the distance and the approach of the Griffith Park Observatory along a ridge to the east. In the street, thirty-five stories below, pedestrians and vehicles appeared minuscule and unreal.

Templeton and I sat side by side, spreading out our notes and going over our game plan.

Our timing during the rest of the evening would be crucial, and we'd planned a framework for the interview with our minds on the clock.

The deadline for breaking news at the *Sun* was 11:30 P.M., although the editors could do a makeover in extreme emergencies two or three hours beyond that. But that was costly and complicated, requiring clearances from the top, which we wanted to avoid.

That meant Templeton needed to file a solid story no later than eleven to allow for editing, then moving from the copy desk to production. From there, it would pass through paste-up to plating before the presses rolled.

At that moment, Harry was at the *Sun,* laying out the pages, selecting and captioning photos, and writing the headline and deck. He planned a forty-two-point headline across the top of page one, with a three-line deck, a one-column lead running fifteen inches, and thirty inches of jump inside. That would give us a total of forty-five column inches for nothing but copy and subheads.

If we didn't get the story, Harry would go to an optional layout, leading with another piece, and hurry that version into production. He was already on thin ice at the *Sun;* if the brass found out he'd kept me involved on a story that had gone so far and failed, as they undoubtedly would, Harry would be gone. Templeton was young and could survive; but in the newspaper business, Harry Brofsky would be finished.

If we pulled it off, got what we needed from our interview and met our deadline, Harry would have the scoop of a lifetime and regain much of the luster and confidence I'd robbed him of six years before. Templeton would suddenly be a star reporter in a city of three million people, on her way to choice assignments. And Gonzalo Albundo would be out of jail and back with his family.

The chance of all that happening depended on how well Templeton and I had prepared for this interview, and what we'd be able to entice from our subject, with Templeton's tape recorder running.

She plugged it into a wall outlet and set it inconspicuously to the side, next to the wine list, with the microphone aimed at our visitor's chair.

Shortly after eight, he arrived.

Forty-three

TEMPLETON and I looked up from our coffee and notes, then stood to shake hands as Paul Masterman, Jr., approached our table.

I noticed that he'd just shaved and, with a recent haircut, looked particularly fresh-faced and attractive.

He was dressed in two-tone saddle shoes, beige tropical wool slacks, and a short-sleeved silk shirt that displayed the beautifully veined arms I'd admired with such unrepentant desire during each of our two previous meetings.

We'd asked him to come alone, without a publicist or campaign manager in tow, so he'd feel free to talk about his father more openly. He'd agreed, in the forthright manner that had so impressed me from the start.

He took a chair on the inside by the window, directly across from Templeton, who sat on my right. She explained that I was there because I'd assisted with the research and had a few questions of my own.

"I hope that's not a problem," she said.

He turned his emerald eyes from Templeton to me and smiled in his boyish way.

"No problem at all. It's always nice seeing Ben."

We ordered dinner, and Templeton asked permission to tape.

"I prefer it," Masterman said. "As Dad always says, there's nothing worse than being misquoted."

She turned the recorder on, and we made small talk over our salads, admiring the view.

The restaurant floor had made nearly two revolutions in the two hours or so that Templeton and I had been there. Our window now gave us clear sight lines west across the city to a sunset glowing orange like a distant fire burning on the surface of the cool blue sea.

Templeton eased the conversation in the direction we wanted to go by asking Masterman if there were plans for more TV spots. She pulled out her notebook, knowing that detailed backup notes could be vital if there was insufficient time later to transcribe her tapes.

"We'll probably shoot one or two more," Masterman said. "Possibly up north, if the opportunity presents itself."

"When I talked with your dad," Templeton said, "he was really proud of your involvement in the campaign. Proud of you in general, in fact. The ideal son, is how he put it."

The color rose from his neck to his face.

"Did he really say that?"

"It must feel especially good to hear that," I said, "given your parents' divorce, and the strain it put on your relationship with your father."

He glanced at Templeton's tape recorder before he spoke.

"Divorce is never easy. But Mom and Dad did what they felt they needed to do, and it's worked out for the best."

"You mentioned to me before that you've worked hard to rebuild broken bridges with your dad."

"And there was that Father's Day piece you wrote in the *Times* last year," Templeton said.

"It's true, I've been on something of a mission the past few years, determined to build a close relationship with Dad. With his love and support, we made it happen."

"He must have been particularly pleased," Templeton said, "when you arranged Wednesday's taping at The Out Crowd bar."

He shrugged. "No more than usual, really."

"But you were right on top of that one," I said. "And with the election so tight, reaching gay voters has been a priority."

"I guess that's true." He shrugged again. "But that's my job. It's what Dad expects."

"And meeting his expectations is important?"

He looked at me a long moment before he replied.

"I want to be the best son I can for him. I want him to know he can depend on me completely."

He softened his next words with a smile.

"That's not so hard to understand, is it?"

"Not at all." I returned his smile, for the same purpose. "Although there's always the danger that when you try so hard to please, you surrender your own identity in the process."

His smile tightened. I realized I'd said more than I needed to. Templeton picked up the thread I was close to breaking.

"Since that TV spot was so vital to your dad's campaign, why don't you tell us exactly how you coordinated it so smoothly."

His eyes stayed on me for a second or two, as if held there by my last words, but finally turned toward Templeton.

"Pretty much the same as all the others," he said. "I read a news story about it in the paper, and it seemed like it had elements that might help us get our message to the gay community. Dad's been misunderstood on certain issues of importance to gays, so we jumped at the chance."

"I'm not too familiar with these film things," Templeton said. "Could you take us through the process step by step?"

"The moment I read about the murder, I contacted the city's film permit office. I put in a request for a permit to block off part of the street in front of The Out Crowd the next day. Then I got on the phone to get a crew together."

"You mentioned reading about it in the paper," Templeton said. "Was that my piece in the *Sun?*"

"I believe it was. I thought it was an excellent article, by the way."

"It couldn't have been the *Sun,*" I said off-handedly. "Billy Lusk was killed just after midnight on Tuesday morning, past the *Sun*'s deadline. Templeton's story didn't run until the following day, Wednesday."

"That's right," Templeton said. "I didn't think of that."

A busboy cleared away our salad plates.

When he was gone, Masterman said, "I guess it must have been the *L.A. Times,* then."

"That's not possible," I said. "The *Times* has out-of-state editions. It has an even earlier deadline than the *Sun.* So there's no way the *Times* could have covered the murder in its Tuesday morning edition."

"Then it must have been the TV morning news."

Masterman said it with his trademark shrug, which was beginning to seem more like a nervous tic than a sign of relaxation.

The waitress arrived with our dinners, handed them out, and left. Masterman had ordered a small steak and reached for the proper knife.

"Actually," I said, "the story wasn't on any of the TV newscasts until late Tuesday afternoon."

Masterman paused as he cut his steak, without looking at us.

"Is it really so important where I saw the news report?"

"Details make the story," Templeton said. "We just want to get them right."

She smiled and took a bite of her omelette.

Then: "So how did you hear about Billy Lusk's murder, Paul?"

He shrugged yet again.

"Must have been on the radio."

He quit cutting his steak, as if he lacked the concentration to finish the job, and speared a tiny roasted potato with his fork.

He laughed lightly and said, "I check so many news sources, I can't really keep them straight."

He popped the potato into his mouth.

"It couldn't have been the radio," I said.

"Why not?"

"The earliest radio news report indicating the murder was gay-related was on KFWB. That was at noon."

"Four hours after you filed for a film permit," Templeton said.

"No kidding." The potato made a lump against Masterman's cheek while he chewed. "You guys really did a lot of background for this story, didn't you?"

"Harry Brofsky calls it fishing," I said. "You never know what you'll catch."

Masterman laughed again, but it was the kind of laugh that has nowhere to go.

"It takes at least twenty-four hours to process an application for a city film permit," Templeton said. "Unless you want to pull rank to push it through, which might call attention to it."

"We checked with the film permit office," I said. "You phoned in your request on Tuesday morning, just after they opened at eight. That enabled you to start the permit process, have the copy written, get your crew together, set up your equipment the next day, and be taping by late afternoon.''

Beyond our windows, darkness transformed the city, camouflaging the congestion, cloaking the boundaries, turning the freeways into streaks of comet light. L.A. twinkled innocently now, not like an urban jungle divided by poverty, race, and fear, but like a vast planetary system full of hope and promise, waiting to be explored.

Paul Masterman, Jr., didn't seem to be enjoying the view, however. He was staring at the steak in front of him as if someone had placed a turd on his plate.

''Why did you check with the film permit people?''

Once again, he spoke without looking up.

''Blood rare,'' I said.

''What?'' He abruptly raised his eyes.

''It looks like they cooked it blood rare. Is that the way you wanted it?''

He looked at me like I was crazy. Then he said, ''Yes, it's fine.''

He swallowed so tightly I could hear the contractions in his throat.

The next question was Templeton's.

''So, exactly how did you know a gay man had been murdered at The Out Crowd, Paul? That is, prior to that first news report at noon on Tuesday?''

''I'd . . . I'd have to check with people in the campaign.'' A bead of sweat rolled slowly down from under the dampening curls on his forehead. ''Someone must have mentioned it to me.''

''I've talked with your coworkers,'' Templeton said. ''They all insist the idea of shooting a campaign spot at The Out Crowd originated with you. They were very generous about giving you the credit.''

He put down his fork and steak knife and drank some water. His shirt was spotted with perspiration against his lean chest.

Finally, trying to make it sound like it didn't matter: ''Is this going to be part of your story?''

The floor of the restaurant continued its silent, imperceptible spin. Our table was again positioned next to the window that faced northwest. I fixed my eyes on the distant glow of the Dodger Stadium night lights, then followed the contour of the hills down to

Silver Lake, trying to pinpoint the neighborhood where The Out Crowd was located.

Templeton slipped a new tape into her recorder. I glanced at my watch.

It was 8:55. We didn't have much cushion. It was time to force the issue.

I looked at Masterman and said straightaway, "Billy Lusk was blackmailing you, wasn't he, Paul?"

He raised his head up, this time with badly troubled eyes.

I knew then what had made him so attractive to me the first time I'd met him, beyond his good looks and the integrity I'd thought I'd seen in him. Beneath the mask of self-assurance he'd copied so well from his father, he'd been confused and afraid. In trying to keep what he thought he needed to make everything right in his life—his father's respect—he'd crossed a terrible line, then found himself in deep trouble because of it. I'd always been soft for young men in trouble. I suspected I always would.

"I didn't know Billy Lusk," he said.

His voice cracked like a schoolboy's. He reached for his water again.

"We figure you met him at USC," Templeton said, "during one of his several enrollments there as a film student."

"Derek Brunheim mentioned to me that Billy had been a Trojan," I said. "It didn't register at the time."

"This is crazy. I'm telling you, I never even heard of him before that night." He cleared his throat. "That is, Tuesday morning. Or afternoon. Whenever it was."

I pushed my plate aside and leaned forward on my elbows, making him look at me.

"What happened, Paul? Did Billy catch your eye? Or did he go after you, charming and seducing you as he had so many other men? Did he get you at a time when your parents were at war with each other and your father was being a bastard and you felt angry and rebellious?"

"Or alone and needy," Templeton suggested.

"I told you! I didn't know William Lusk!"

"You'd planned to follow your father into politics," I said. "It's what you've been pointing toward for years. Then Billy Lusk came out of the woodwork, saddled with an expensive cocaine habit, demanding money to keep quiet about the affair you had with him.''

Masterman pointed a finger at me and screwed his face up with fury, looking and sounding exactly like his father's son.

''I think you should be very careful about the accusations you make. Slander is actionable. And you don't exactly have the best reputation for telling the truth.''

''You knew how your father felt about homosexuals,'' Templeton said, softer and more sympathetic. ''You knew that with one phone call to the senator, Billy could destroy what you had worked years to build.''

''Even if he didn't disown you as a son,'' I added, ''your work on his campaigns would be finished. You'd be too serious a political liability. And your chances of ever rising to national office would be a long shot.''

He stood up.

''This interview is over.''

He pulled out his wallet, removed some bills, and tossed them on the table, presumably to cover his meal.

By then, I was standing beside him, with a hand around his upper arm and my mouth inches from his ear. The bicep under my fingers was small and hard, like a baseball. I could feel damp heat radiating from his armpit.

''We can go to the police with what we have,'' I said.

He stood motionless, no doubt trying to maintain a calm exterior while frantically sorting things out inside.

''Sit down, Paul. Let's work things out.''

He sat. I moved back around the table and took my chair next to Templeton.

When he spoke again, his voice was light, almost friendly.

''It doesn't look like you have anything, really.''

He used his napkin to blot perspiration from his face, then spread it in his lap.

''I'm a married man. I'll be a father in a few weeks.'' He laughed and threw up his hands. ''Hey, guys, I'm heterosexual.''

''You certainly wouldn't be the only married man who's been sexually involved with other men,'' Templeton said.

He turned toward her tape recorder and said emphatically, ''I'm telling you, I never met Billy Lusk in my life.''

Templeton reached into her file folder, came up with a copy of the photograph I'd found in Billy Lusk's collection, and passed it across to Masterman.

"Ben found it with a couple of hundred other photos," she said. "Photos that Billy Lusk took of his lovers over the years, after having sex with them."

"It was kind of a hobby of his," I said. "You were asleep and never knew he shot it. He was probably holding it back to use as ammunition if you resisted his demands for money. Or for down the road when he wanted more."

"Or maybe he told you about it," Templeton said, "which finally drove you over the edge."

The blood was gone from Masterman's face, and his breathing was erratic.

"Obviously, that's me. But . . . but it doesn't prove I knew Billy Lusk."

Templeton handed across a blowup of the photo.

"If you look in the upper left hand corner, on the nightstand, you'll see a framed photo of Billy with his best friend, Samantha Eliason. There were only two copies made."

"Billy always kept his on his bedside table," I said. "Samantha has the other one."

"I'm afraid that puts you in Billy's bed," Templeton said.

"OK!" Masterman shouted.

A couple dining at the adjacent table looked over. He lowered his voice and leaned toward the middle of the table.

"OK. Maybe I slept with him once. But one foolish act, one moment of poor judgment, doesn't make me a murderer."

"It gives you a motive," I said.

"Motive is insufficient when there's an ironclad alibi."

"You mean you have an alibi?" Templeton said, sounding surprised.

"If you check, you'll find that when Billy Lusk was murdered, I was at a campaign appearance with my father. At a union hall several miles away."

I threw a sheepish glance toward Templeton.

"That would make a difference," I said.

His eyes went again to Templeton's tape recorder.

"I'm not sure I should say anything else."

"If you can explain things to our satisfaction," Templeton said, "we won't have much of a story."

"But if all you can give us is a 'no comment,' " I said, "we'll have to go with what we've got."

"You wouldn't write about what I did with Billy Lusk," Masterman said. "That's invasion of privacy."

"Not at all, Paul. If you're not a public figure, your father certainly is. Considering his stand on gay rights issues, and your involvement in his campaign, I'm afraid your own sexual history is both pertinent and newsworthy."

He shook the photograph. "You wouldn't print this."

"Unfortunately, the *Sun* isn't known for its high standards," Templeton said. "We'd do just about anything to attract readers from the *L.A. Times.*"

He stared at us, incredulous.

"God, you people."

Templeton stretched her hand across the table and touched him reassuringly on the wrist.

"We just want your side of things, Paul. If you can convince us there was no problem between you and Billy, we'll consider dropping the whole thing."

His eyes roved our faces while his mind worked behind them. Then he placed his fork and steak knife in the middle of his plate, pushed it away, and folded his hands tightly in front of him on the table.

"We left Dad's office shortly after eleven so he could make one last campaign stop that night. We got to the union hall around eleven-thirty, and he started speaking a few minutes after that. I was there with him, along with several others. I can tell you exactly what he said."

I glanced at my watch. It was a few minutes after nine.

"Why not sum it up for us, as succinctly as you can."

He summarized his father's speech, which focused on the financial impact of illegal immigration on state resources and his plans to tighten and enforce immigration laws.

"You see, I couldn't possibly have been at that bar when William Lusk was murdered. Or I'd have no idea what my father told his audience that night."

Templeton stopped scribbling in her notebook.

"The problem is, Paul, you just told us what your father *planned* to say, based on the text of his prepared speech. But a few minutes into that speech, he saw a large number of Hispanic faces in the auditorium and decided he'd better switch topics. The speech he actually delivered focused on his plans to create jobs and revive the economy.''

"But you wouldn't know about that,'' I said. ''By that time, you were in your car driving to The Out Crowd.''

''A security guard in the parking lot recalls your driving away shortly before midnight,'' Templeton said, ''and returning thirty or forty minutes later. He's signed an affidavit for us to that effect.''

"Your father's notoriously long-winded at the podium,'' I said. ''He talked for almost an hour that night. Long enough for you to drive the four miles to The Out Crowd, take care of business, and drive back again.''

"You called Billy from the pay phone across the street,'' Templeton said, ''and asked him to meet you out back. You were waiting for him when he came out.''

"That's when you shot him with your father's thirty-eight,'' I said. ''We know he kept a thirty-eight because he mentioned it last year in a speech to the NRA.''

''No,'' Masterman said weakly.

"You then raced back to the union hall. You joined in the applause for the final few minutes of your father's talk, when he delivered his usual closing, urging his audience to help get out the vote on election day. You each left in separate cars that night, and didn't get a chance to talk. You had no way of knowing he'd changed speeches.''

Masterman gripped the edge of the table, trying to steady himself.

''That's ridiculous.'' He laughed again, but it couldn't have sounded more false, more anxious. ''How could I possibly know that William Lusk was going to be in a gay bar in Silver Lake?''

''Because you invited him to meet you there,'' Templeton said.

She pulled a photocopied sheet from her file and handed it to him.

''A source at the phone company was able to get me a copy of all the phone calls made from your father's office during the past week. You'll notice that we've highlighted one call in particular. It's to the home of Derek Brunheim, Monday night at three minutes past eleven. The call Billy got just before he went out.''

"You have no right to those phone records,'' Masterman said.

"Apparently, you've forgotten about sunshine laws,'' I said.

"Public officials are required to file a record of all calls made at public expense with the city or county, which automatically become available to the press. If we don't have a right to these records now, we would have gotten them eventually."

"And the police can get them any time they want," Templeton said. "As well as those of Derek Brunheim, which we suspect will show a number of calls made to you in the recent past, as Billy pressured you for money."

The waitress stopped to ask if there was a problem with Masterman's steak, since he hadn't eaten a bite. He mumbled that it was fine. She warmed our coffees and went away.

"But if I murdered Billy Lusk, why would I want to shoot a TV spot there the very next day? It doesn't make sense."

"It does if you were obsessed with pleasing your father," I said. "You suddenly had the opportunity to arrange the gay spot he wanted so badly, and you took it."

"Besides," Templeton said, "many murderers show a compulsion to return to the crime site, even with the police still on the scene."

"When the police check," I said, "we think they'll either find your father's thirty-eight is missing, or that ballistics match it to the murder weapon."

Masterman stared numbly at the photo. In it, his face and body were leaner and more youthful by several years, and there was an aura of innocence about him as he slept.

"I only went with him once."

His voice was barely audible. He looked first at Templeton, then at me, imploringly.

"I'm not gay. I was just experimenting, that's all. It was one time."

"You knew that if you paid Billy what he asked, it wouldn't stop there," I said. "To go to the police would have led to his arrest and made it a matter of public record, which meant the media could get hold of it. You figured the only way to stop him was to kill him."

"All right, I killed him!"

Masterman raised his voice, fighting tears. He clenched his fists so tight the blood went out of them.

"He was scum. He didn't care who he hurt. I have a chance to do so much good in the world. He didn't care about anyone but himself."

He spoke less hatefully than passionately, as if he really believed he might convince us to bury the story, forget what we knew, let him get on with his life.

"For God's sake! I have a wife! A baby on the way!"

His voice became a whimper.

"Don't do this to me."

I was watching him closely, and when he grabbed the steak knife I was already reaching across the table. He had the blade aimed at his heart as I clasped my bigger hand around his. I squeezed tight, locking the handle of the knife deep inside his fist. The tip was poised an inch from his chest.

Without loosening my grip, I worked my way around the table to sit beside him. I told Templeton to call 911.

"Ask for the detective in charge of the Billy Lusk investigation. Tell him what we've got. Tell him we'll cooperate only if they promise to sit on this and hold off booking their suspect until nine tomorrow morning."

I wanted to be sure Harry got his scoop clean, with the story on the street ahead of the *L.A. Times* and the local morning news shows, which were notorious for combing the morning papers for news leads.

Templeton said, "I'm not sure I'm comfortable cozying up to the police."

I glanced at the blade protruding from Masterman's closed fist.

"Would you rather help this man commit suicide?"

She grabbed her notebook and left to make the call, leaving her tape recorder behind, still running.

The time was 9:17. I expected Templeton back within five minutes. If all went as planned, she'd be at the *Sun* fifteen or twenty minutes after that, putting her story together in time to make her no-fuss deadline. The police could talk to her after Harry locked it, with the presses rolling. The early edition would be in news racks and on doorsteps across the city as the sun came up, about the time Gonzalo Albundo was being processed out of Central Jail.

I used my other hand to work the knife free and flung it across the table to the floor. The couple next to us hadn't stopped staring, and diners at other tables had joined them.

"Gonzalo Albundo must have seemed like a miracle to you," I said.

Masterman opened his mouth to speak, but nothing came out.

''A troubled boy out of nowhere,'' I said, ''willing for some crazy reason to take the rap. He must have seemed like a gift from God.''

But Masterman wasn't concerned about Gonzalo Albundo.

''When did you know it was me?''

He sounded beaten, pitiful. Yet I also thought I heard a certain calculation.

''Something felt odd the first time I met you at The Out Crowd. When I saw the film permit. It struck me that the shoot had been put together rather fast.''

''That's when you suspected me?''

''It was just a question mark. We started checking, and things started pointing your way.''

He stared at the Polaroid.

''And the photo clinched it?''

''It linked you directly with the victim and suggested motive. It made the pieces fit.''

We were so close I could see two or three tiny hairs on one cheek that he'd missed while shaving. His wife should have noticed, I thought; I would have.

He kept his eyes intently forward and his head slightly lowered, like a trapped animal waiting for a chance to escape.

''Yet you remained friendly,'' he said. ''Even after you became suspicious.''

I reached over with my free hand and shut off Templeton's tape recorder. At that moment, I ceased being a reporter.

''Like I said, I wasn't sure at first. It was just a notion. Then I wanted to look elsewhere for suspects. Hoping I was wrong, hoping I'd find a better one to replace you.''

''Why?''

''Probably because I liked you so much.''

He raised his head alertly, the movement so slight I almost missed it.

''Or maybe I was just buying time,'' I said. ''Giving myself a chance to spend some time with you while I could.''

He looked over at me, his eyes suddenly alive with hope.

''I like you, too, Ben. I always felt something special between us. A bond. A connection.''

''I thought maybe you did.''

He looked away, dropping his head pathetically. I slipped my hand inside his and intertwined our fingers.

"No matter how hard we try otherwise," I said, "we end up being a lot like our fathers, don't we?"

"He's had some problems, but he's not such a bad guy, Ben. There's a whole side of him that no one knows."

"There always is."

"This will destroy his political career. You know how TV is. They'll replay that gay spot forever on the news. Rub his nose in the gun control issue. Make him look like a fool."

He turned his eyes plaintively to me again.

"Whatever you think of his politics, it's not fair."

"I suppose not."

"And my mother." Tears brimmed in his eyes. "This will kill my mother."

Perhaps he thought there was some remote chance that I'd destroy the taped interview and convince Templeton to abandon the story; that I was that crazy for him. It was a wild notion, but he had nothing to lose, and his level of desperation at that moment must have bordered on madness.

"My wife. My daughter. Try to think about them."

"Believe me, Paul, I have."

He looked over at me, studying my face for weakness, praying for a way out.

"This will destroy our family, Ben."

I wanted to tell him that the seeds of destruction had been sown in his family long before Templeton and I had found him out, long before he had murdered. That there are times when it's better to chop off poisonous roots and start fresh, creating a new family, on different terms, with different values. That's what Maurice and Fred had taught Jacques, and what Jacques had tried to show me. It had taken me a long time to understand that there's more than one kind. That the only true family is the one that nurtures and protects. And that anything else is a lie.

There was a lot I would have liked to talk about with Paul Masterman, Jr., but it was too complicated now, and too late.

"Gonzalo Albundo has a family," I said. "So did Billy Lusk."

My words apparently found the decent part of him, the small part that had survived whatever had destroyed the rest. Hope dimmed in his eyes, and he sagged with remorse that no longer appeared calculated for effect.

I brushed the back of my hand gently across his face, the way my mother had always touched mine after my father had delivered a beating. I ran my fingers through his thick curls, then pulled his face toward mine and kissed him on the lips.

"The police are on their way, Paul. You should think about who you're going to call from jail."

He began to tremble uncontrollably, and looked at me with the most frightened eyes I'd ever seen.

It was the kind of hopelessness I'd seen in Jacques's eyes, when his lungs had no longer worked and he'd struggled to get a breath like a man drowning in a sea of oxygen. When he'd sensed correctly that his life had come down to its final hours, and I'd packed him into the Mustang for our last ride to County Hospital.

I hadn't been there to see his eyes at the end, but I could imagine them now, as he'd called out for me and I hadn't come, because I'd lacked the courage to share with him life's last and most intimate act, and in my cowardice, had let him die alone.

The waitress, looking uneasy, stopped at our table to ask if everything was all right. The host stood a short distance away, watching us closely, so there must have been complaints.

I asked the waitress if she was a regular reader of the *Los Angeles Sun.*

"To be honest," she said, "I get most of my news from the TV."

"You really should do more reading," I said, and asked for the check.

The restaurant continued its silent rotation above the starry landscape. Masterman and I sat there passively, like two lost shuttle pilots back in the hands of ground control, coming slowly down to earth.

He bent his head over the table and wept. I continued to hold his hand, first stroking his arm, then running my finger along the soft ridges of his lovely veins.

For a few minutes more, until they came to take him from me, he was mine.